THE INN AT EVERGREEN HOLLOW

EVERGREEN HOLLOW CHRISTMAS BOOK ONE

FIONA BAKER

Copyright © 2024 by Fiona Baker

All rights reserved. This book or any portion thereof
may not be reproduced or used in any manner whatsoever without
the express written permission of the publisher except for the use
of brief quotations in a book review.

Published in the United States of America

First Edition, 2024

fionabakerauthor.com

JOIN MY NEWSLETTER

If you love beachy, feel-good women's fiction, sign up to receive my newsletter, where you'll get free books, exclusive bonus content, and info on my new releases and sales!

CHAPTER ONE

Greenery, flowers, mistletoe, music...

Nora Stoker hummed along to herself as she ran down the checklist on the clipboard in her hand, the soft sound of strings playing "*Ave Maria*" filtering from the ballroom just beyond the doors.

Christmastime weddings were, in her opinion, both some of the most beautiful and the most difficult to pull off. They needed to be elegant while still evoking that holiday warmth, without any of the tackiness that could come from being *too* on-the-nose with the decorations and music.

But, as always, she thought that it had been executed flawlessly. There was abundant greenery with hints of gold and soft lighting, the occasional red of roses and poinsettias, and the final touch, a single sprig of mistletoe hanging above the doors where the happy couple would exit after saying their vows. A small detail that she was proud to say she had thought of herself.

After all, that was why brides came to Metropolitan Events for their wedding planning. They were known for those small touches that could make even the largest event feel personal.

She checked off the last item on the list, looking around for one of the ushers. She spied one of them, a tall brown-haired young man in his early twenties standing stiffly in the black-and-white uniform of the hotel. Her heels clicking against the tile as she walked quickly in his direction. She was dressed similarly, in slim black trousers and a cream-colored silk shirt with pearl buttons, the sleeves now rolled up and buttoned at her elbows after a morning of running around and checking off every item on her list.

Nora tucked a single wayward bit of light brown hair behind her ear, smiling pleasantly at the usher as she approached.

"Is everything set for the bride to walk down the aisle? We have less than an hour until the ceremony."

The usher nodded. "Valet is out front, starting to

receive guests, and there are ushers ready to escort everyone to their seats. The string quartet is set up just as you asked, and caterers are here and starting to prep for the cocktail hour, just as soon as the ceremony is over. The bride's photographers have already arrived. Two were down here for guest arrivals, one was with the groom and his party, and another was with the bride and hers. And there were two videographers as well, one to document guest arrivals and another going back and forth between the bride and groom."

Nora nodded as he spoke, running down her list again to double-check each item. "All right. I'll be ready as soon as the bride arrives, then. Make sure everyone is on headset, I need to be able to fix anything that might go wrong on a moment's notice."

"Nothing will go wrong, ma'am." There was a confidence in his voice that told Nora that this was likely the first wedding he'd worked.

She, on the other hand, had coordinated more than she could count by now. Something *always* went wrong. It was her job, once the ceremony began, to ensure that those mishaps were so flawlessly corrected that the bride would never know. That there would never be any evidence of it.

It was imperative that it *seem* as if nothing ever went wrong.

It was a job that she genuinely loved. Since she'd graduated with a degree in hospitality from Boston University, she'd worked for Metropolitan Events, coordinating weddings and parties and proms with an enthusiasm that always made her feel secure that she had made the right choice for her career.

She'd coordinated fancy events for corporations and other businesses too, but her favorite clients were always the individuals. The newly engaged couples, the mothers planning a quinceañera for their daughters, the schools looking to throw a prom or winter dance. It always felt so satisfying to know that she had played a key role in making memories that would last someone a lifetime, no matter how much work it entailed.

And it was always a *lot* of work. She'd been up since before six, getting ready to go to the venue and triple-check everything. But the result would be a perfect day for a new bride, and Nora never doubted for a second how much she loved it all, from start to finish.

As the guests began to file in, Nora took up her position halfway down the aisle and to one side of the room, blending in with the decor as she watched to ensure that no last-minute interceptions were needed.

The guests were filing down the green and gold velvet runner that ran the length of the aisle, being ushered to their appropriate seats—one side for family and friends of the bride, the other for the groom, closest family in the front two rows. Nora could hear the bride's mother commenting on how tasteful the decorations were, and she felt a flush of pleasure as she glanced toward the ballroom doors, knowing that the bride would be entering in less than five minutes.

Everything had been planned, down to the second. And right on cue, as the last of the guests took their seat, Nora heard the music change.

The bride was stunning. For a moment, Nora couldn't help but picture herself on her own upcoming wedding day, as she saw the pretty brunette in the long-sleeved and full-skirted Mikado silk gown start to glide down the aisle.

She'd picked out something more appropriate for an early summer wedding, a thin silk and lace dress, but she felt an eager flutter of excitement in her stomach as she watched the bride approach the altar and the smiling groom. It had been difficult in the bustle of the last few months to find much time for planning, but she couldn't wait for the slower month of January to get back to it.

She could picture her own fiancé standing there, smiling brightly at her as she approached, maybe even welling up with the faintest hint of tears.

A sharp bark broke her out of her momentary reverie, and Nora's head snapped immediately toward the source of the disturbance. In the front row, she saw the culprit: a small black Scottish terrier with a plaid collar standing up on his hind legs, front paws firmly placed on the seat in front of him.

The yipping began just as the officiant began to say the familiar words, "Dearly beloved..."

Nora darted forward, intent on the first of the promised mishaps.

She'd had a feeling something like this would happen when one of the bridesmaids, who owned the terrier, had insisted on bringing the dog to the ceremony. Despite Nora's gentle suggestions that the venue didn't usually allow animals and that it might be best to leave the dog at home, the bridesmaid had whipped out emotional support animal paperwork instead, promising in the same breath that the mother of the bride would be happy to hold onto the little terror for the duration of the ceremony.

As if to add insult to injury, Nora saw that it was

not the mother of the bride holding the dog, but one of the bride's cousins, who was clearly having trouble holding onto the small creature.

The dog was squirming now, readying itself for another volley of yips as the bride began her vows, and Nora moved swiftly down the aisle, thanking her lucky stars that the dog was situated only two seats down from her side of the room. It might have been so much worse if she'd had to make her way down the aisle to get the dog in full view of the videographer.

Just as she reached the edge of the seats, the small terrier twisted out of the cousin's hands, launching itself into the air like the world's furriest bottle rocket. Nora gasped, nearly breaking into a run as she grabbed for the dog, her hands closing on the wiry fur just as the small terrier nearly made it to the front row.

"Come *here!*" she whispered under her breath, tucking the writhing animal under her arm. A few guests had begun to look around, but she had managed to get the dog before it burst out onto the aisle—or worse, ran under the bride's skirts or upset the decor—and Nora darted for a side door, narrowly preventing the wedding from being entirely disturbed.

"Just another day on the job," she murmured, closing the door silently and reaching for the small earpiece tucked into her ear. "That's why they come to Metropolitan Events, isn't it?" she cooed to the dog, walking a few more feet away from the ballroom. "Where else can you get a wedding planner and an animal-catcher all in one?"

The dog let out another sharp bark, nearly squirming out of the crook of Nora's arm, and she pressed her earpiece to call the caterer. "I've got a dog here in need of a treat," she said, cradling it against her blouse as she scratched between its ears. "Can you bring me a piece of bacon, maybe? Something it might like."

"Of course. Give me just a minute." The tinny voice of one of the caterers responded almost immediately, and Nora walked to one of the benches lining the lobby, sinking down as she held the small dog in her lap. She'd never admit it out loud, but the opportunity to sit was actually one she was grateful for. Her feet were starting to ache.

Maybe I should go and get a pedicure tomorrow, she thought, craning her neck this way and that as she waited on the caterer. *Maybe a full massage too. An early Christmas present to myself.*

One of the caterers swept around the corner, a

blonde woman with her hair caught up in a net, dressed in the same crisp black and white they'd all opted for. There was a small dish in her hand, and Nora gratefully took it. "Thank you." She fished a small piece of bacon out of it. It was sticky, and she smelled the faint scent of maple. "This ought to keep the little guy happy for a minute."

"No problem." The caterer smiled at her, disappearing back the way she'd come, and Nora fished another piece of bacon out of the dish.

"How's this?" She nibbled at one of the pieces herself as the dog ate. It had been hours since she'd had a quick breakfast of black coffee and an apple-cinnamon muffin from the grocery-store bakery, and she let out a soft sigh of pleasure at the taste. It was smoky and sweet all at once, with just a hint of saltiness, and Nora wondered what it was actually meant for. Whatever it was, she hoped she'd get a chance to try it at the reception—although as busy as she stayed during these events, she rarely got a chance to eat until afterward.

The dog scarfed down the bite, and then another, curling onto Nora's lap as she fed it one small treat after another. The weight of the small animal was soothing, and she felt a small pang of nostalgia for the days when she used to have a childhood pet.

She'd thought about getting a pet now and again. Something lower-maintenance than a dog. As much as she loved them, she worked too many hours to make dog ownership feasible. A cat, maybe, although even they needed attention from time to time, and when she wasn't working, she was usually with Rob.

He was firmly against the idea of getting any kind of pet too, and since they'd be living together soon, that made it all pretty much a moot point. His arguments were sound too. They worked too much, he didn't want what little time they had together taken up with caring for an animal, it was expensive, it would prevent them from vacationing as easily as they otherwise would.

Not that we've gone on many vacations, Nora thought as she stroked the small dog's back.

They both worked constantly. The last time they'd gone away together was three years ago, on a little cabin getaway that had left them both itching for Internet access to check their email. The isolation had made them grouchy and irritable, and they hadn't planned another vacation since.

From a lack of time, she told herself again and again. *Nothing more.*

From the ballroom, she could hear the music picking up again, a clear sign that the happy couple were about to exit as man and wife. Nora fed the last of the sticky bacon bits to the dog, her earpiece crackling as the staff began passing instructions back and forth for pictures and the cocktail hour, and she stood just as she saw the dog's owner hurrying in her direction.

The bridesmaid had her gold skirt in one hand, rushing over with an expression on her face that was both chagrined and grateful all at once.

"Thank you *so* much," she gushed, reaching for the dog. "You really saved the day. Smoky didn't mean to be noisy, did you, baby? No, you didn't." She cooed at the dog, giving Nora another grateful smile.

"All in a day's work." Nora smiled in return, and she meant it. It had been worrisome and a little frustrating, but in the end, it didn't matter. The crisis was averted, and nothing had marred the perfect day that she'd helped to arrange.

By the time midnight rolled around, the bride and groom leaving the venue in a shower of sparklers, Nora was both exhausted and utterly pleased. There had been a few other small mishaps—a forgotten card for one of the cameras, an appetizer that had only two pieces per guest available instead of three—but each time, she'd managed to find a workaround. She watched as the guests started to file out toward the valet, making her way to the ballroom to ensure that cleanup had started. The venue would need to be cleared out by two a.m., but she didn't need to stick around that long, just ensure that everyone who would be doing the job was present and already working.

Once that was finished, she fetched her heavy wool coat from the coat check as she prepared to leave, winding a cashmere scarf around her neck and reaching for her valet ticket. She stepped outside into the frigid night air, only to stop in utter surprise at the sight in front of her.

"Rob?" Nora's eyes widened as she saw her fiancé, Rob Smith, standing on the curb. He looked as handsome as ever, his brown hair ruffled in the cold Boston wind, cheeks flushed from it, wrapped up in a cashmere peacoat and slim designer jeans. "What are you doing here? I thought you'd already be on the way to the airport for your business trip."

Since long before they'd met, Rob had worked as a sales executive for a moped manufacturer. It wasn't the most interesting of jobs, exactly—she often felt her eyelids start to droop when he started talking about spreadsheets and quarterly sales—but she knew he didn't particularly love hearing her go on about floral arrangements and themed menus either. He traveled often, and she'd been expecting a week alone while he was in Chicago for meetings. They'd said goodbye that morning before she left for the wedding, and Nora had thought he would be gone by the time she got home.

But he was standing there, unexpectedly, and her heart fluttered. There was a time when him going out of his way to surprise her with something sweet and romantic—like flowers or an unexpected kiss goodbye on his way to his flight—wouldn't have been unusual. It made her feel warm all over to think that he might have made the effort to do something like that for her again.

The past few months had been so devoid of romance, with how busy their schedules had been. They'd been like ships passing in the night, Nora had often thought, with date nights becoming fewer and fewer, and nights in together skipped in favor of early bedtimes or long nights for Rob at the office. Some of her friends had started to question if it was normal for things to wane so much, with a wedding on the horizon. Shouldn't they be even *more* excited and eager to spend time with one another?

Nora had reassured them, and herself, that it was

fine. Everything was perfect. Yes, they hadn't quite settled on where they'd be living after the wedding yet, and yes, Rob got frustrated every time she brought up wedding plans, telling her it was her job to do it perfectly, so she might as well make all the choices. But everything *else* was perfect. Everything since college had been right on track, every box on the list checked, right down to meeting a handsome man with a good job who always said all the right things to her friends, remembered birthdays and anniversaries, and brought his mother flowers and wine when they went home to visit. He wasn't exciting, but he was what she wanted.

Excitement wore off. Stability and companionship were more important than anything else. But Nora couldn't help relishing the flutter of excitement she felt as her pace quickened and she walked toward Rob, eager for him to pull her in for a kiss and whisper something sweet in her ear, the kind of thing she'd been missing.

But he wasn't smiling. She could see that as she got closer. His face looked tense and serious. Grave, even, as if something had happened. The excited fluttering in her stomach curdled, turning to a crawling sensation of unease. Rob rarely looked like that. She couldn't really remember the last time.

"I'm headed that way." His voice was eerily flat. "But I had something I needed to talk to you about, first."

The sound of his voice made her stomach twist. He never spoke to her like that, without any inflection, as if he were reciting a grocery list instead of talking to the woman he loved.

"What's up?" She tried to keep her tone light, to not let on how the knot in her stomach was tightening. She'd been with Rob for nearly five years. It was impossible to be with someone for so long, and not know them nearly as well as she knew herself. Something was wrong. She braced herself for him to say that he was going to see his parents, that one of them was ill, or that something had happened with his job.

"I've been thinking about it for some time." Rob scuffed the toe of his designer boot against the curb, a nervous gesture that made Nora feel faintly sick. Rob was fastidious about his clothing. A careless gesture like that wasn't like him at all. "Nora…"

He let out a sharp breath that puffed between them, a small cloud in the frigid air. "There's no easy way to say this. But with the appointments we have next week, I just can't let this continue on without saying…"

"What?" The word came out more sharply than she intended it to. That sick feeling spread. She thought she knew what he was going to say, and she couldn't decide if she wanted to put off the moment when she'd hear it forever, or get it over with. She didn't really think that she was going to get a choice.

"I think we need to break off the engagement." Rob said the words in a rush, each one punctuated by another puff in the cold air. "I—no, we need to. I'm saying it. We need to break—"

"I heard you." Nora's voice sounded strangled, the sudden lump in her throat trying to block her speech. Somewhere behind her, she heard the valet's footsteps, but she couldn't bring herself to focus on anything other than Rob, on the awful thing that he couldn't actually mean.

But if it was somehow a joke, that was even worse.

"Why?" She sucked in a breath, the cold air jolting her back into her senses. "Why now? Why on earth haven't you talked to me about this before, Rob? This is the first I'm hearing of it, even though you say you've been thinking about it for a long time."

Rob chewed on his lower lip, shifting from one foot to another. "It's just been on my mind, Nor.

We're just... we're not all that suited to each other, you know? I thought about it when we went off to that cabin. You planned everything, all on your own."

"It was meant to be a surprise!" Nora's eyes widened, a mixture of hurt and anger tangling up in her chest. "You always said you liked that I was a planner, that it meant I could just pick, and you knew it would be good."

"Well, it wasn't. We both agreed on that, after. And I hate surprises." Rob's gaze took on a stubborn look that Nora had seen before, from time to time. "I just think—"

"Rob, that was three years ago." Her chest felt so tight she could barely breathe. "You've been thinking this all that time. We got engaged *after* that! At Thanksgiving last year."

"I know." He ran a gloved hand through his hair. "Things were so good, for the most part. I just kind of ignored what kept bothering me."

"*What* kept bothering you?" Nora felt tears burning at the back of her eyes, but she refused to let them fall. Not here, not right now. She never cried in public. She would let herself fall apart later. "You never talked to me about any of this. I thought everything was fine."

"It *was*." Rob let out another sharp breath. "Look, I've just realized that we're not meant for each other. There are lots of little things. I think we'll be happier if we just go our separate ways."

It's all so vague.

A pit opened up in Nora's stomach, a horrible suspicion forming. At the last office party, she remembered a pretty blonde in a blue dress who had gushed over Rob's sales numbers. He had smiled broadly as he introduced the woman and mentioned how hard she was working. And if Nora remembered correctly, the woman had just been made partner two weeks ago.

"Is this about Julie?" She swallowed hard, remembering the proud way he'd looked at her. She'd mentioned something about Rob giving her a glowing recommendation right as she was up for a review with the other partners in the company.

Rob's lips pressed together tightly. "I don't have time to go over this, Nora. I really do need to go and catch my flight. I just didn't want to leave without talking things over with you. I really am sorry."

It sounds like a sales pitch. Like he practiced it. Nora felt the pit in her stomach widen, that sick feeling spreading. She could imagine Julie on the flight to Chicago, in Rob's hotel—Rob wanting to neatly break things off so he didn't have to feel guilty, like a cheater. When in fact, it didn't matter, if he'd been *wanting* to cheat this whole time.

Nora swallowed hard. She couldn't think of anything to say. The last thing she wanted to do was beg for him to stay, but she couldn't just say goodbye either. It seemed preposterous that just this morning he'd kissed her as she walked out of his apartment, like everything was normal, and now he'd caught her completely unaware. She had truly never seen this coming.

It didn't matter anyway. He was already walking away, as if he'd delivered his message, and had nothing more to say. Nothing more than a few sentences, after years together.

She stood there, frozen both literally and figuratively, watching him leave. Tears burned her eyes, and she dipped her head, not wanting anyone else to see as she tried to surreptitiously wipe them away with the back of her glove. She couldn't quite believe it was really happening.

Rob hadn't been a Prince Charming. He hadn't swept her off her feet or romanced her until her head spun or fulfilled any wild fantasies. But he'd been handsome, ambitious enough, stable, secure. He'd had a similar five-year-plan.

He'd fit perfectly in the checklist—boyfriend, then fiancé, soon husband and later a father. He'd wanted kids, eventually. They handled finances the same way. Decisions had always been made easily. If he didn't have an opinion, he let her choose. He'd fit her vision for her life so perfectly. She had always assumed that she did the same for him.

Now a piece of her puzzle had been forcibly removed, and Nora felt, suddenly, that the entire plan was beginning to crumble.

Someone cleared their throat behind her, and she knew it was the valet. She turned, feeling numb as she took the keys and handed him a cash tip, mumbling her thanks as she strode toward her sleek, sensible Camry. The interior smelled of warm leather and the upholstery shampoo that they used to detail it at the dealer, and she closed her eyes, trying not to think about the day she and Rob had gone to pick it out together. He'd said it fit her perfectly. Sleek, neat, put-together. She'd taken it as a compliment. But now, everything he'd ever said began to shift and re-frame itself in her mind, making her question all of it.

Julie probably drove a sports car. Something quick and fun and bright. Something *exciting*.

The tears began to fall as she sat there, the car

idling as she looked at the venue where she'd just facilitated a beautiful wedding. Where, just a few hours ago, she'd been imagining her own. It had been bright and full of laughter and cheer, but she saw the lights beginning to go out as the cleanup crew finished, and she felt a hollow ache in her chest. Everything felt hollow now.

The week had gone so well. She'd been looking forward to a relaxing weekend, maybe even a little wedding planning, and then an exceptionally productive week to follow while Rob was out of town. She'd been looking at reservations for when he returned, a nice dinner to celebrate the deal that she'd been certain he was going to close. The holidays were right around the corner, and she'd thought of going to get a Christmas tree for her apartment with him, maybe decorating together afterward.

He hated decorating. She always thought he'd enjoyed it when they did it together, but now she thought that maybe he'd always been pretending. That nothing was really as it had seemed, all these years.

As she drove home, Nora was certain that she'd never felt so lost.

CHAPTER TWO

The glaring morning sunlight that woke Nora only served to make her splitting headache that much worse.

She'd cried herself to sleep, long past when she normally would have gone to bed. She could feel the aftereffects of it as she slowly pushed herself up against the pillows, rubbing her hands over her face. Everything felt hopeless.

She hadn't slept well at all. The night had been broken up by restless dreams of Rob telling her he was breaking off their engagement, but this time at the altar, embarrassing her in front of everyone. Dreams of her walking into her office for a meeting with a new couple, only to find Rob and Julie sitting there, an engagement ring matching her own on

Julie's slender finger. She'd woken each time, sobbing, and then fallen back to sleep.

The engagement ring in question was sitting on her nightstand. She'd torn it off her finger right before falling into bed in a fit of tears and anger, and now she picked it up, turning it so the diamond caught the light. Two carats, an oval solitaire set in rose gold. Somewhere in Rob's apartment, the band that they'd picked out to go with it was sitting in a small velvet box—a thin pave and rose gold diamond ring. His matching gold band would be next to it, waiting for the big day.

A day that was never going to happen now.

Fresh tears welled in Nora's eyes, and she threw back her plush duvet, sliding out of bed. Her bedroom was her sanctuary, carefully designed and decorated to all of her personal tastes, just like the rest of her apartment. She'd thought about discussing the possibility of keeping it, when she and Rob finally had time to look at where they'd live after the wedding. The apartment had felt hard to let go of.

She'd picked out every piece of furniture in it— some new and designer, some vintage, all of it flowing seamlessly. The bedroom was all dusty rose and cream, and Nora closed her eyes as her feet sank into the soft woven rug at the edge of her bed. She had designed her apartment to feel like an escape, like a cloud she could sink into at the end of a long day, comfortable in her own space.

Now, it felt like a reminder that she was going to be alone. Not just when she wanted to be, but *all* alone, all of the time. Maybe forever.

Thirty-five felt like a daunting age to start over.

Nora padded to the bathroom, flicking on the light. Looking in the mirror did nothing to make her feel better, as it reflected puffy red eyes and a tired complexion from the makeup she'd forgotten to take off. She turned the faucet on warm, rubbing cold cream over her face to take off last night's foundation, contemplating a shower. That might make things feel more manageable, she told herself. That and a cup of coffee.

Her phone buzzed on the counter next to her, making her jump a little as the cheery tone followed it. For a moment, her heart leapt, thinking it might be Rob. He'd text her and apologize, saying he didn't know what he'd been thinking. That he'd been out of his mind. That it had been a mistake.

Nora swallowed hard as she picked up her phone. The text wasn't from Rob.

MELANIE: Long time, no talk! How's it going?

Nora bit her lip. She hadn't heard from Melanie Carter in a long time. But that was the kind of friendship they'd always had, and the reason why Melanie was the only friend she still had in Evergreen Hollow, where they'd both grown up. Everyone else had drifted away with time and long gaps in communication and life changes, but she and Melanie had always been able to go a long time without speaking and then pick up where they'd left off as if no time had passed at all. It was something she cherished.

The sight of Melanie's name on her phone felt like a warm hug, a reminder of happier, more comforting times. They'd known each other since they were kids, and even if they didn't know *everything* about each other anymore, Melanie always seemed to understand her. It was the reason why, before she could stop herself, she started to text back the truth instead of a pretty lie.

NORA: Not great.

Nora looked at the blunt two-word text. The water was steaming hot, splashing from the faucet, and she turned it down, running it over her fingers before splashing it over her face. Her phone buzzed again, more insistently, and she glanced over to see that Melanie was calling her.

Video calling, actually.

Nora winced, grabbing a hand towel and drying off her face before answering the phone. Melanie's expression, the moment the video call turned on, was more reflective than the mirror she'd been looking into just before.

"You look awful!" Melanie burst out, her brows pinched together with worry.

Nora laughed wryly, the sound coming out more bitter than she'd expected. "That's only natural after getting dumped by your fiancé while he's rushing to catch an airplane, I think." She sank onto the edge of the tub, running a hand through her hair. "It seemed like he couldn't get away from me fast enough, honestly."

Melanie shook her head, her short blonde hair flying wildly around her face. Nora could see that she was sitting cross-legged on a yoga mat—probably post-morning-run. She'd always been the most enthusiastically athletic person Nora had ever met, even in winter when everyone else opted for cookies and time on the couch.

"A man who would leave you like that is *not* worth crying over," she said emphatically. "And I can tell you've been crying. He's an idiot, Nora."

Nora nodded, swallowing hard against the tears

that threatened to well back up. She dashed the back of one hand across her eyes, walking out of the bathroom and toward the kitchen with the phone still in one hand. She needed that cup of coffee.

"I feel lost," she admitted, her voice still quavering a little. "I don't even know what to do with myself for the holidays now. I've spent all the Christmases that Rob and I were together with his family. *Four* of them, Melanie. I'd just planned for that like always. I didn't think—"

She half-expected Melanie to make sympathetic noises and feel sad on her behalf, but instead, Melanie perked up as if Nora had just made the best suggestion she'd heard all morning.

"Just come home for Christmas, then!" Her voice took on a bright, excited note. "A change of scenery might be just what you need. A *complete* change. I hear you making coffee. You can come see the shop! It's so pretty this time of year. You'll love what I've done with the place."

Nora couldn't help but laugh at that. Years ago, Melanie had saved up to buy The Mellow Mug, the coffee shop and bakery that she now owned. It was her pride and joy, her baby, and Nora could hear Melanie practically vibrating with eagerness.

"You work so hard, all of the time," Melanie

insisted. "I know you have a ton of vacation days built up. You never take any of them. Don't tell me otherwise, I know better. You could take some time off and come for the whole month of December!"

"I don't know." Nora bit her lip again, chewing restlessly on it as she poured a splash of sweet organic creamer—a weekend treat—into her coffee mug and sank onto one of the plush velvet stools at her counter. "I have clients."

"Someone would help you. You could do remote meetings if you needed to—but really, Nora, you *need* a vacation. No one at your office is going to begrudge you that. How many times have you taken off in all the time you've worked there?"

"Three." Nora mumbled it around the edge of her coffee cup, propping the phone up against a recipe book. A recipe book that she'd pointedly never had time to use.

"*Exactly.* This is practically bereavement. You've been *dumped* by your *fiancé*."

"Gee, rub it in." Nora took another sip. It was so much better than her usual morning coffee. She hated it black—she didn't know why she drank it that way five days out of seven, except that it meant fewer calories, and Rob was always on her about how unhealthy even organic creamer was. But her usual coffee, even the expensive kind, always tasted so bitter. This was sweet and rich and velvety, with a hint of hazelnut. Melanie's coffee would be even better. A real latte, the kind she never took the time to make and always felt guilty splurging on.

"Sorry." Melanie looked briefly chagrined. "I'm just saying, it would be good for you. A whole month off, away from everything. Come on, Nora. You know I'm right."

"I don't know," Nora repeated. "I love my parents and my family—but you know how I feel about Evergreen Hollow. I always felt stifled there. I haven't talked to Caroline in years. She's lived there her whole life, even after Margo and I took off. You know what she's going to have to say if I just turn up out of nowhere, and after what happened with Rob..." Nora winced just thinking about the biting questions her older sister would have. "I don't know if I want to deal with all of that right after a breakup. It feels like a lot to take on."

Melanie paused, a sympathetic look warming her expression. "I know, Nora. Caroline has always been a lot. But you don't have anything to lose, right? What's the worst that could happen? And the best is that you get a vacation with family and friends."

"Okay." The word burst out of Nora's lips before

she could talk herself out of it again, her hands wrapping tightly around the warmth of her coffee cup. She wasn't entirely sure what had come over her, except she felt that Melanie was absolutely right about one thing.

She needed a change. A *big* change. And going home for the holidays would certainly be that.

"I'll talk to my boss about the time off. And I'll book a ticket. Midweek, maybe." Nora took another sip of her coffee, trying to disguise her nerves. Going home shouldn't feel like such a monumental task—but she knew why it did.

"*Yes!*" Melanie fist-pumped the air, bouncing up and down on her yoga mat. "I mean, I'm sorry this is why you're coming home. But I'm *so* excited to see you in person again, Nor! Seriously, we're going to have the *best* time."

Nora forced a smile. "We will. I'm sure of it."

"Okay! See you soon!"

The video call clicked off, and Nora set the phone down, that uneasy feeling in her stomach returning and hearkening back to the night before. She felt entirely uncertain that going home was a good idea. It seemed like a decision fraught with landmines, with possibilities of everything feeling so much worse than it already did.

But it was too late to change her mind, she knew. She couldn't begin to imagine the disappointment on Melanie's face if she called her back and told her it was impossible.

She was committed.

CHAPTER THREE

The small bell above what *should* have been the door of the Sugar Maple general store chimed as Aiden Masters walked in, lugging the newly hewn door that he'd brought along with him. The smell of cedar, cardboard boxes, warm bread, and fried food filled his nostrils as he set the door down with a heavy *thud,* leaning it carefully against a bare space on the wall as he walked to the front counter and knocked heavily against it.

"Leon?" he called out, looking around for the owner, who appeared a moment later. Leon Woodrow hadn't changed a bit in all the time Aiden had known him. He had iron-gray hair, from his head to his eyebrows to his bushy beard, and he almost always wore a cheerful smile on his wrinkled face.

"Aiden!" Leon grinned, clapping the younger man on the shoulder and looking over it toward the door. "Thank goodness you've brought it over. My wife hates the one we've been using as a replacement. I can already see that's good work you've done, and quickly too."

"Well, I've been having to stay on top of things." Aiden raked a hand through his dark hair, feeling what might be a wood shaving catch on his fingertips. "Most of my energy's been going to help rebuild the roof on the town center. Lord knows nothing gets done if that building isn't functional. And with the festival coming up..."

"The whole place would go up in a puff of smoke if that festival didn't happen," Leon said with a grin. "That storm right after Thanksgiving really wreaked havoc. Haven't seen one like that in a decade or more. Luckily we've got our own personal handyman to help clean up the mess."

"I do my best." Aiden returned the grin, glancing back at the door. "It shouldn't take me long to get the hinges on and get you all squared away."

"Hmm." Leon rubbed a hand over his beard. "You think the event center's going to be repaired in time for the festival? I could talk to Bethany about alternate locations if need be."

"And watch the top of her head blow right off?" Aiden smirked. "Trust me, I'll do everything in my power to make sure the roof is sound for the festivities. And I'll help with whatever else is needed too."

There was no doubt in his mind just how important it was. The festival had been a focal point of the town for as long as he'd been alive, and his parents. His grandparents too, up to a point. It had changed shape over the years, grown and gotten bigger, but the idea was always the same. It was an unabashed celebration of the holidays, with everyone in Christmas outfits, a festive costume contest, a gift drive, booths and games and food. There was something for everyone, young and old, and Aiden wasn't immune to the nostalgia and cheer of it all. He'd miss it too, if something happened to shake up what was undoubtedly a foundation of Evergreen Hollow.

Leon shook his head. "We're lucky to have such a talented resident carpenter." He leaned back against the counter, arms crossed over his chest as he watched Aiden start to take out new hinges for the door, measuring where they needed to be attached. "Not every town would bounce back so quickly."

Aiden waved a hand to brush off the

compliment, unable to speak through the handful of nails he'd slipped between his lips, hammer in one hand and hinge in the other. For a long moment, the only sound in the quiet of the morning surrounding the general store was the heavy *thud* of the hammer as he secured the hinges, moving them this way and that and adding a little WD-40 when one dared to squeak. He double-checked the measurements, then hefted the door up, waving Leon off again when the older man started to move as if to offer help.

"I grew up in Evergreen Hollow." Aiden lined the door up, peering at it. "Always intended on coming back, even when I went to Albany to that trade school. Never had any plans to stay gone for too long."

"You'd probably be making better money there." Leon lifted one shoulder in a shrug. "Or you could be up in New York City, working on some big-scale projects. Living large. You've got the talent for it, that's for sure."

Aiden snorted. "All that noise and chaos? Not for me. I like it here." He slid the hinges in place, starting on the fastenings. "Besides, there's nothing more fulfilling than keeping up my hometown. Seeing all these buildings in good shape, still standing, knowing I've got a part in literally building the history of it..." He shook his head. "It's a better feeling than working on any skyscraper, that's for sure."

"Well, we're fortunate you came back. Don't know what we'd do without you. Bethany complained about that temporary door every day it was up, said it couldn't compare to the work you did. Let in a draft, she said."

"Well, this one won't." Aiden grinned. "Besides, I'm the lucky one. Normally this time of year is slow, but not now. I'll have as much work as I need to keep my hands busy until springtime."

"Maybe you should think about trying to find some other ways to occupy your time." There was a distinct gleam in Leon's eye that Aiden recognized immediately—the gleam of a happily married man who would like nothing better than to set someone up. "Gracie was in here the other day, when you were measuring that door frame. I know she'd be tickled pink if you asked her out on a date sometime. Maybe to Marie's. Place that fancy, a girl can't help but have a good time."

There it is.

Aiden chuckled, rolling his eyes lightly as he moved the door back and forth.

"Appreciate the offer," he said finally, reaching

up to tighten one of the screws. "But I can't say I'm really all that interested in dating just now."

"You might think differently if you tried." There was that fatherly tone in Leon's voice that Aiden knew well, the one he used with anyone a hair under forty. "Bethany and I don't always see eye to eye, but my life wouldn't be a thing without that woman. I'm grateful every day I have her. I can tell you, you get to a certain age and your outlook changes."

Aiden glanced over his shoulder. "I'm not opposed to the idea of finding love," he clarified, leaning down to fish another tool out of his carpentry bag. "I just don't think being set up is the way, you know? I feel like when I cross paths with the right woman, it'll just hit me. I'll know I found her. Until then..." Aiden shrugged. "I'm fine with waiting."

"An old romantic." Leon laughed, circling around behind the counter. "Well, there's something to be said for that. I can't argue with you there."

"I just figure it'll happen if the time is right." Aiden closed the door, moving on to the locks. "You got a new shipment of that beef I like in yet? Thought I might drop by Melanie's bakery, get some of that sourdough for sandwiches for the week."

"Sounds like I need to get the deli counter up and running." Leon grinned, fishing out the keys to unlock it. "It's been quiet as a church mouse all morning, and I've been taking advantage of it. Haven't opened up but half the store so far."

"Everyone's busy bouncing back from the storm." Aiden flicked the deadbolt this way and that, making sure it would hold. Evergreen Hollow wasn't exactly the kind of place where theft was a real concern—plenty of folks didn't even bother locking their houses—but he liked to be thorough. Leon could decide how much he wanted to make use of the locks—he'd ensure they were in good working shape, just in case. "I know Joe is coming by at some point to stock up on tools. We've been going through hardware like nobody's business, working on the event center. And I think his lever broke yesterday. He'll need a new one. But he likes to get all that himself, so—"

Aiden shrugged, finishing the last of the repairs and tucking his tools away.

He had plenty of carpentry supplies he'd have been happy to offer up in service of repairing the center, but Joe had turned him down. He saw the wisdom in it—it put money in Leon's pocket and went right back into the town, but he wanted to help in any way he could. Seeing the town so beat up from that storm felt like a personal injury. One he was eager to treat.

"I'm going to head out and see what they need," Aiden said, clapping Leon on the shoulder as the older man brought him a paper-wrapped package of deli meat. "How much do I owe you?"

"On the house, for how quick you got that door here." Leon pushed the package into Aiden's hands, the expression on his face clear enough that Aiden knew he wouldn't be taking no for an answer. "I'll call you if there are any issues with it."

"You do that." Aiden nodded, picking up his bag, and headed out into the crisp winter air.

It was frigid, here in Vermont, a month before Christmas. But he loved it. The invigorating cold, the beauty of the landscape, the cheer that seemed to permeate everything. Even with the semi-disaster that the storm had been, everyone was picking up and carrying on, making sure to help each other as they put Evergreen Hollow back together. It was just one more reason why he loved the town as much as he did.

There was no doubt about it, he'd always made the right decision coming back.

Evergreen Hollow was always going to be his home.

CHAPTER FOUR

Nora's flight arrived in the tiny airport just outside of Evergreen Hollow a little before one in the afternoon, just in time for her to look out of the small plane window to the endless white expanse beyond and wonder for the thousandth time just how big of a mistake she might have made.

She hadn't even *really* made it to Evergreen Hollow yet. It was still two hours by car, which would leave plenty of time for her to ruminate on whether or not this had been a good idea. Although Melanie had promised to pick her up, and Nora felt certain that would involve an endless stream of distraction in the form of catching up.

That thought was definitely a relief.

She retrieved her luggage from the tiny baggage

carousel, keeping an eye out for Melanie as she strolled through the airport to the front doors. The whiff of coffee from the small stand near the entrance was tantalizing, but she knew Melanie would never hear the end of it if she got coffee from somewhere other than The Mellow Mug. Knowing Melanie, she'd bring coffee *with* her.

The sharp, cold Vermont air hit Nora the moment she stepped outside, and she breathed it in, sucking it deeply into her lungs. She'd been outside for two seconds, and she already felt overwhelmed by a nostalgia that she'd left behind years ago. *Was it a mistake to come back?* The question that had been rattling around in her head for hours took root more firmly, growing tendrils that sank in and made her stomach a little queasy.

Only time would tell. There was nothing to do now but find out. And the truth was that she had no idea what else she would have done with her holiday. Sitting in her apartment alone, no matter how beautiful and cozy, would have felt like an even bigger blow.

Nora heard a shout that sounded like her name, and jolted out of her worry to see Melanie jogging toward her, wrapped up in a thick infinity scarf and long-sleeved running clothes. She looked exactly like

Nora remembered her—blonde and pink-cheeked and always in motion, every bit the athletic runner that she'd always been.

Nothing changes here. Not even the people.

To everyone in Evergreen Hollow, that was the *point*. The appeal. The familiarity of it, the friendliness, the knowledge that things would always be the way they had always been. A rhythm to life that Nora had always found suffocating. Her ambition had always felt out of place. Her desire for a certain lifestyle felt like she was spoiled, here. In Boston, it just felt like she fit in.

Melanie waved excitedly, skidding through the snow as she came to a halt in front of Nora—with a steaming cup in her hand, exactly as Nora had thought. She thrust it into Nora's, reaching for one of the bags.

"Here, I'll help you with this. I can grab two, actually. I added weights to my routine, did I tell you? I don't think I did. Not like—a *lot* but a couple of times a week—I think I'm getting some muscle!" Melanie lifted one arm, flexing it playfully as she grabbed two of Nora's suitcases in exchange for the latte.

"I can see it." Nora appreciatively lifted the latte to her lips, breathing in the minty chocolate steam, grateful for the caffeine. "How on earth did you manage to keep this warm? It's two hours from the cafe."

Melanie grinned, hoisting the bags into the back of her Jeep and tapping a finger against the edge of the mug Nora held, her eyes bright. "They're insulated travel mugs. I've been selling them in the shop and they've been *flying* off the shelves—they're freaking magic. They'll keep literally anything hot or cold for up to eight hours. Everyone loves them."

"I'm so happy you discovered them." Nora clutched the mug tighter, taking another sip. "I knew you'd sense it if I drank airport coffee, so I've been hanging on by a thread."

"Only the best for you!" Melanie swung into the Jeep and Nora followed, sinking back into the passenger side as Melanie started the engine. The instant the truck came on, Christmas music flooded the cab, and Nora instantly felt herself react. She very nearly reached out and switched it off.

For all the holiday cheer she'd had the day of her last event before leaving, she felt as if she'd turned thoroughly into the Grinch. The breakup had shattered her holiday spirit, but Nora clenched her hands around the mug, forcing herself not to turn it off. She knew it would ruin the mood in the car, and she didn't want to do that. Not when Melanie had so eagerly gone out of her way to pick Nora up, insisting that she couldn't get an Uber, that there probably wouldn't even *be* an Uber. Maybe a bad taxi, and she couldn't allow that. Not when Nora was finally coming back to visit.

Nora caught the sympathetic glance Melanie immediately shot her way. The flinch at the music hadn't been missed, and Nora instantly felt guilty.

"I'm really happy you're back." Melanie took her eyes off the road to look at Nora for just a moment before returning them to the highway. "I hope this is going to be good for you. Wipe all that bad stuff away. How long has it been anyway? I've lost count."

It wasn't meant to make her feel guilty, Nora knew, but she felt a small stab anyway. "A really long time," she admitted, taking another sip of the coffee. Her family and Melanie had been to visit her in Boston over the years, but she hadn't returned the favor. No matter how many times she told herself she would, she kept putting it off. "There was that one time, right after graduation. So, like, twelve years? A little more?"

That one time had been enough to make her keep pushing off a return, again and again. She'd felt so stifled as soon as she'd come back, trapped within the town limits like a bird in a cage. No one had understood why she'd gotten a degree in event planning or why anyone would spend tens of thousands of dollars on throwing a party instead of using a perfectly good rec center or church hall.

It didn't make sense why Nora's clients would hire Michelin-starred chefs instead of having family cater their graduation or reunion or even a wedding reception. Why flowers cost as much as an entire car for some of the residents in Evergreen Hollow. It felt to Nora like they were all judging her for having dedicated her life to something that to them, seemed shallow and wasteful and spoiled. And she felt like they didn't understand how happy it made her, to turn all that extravagance into something beautiful and elegant and memorable.

I wonder if I'll feel the same way now. Nora bit her lip, looking out at the snowy expanse stretching out on either side of the road, studded with maples. That worry that it might have been a mistake to come crept in again, but Melanie glanced over at her, seemingly picking up on her friend's worry.

"Was it too hard to get off work? I know the holidays must be busy."

"Not as much as you might think. Mostly winter weddings, and New Year's Eve parties. But I managed to get my work covered." It hadn't been *as* easy as Nora made it sound. Her years of never taking off work had created an expectation that her boss hadn't been thrilled to see change. But she'd had the paid time off, and in the end, she'd been there long enough that she had the ability to put her foot down, just a little. "January is always a slow month, so I can catch up when I get back on any of the busy work that might pile up."

And not think about my canceled wedding. She shoved the thought out of her head, hard. She'd had January penciled in for months as the time she'd use to really dig into wedding planning, come up with all the options and lay them out for Rob so he could just tell her what he liked best and help her narrow it all down. She'd even considered trying to arrange a little getaway for them, something less remote this time. Maybe even a tropical vacation where they could both get a tan and work on the wedding planning with a drink in hand.

The whole time she'd been dreaming about that, he'd been thinking of his escape route from their relationship.

"Tell me about busy work." Melanie shook her head. "I've got a few employees home on Christmas break from college, but I feel like every day there's more to do. And taxes coming up—it's always something. I feel like I can never entirely get through my to-do list."

Nora felt a smile spreading across her lips, the first she'd managed in a while. "I love lists. Maybe I can help."

Melanie swatted her, the Jeep swerving a little. "You're on *vacation*. I know that's a foreign word to you, but you're going to learn it while you're here. I didn't ask you to visit so I could put you to work."

Nora threw up her hands. "I'm just saying. I love paperwork."

"I know you do."

Nora felt herself relax a little, bit by bit, as they approached Evergreen Hollow. For all her worries, it was good to see her friend in person again. To laugh and tease each other, the way they used to. It had been *years* since she'd seen Melanie, years that had slid by so quickly she would have sworn it hadn't been all that long—but now that she was here, she realized just how much time really had gone by.

Too much.

This, at least, was a very good reason to have come back to visit.

Still, Nora felt that nervous clench in her stomach again as the town started to come into view.

Another wave of nostalgia hit her—she recognized it all. All of the snow-topped roofs and rustic storefronts and the one black-and-cream stone restaurant that served as the place for a fancy night out in Evergreen Hollow, Marie's. They'd gone there for dinner when she'd come back after graduation, and she had spent the entire night mentally comparing it to her favorite three-star haunt in Boston. Another swell of guilt gripped her at the memory.

Melanie kept driving through town toward The Mistletoe Inn—the small bed and breakfast that Nora's parents had owned and run since before she was born. Her sister Caroline helped run it now, and Nora felt another quiver of unease at the thought of Caroline. She knew very well that Caroline was going to be the hardest sell on her brief return home. Caroline wasn't going to just let her wave away her absence for the last several years.

As Melanie pulled into the driveway, Nora saw the inn, exactly as she remembered it. It was quaint and homey, a large log cabin-style building with a gabled shingle roof and a large wrap-around porch. Snow was built up on the sides of the pathway leading to the porch steps, where it had been shoveled out of the way.

The place was fully decorated for Christmas. Lights were strung along the rooftop edge and the porch, a cluster of reindeer stood out in the snow, and the trees out front were strung with more lights. Holly bushes brightened up the space next to the stairs up to the porch, and a huge wreath hung from the front door, a glimmer of a beautifully decorated tree visible through the front window.

A rush of memories hit Nora as she sat there, unable to move from the Jeep for a moment. She'd helped decorate this place with her parents and sisters, year after year, Christmas after Christmas.

It had stayed almost entirely the same, even down to the huge snowman sitting near the edge of the front yard, holding a rustic wooden sign with ***Evergreen Snowman Festival*** written in curly dark green script across it.

She remembered making that snowman every year with her mother and sisters. It had been fun when she was a kid—something that she looked forward to, along with the homemade hot chocolate her mother always made afterward—but now she looked at it and thought that it seemed dated.

Surely putting out the same decorations, year after year, with that sign that had begun to look weathered around the edges in a way that wasn't as aesthetically pleasing as one might think, seemed like a tired tradition.

Nora knew if she said that aloud, she would be met with almost universal disagreement. That sameness, that sense of familiarity, was what everyone in Evergreen Hollow clung to. It was part of what had driven her away.

The front door opened with a jingle of bells attached to the wreath hanging from it, and Nora's mother hurried out, a bright smile spreading across her face.

Nora slid out of the Jeep, her mother's appearance jolting her out of her momentary paralysis. Rhonda had had a hip replacement years ago, around the time that Nora moved to Boston. It hadn't given her any trouble in the many years since, but the idea of her going down icy steps in a hurry to see her daughter was enough to propel Nora out of the Jeep and toward the porch.

Rhonda was already at the edge of the steps by the time Nora made her way there. She was a petite, bright-eyed woman, still graceful from her career as a ballerina in her younger days, her frame still delicate.

Nora saw the necklace that she always wore dangling against her bright-red wool sweater—three hearts with the initials of each of her children on them—and Nora felt that wave of nostalgia again. Her mother was as unchanged as everything else— still the same short gray bob with a hint of curl to it, still the complete lack of makeup on her lightly lined face, still the commitment to Christmas-colored sweaters for the entire month of December.

It was all the same, and Nora couldn't decide if it made her feel comforted, or made her want to run. She was leaning toward the latter.

"Nora!" Rhonda wrapped her arms around her daughter, squeezing tightly. She smelled of vanilla and sugar—not anything store bought, but the distinct scent of baking. "And Melanie! Thank you so much for getting her from the airport. I would have done it myself," Rhonda added, detaching from her daughter briefly to look her over, "but Melanie insisted. It was important to her, so I figured I would make sure things were ready here for you. Your room is all made up, and there are cocoa and cookies inside! Melanie, you should stay for a little while too. The shop will manage without you for another hour."

Melanie shot Nora a glance that Nora fully understood. No one turned down cookies when Rhonda offered them, or any of her hospitality for that matter. There was nothing in the world that gave Rhonda Stoker more joy than doting over guests at the inn, and neither of the girls would have done anything to deny her that.

"Where's Dad?" Nora asked, as she sank down into one of the armchairs by the fire in the small living room.

The tree that she had spied through the window outside was decorated exactly as she remembered, with a handful of new ornaments sprinkled in. The living room was warm and cozy, with a long sofa in front of the fire piled with soft-looking pillows and plaid wool throw blankets, and a smattering of equally soft armchairs divided into groups of two and three, with small wooden tables tucked between them for drinks or food to be set on. One chair was near the tree, an extra pillow on the seat, and Cloud —the inn's fluffy gray cat—curled up on it asleep.

"Out fishing." Rhonda waved a hand. "He'll be back for dinner, he said. He was going to stay and wait for you to get here, but I told him to go on, we'd have some time just us girls to catch up. Now, you sit down and get comfortable, and I'll be right back."

'Cookies,' as it turned out, meant a China platter of sweets that Rhonda set on the table in front of the three chairs, along with three steaming mugs of hot cocoa with fluffy marshmallows floating on top. Nora knew the hot cocoa was a mix Rhonda would have made herself, combined with local milk, the marshmallows from the confectionery in town. If it could be made, grown, or bought in Evergreen Hollow, the residents always preferred it. Local was better, as far as they were all concerned.

"These look amazing," Melanie gushed, reaching for a piece of maple sugar candy. The pile of candy was nestled between pillowy snickerdoodles and a handful of delicate-looking meringues, along with fudge brownies topped with thick chocolate icing and traditional sugar cookies decorated by hand. "I know why I can't come by all that often, I'd be ten pounds heavier by the end of Christmas! No one makes sweets like you do, Mrs. Stoker."

Rhonda laughed, settling into her chair next to Nora and reaching for one of the meringues. "Well, I spent all that time in my younger years wishing I could eat sweets. Ballet is so unforgiving when it comes to that. So now, I can eat what I please. And I love seeing others enjoy it."

Nora knew exactly how sincere her mother was on that point. Running a bed-and-breakfast was no small task. There had been times over the years when both her father and her sisters had encouraged Rhonda to remove the "breakfast" facet of The

Mistletoe Inn, offering maybe just something continental—a spread of muffins and tea—or let the guests fend for themselves altogether. But Rhonda had always refused, saying that cooking a big morning meal for the inn's guests was one of the things that made her the happiest.

She wondered, sometimes, what would happen when the inevitable day came that Caroline took over entirely. She couldn't imagine her no-nonsense older sister enthused over spending hours in the kitchen preparing breakfast and treats for the guests, when there were plenty of more efficient options. But Nora also knew that Caroline loved the inn. She wasn't sure, exactly, what plans Caroline had for it in the future.

After so long away, she wasn't entirely sure that it was her place to ask.

"I'm so excited to have you here for the holidays." Rhonda beamed at her daughter. "I thought you would be spending it with Rob's family. It's such a wonderful surprise."

Nora swallowed hard, the bite of brownie suddenly sticking in her throat. She took a gulp of hot chocolate, nearly burning her mouth in the process. She wanted to savor it all, since she never let herself have treats like this at home—and even if she did buy sweets, they were never quite the same.

But the mention of Rob made her nearly choke.

"We broke up." She blurted it out, wanting to get the news out as quickly as possible, and get past it. "He broke off the engagement. But really, it was a long time coming. We agreed..." She swallowed again, not wanting to lie. "Things just weren't working out," she finished lamely, setting down her cocoa again. "But I'm okay, really. Better I know now than after we're already married. I can cancel wedding plans."

Melanie nodded, and Rhonda smiled. "That's a very wise way of looking at it," she said gently. "You'll have such a nice time here too. We have so much to catch up on. You won't even think about it. There's nothing like the holidays to brighten everything up."

Nora saw the shine in her mother's eyes, that building excitement that she knew could overflow into ideas that hadn't been discussed yet. "Don't get any big ideas," she warned, softening the words with a smile. "I'm not moving back. I'm just here to regroup and get my head on straight. I still have my job and apartment and everything back in Boston.

And I love it all. I might have moved there for Rob, but I don't have any intention of leaving."

"Well, we're happy to have you for as long as we can have you." Rhonda reached out and patted her daughter's hand. "There's no pressure. I just want to enjoy every minute I get with you. And you'll be here for the festival!"

Privately, Nora thought that she couldn't care less about the festival. She hadn't enjoyed it since she was a child, and as an adult, it seemed kitschy and even a little tacky, highlighting the rustic homeliness of the town that felt so suffocating to her. The festival had grown over the years, but the overall feeling of it never really changed. But she smiled anyway, nodding because she knew it would make her mother happy to see her interested. Her mother's joy was infectious, and Nora found herself relaxing, just a little.

Despite all of her reservations, it was good to be back.

* * *

Aiden rubbed his gloved hand over his face, trying not to look too closely in the direction of the floodlights that had been set up so that the work on the roof could continue past nightfall. He, Joe Woodham, his close friend Blake Monroe, Avery Smith, Colin Bailey, and a few of the other guys around town who were handy had all stayed long past when they'd normally be done working to try and get more progress on the event center's roof. It wasn't the safest idea, being up on the rafters with the cold and damp in the dark, but the floodlights offered enough of a glow that they could manage it.

With the festival coming up, they were all feeling the time crunch. He wanted to keep things moving, to not let everyone down. He knew Bethany would try to find another space to host it if she had to, but he didn't want to see the look on her face when that news was delivered, when the festival had to be changed for the first time in who knows how many years. Tradition was what kept the town going, a part of their closeness, the sense of family that made living in Evergreen Hollow such a special experience. He was going to do everything in his power to make sure that nothing affected that.

"We should probably pack it in soon." Avery set down a hammer, leaning back on his heels as he looked at the shingles. "I know my wife is going to have dinner waiting, and I'm getting hungry. Temperature is dropping too."

"We've made good progress." Joe glanced over at Aiden. "I think we can pick up bright and early in the morning. As long as the weather holds and there isn't another big storm, we should have it all fixed by the time the festival happens."

"Someone tell the weatherman to predict sunshiny skies," Colin joked, climbing carefully down the ladder. The heavy sound of his boots crunching through the snow echoed in the quiet night as he went to toss his tools back into the box. "It'd be rare for a storm like that to happen twice in as many weeks. I don't think we have anything to worry about."

"Certainly hope not." Blake looked over at Aiden. "Want to grab a beer at the grill or something?"

"Normally I'd say yes, but I think I'm going to call it a night. I want to be up early tomorrow to get started." Aiden headed for the ladder, careful of any icy spots. "Give you a raincheck on that."

"Sure thing." Blake followed him down, the guys all packing up and setting the tools and materials safely inside the entry of the event center before breaking off, heading to their respective vehicles.

Aiden hung back for a moment as the sound of starting engines filled the crisp air, one hand on the hood of his truck as he surveyed the progress they'd made so far. It filled him with a sense of satisfaction, seeing it come along so well. It always made him feel warm and at home, when everyone came together like this to see things fixed. There wasn't any better feeling that he could imagine.

He hoisted his toolbox, setting it in the back of the truck before sliding into the driver's side and turning the engine on, letting it warm up for a minute. The floodlights had all been turned off, leaving the building a dark silhouette in the crisp snow, the glow of the moon faintly illuminating it. His back hurt and his hands had a few new callouses from the long hours he'd been pulling, but it would be all worth it when the festival went off without a hitch.

Aiden drummed his fingers against the steering wheel as he drove back to his house, humming along with the Christmas carols on the radio. He turned past The Mistletoe Inn, glancing over at it—the cheery decorations were always a pleasure to look at—and did a double-take when he thought he saw someone familiar sitting on the front porch, along with Rhonda and Donovan Stoker.

It can't be. He could have sworn he caught a glimpse of Nora Stoker, her dark hair loose around her shoulders, wrapped up in a cream-colored wool peacoat. His heart skipped a little in his chest at the thought, and he slowed down a little without thinking, but he couldn't fully make her out. He didn't want to stop driving altogether and get caught staring, and it was impossible to see for sure.

It was equally impossible to get her out of his head, once the thought of her entered it.

Oh, wow, if it really is Nora...

He hadn't seen her in years. They'd gone to high school together, like every other teenager growing up in Evergreen Hollow, but she'd never so much as glanced his way in all those years. On the rare occasion that he had overheard some conversation she was a part of, it was always abundantly clear that she couldn't wait to leave town. He'd seen her back once since he'd heard she had up and moved to Boston after college, but that had been... what, eleven or twelve years ago?

A long time for someone to be gone, and then suddenly pop back up again.

Surely it wasn't her.

Aiden turned into his driveway, the trip having gone by in a hurry while he was lost in thought. It had to have been one of the inn's guests. It wouldn't be unusual for someone so sleek and polished to be staying at The Mistletoe Inn. Plenty of people from Boston and New York came to enjoy the rustic charm of Evergreen Hollow, especially around the holidays.

He tried to shake off the little bubble of excitement that rose in his chest at the thought of it being Nora, kicking the snow off his boots as he opened his front door.

But a small part of him couldn't help thinking that if there was a chance that Nora Stoker had decided to come home for the holidays…

Well, wouldn't that be something.

CHAPTER FIVE

Nora hadn't set an alarm the night before, against all of her instincts, telling herself that she was on vacation. She woke up at eight-thirty, a full hour and a half later than she usually woke on a Thursday morning, and she told herself that was a small victory.

The sight of the cozy bedroom that she was staying in, first thing in the morning, was so quaint and beautiful that she couldn't help but smile in spite of herself. The bed was a birch four-poster, with soft cream-colored sheets and a buffalo-plaid duvet, made up with four soft pillows and a dark green throw blanket at the end of it. The nightstand and dresser matched, a juniper-scented candle next to the bed, and a wing chair with another green wool throw and a buffalo-plaid pillow next to the large window. The floor was dark, well-cared-for wood, with a sheepskin rug next to the bed, and it all felt so warm and comforting that Nora didn't even miss her apartment at home for a moment.

She'd decorated that to her tastes, made it into a haven, but this reminded her of something else. A feeling of family, of nostalgia, that she thought she could indulge for just a little while.

Then she looked down at her phone, picking it up to see if Rob had called or left her any messages, and her spirits sank again when she saw there was nothing.

He hadn't so much as checked in to ask her what her plans for the holidays were now, if she was staying in Boston, if she was okay. She'd nearly called or texted him a dozen times since he'd ended their engagement, stopping herself every time, but there hadn't been so much as a single message from him. So far as she knew, he didn't even know she'd gone back to Evergreen Hollow for Christmas.

Nora let out a sharp breath, dropping her phone back onto the nightstand and throwing back the covers. She slipped her feet into the fluffy slippers that had been waiting by the bed for her when she came up the night before, trudging to the attached bathroom in her pajamas. The bathroom was equally small and cozy—a standalone shower in one corner with a clawfoot tub below a small window, and a black granite countertop with rustic wooden cabinets below it. There was a porcelain bowl sink and an oval mirror above it, a guest basket filled with soaps and bath oils and lotion set neatly on the countertop next to a wooden shelf with folded towels and washcloths, all in dark green.

Nora rifled through the basket, taking out a bottle of eggnog-scented shower gel. She'd brought her own shampoo and conditioner from home, but she thought she should try to use at least some of the products that her mother went to so much effort to put out, just in the spirit of being home.

She bit her lip as she stepped into the shower, trying not to think about Rob. She hadn't cried over it since she'd boarded the plane to Vermont, and she told herself not to start crying over him again now. There was no point. It wouldn't change anything, and he wouldn't know or care. He didn't deserve her tears, and she knew both Melanie and her mother would say the same thing, if they saw her in the shower fighting back the wave of sadness that washed over her.

Getting ready for the day felt strange. She

rummaged under the sink for a blow-dryer, finding one of the small hotel-sized ones that would take ages to dry all of her thick, long hair. She set about the task anyway, clipping up most of it atop her head and going section by section, spraying heat protectant and detangler until her hair was smooth and straight and glossy.

At home, she would have had a half-dozen more products scattered across her counter, along with makeup, but she'd decided to make an effort to tone things down a little back home. She knew exactly the sorts of looks she would get if she hung out in Evergreen Hollow with perfectly straightened hair and a full face of makeup, but there was only so much she could do. Even with her hair just blow-dried, her face bare except for her thorough skin-care routine, and her skinny jeans and cashmere sweater, she looked out of place.

She looked too polished, too perfect. It was a look she'd spent years cultivating, with expensive skin care and designer clothes and a hairdresser that she trusted with her life to keep her grays covered and her hair perfectly cut and colored, but here it stuck out. The sweater was obviously expensive, the jeans an even dark wash that screamed designer, the tiny diamond studs in her ears that she had thought were subtle when she packed them shouting that she no longer belonged here.

Nora bit her lip, walking back out to the bedroom and sinking back down onto the bed to pull on her black velvet ankle boots—shoes that, she realized now, were entirely out of place in the heavy Vermont snow. The town did their best to keep paths cleared, but it wouldn't be as efficiently done as it was in Boston.

She'd brought Hunter boots, and although designer snow boots seemed to once again scream that she no longer belonged here, she swapped her velvet booties out for those instead.

At least she'd look as if she tried.

She headed down the stairs, the scent of breakfast wafting up as she walked into the living room. The dining room was just past that—a room bordering the kitchen with a long, well-loved wooden table covered in a holiday runner and set with the China that the inn had been using for as long as Nora could remember. A gingerbread-scented candle was burning on the sideboard, and a large window took up most of one side of the room, looking out to the property beyond. It was a vista of pristine snow, dotted with more maples, a winding stone path leading out through them for anyone who might want to take a post-breakfast walk.

There were only three other guests at the table, Nora noticed. An older couple sitting side by side, sipping coffee and talking quietly as they looked out at the view, and a woman who looked to be in her mid-twenties, typing away at a laptop with a mug next to her. Someone on a writing retreat, Nora thought, as she walked quickly through the dining room before anyone could say anything to her, and into the kitchen.

Rhonda was at the stove, pulling what Nora saw was a pan of mini quiches out of the oven. She set them on the counter, beaming at her daughter as Nora walked in.

"So that's what I smelled. They look delicious."

"I made your favorite. Ham and cheese. Here, I'll get you one. No, sit down. You don't need to do anything." Rhonda waved a hand as she reached for one of the China plates, scooping a quiche onto it and walking to the smaller table that Nora had sat down at with the plate and a glass of fresh-squeezed orange juice. "I'll get you some coffee. Creamer?" Ever the caretaker, she was quick to get breakfast together before Nora could protest that she could serve it herself, and not put her mother out.

"Whatever you have is fine." Nora picked up her fork, cutting off a piece of the quiche. It was soft and smelled incredible, and she could remember what it would taste like before she even took a bite. The ham and eggs and cheese would have come from a local farm, and Rhonda had perfected the recipe over years. "I'm not picky."

Rhonda laughed, taking a bottle of creamer out of the fridge and pouring a little into a mug of coffee. "We both know that's not true. But there's nothing wrong with it." She poured herself a cup too, coming to sit down for a moment next to Nora.

"The guests must either eat early or late these days," Nora remarked, taking another bite of the quiche. "There was hardly anyone in the dining room. Oh wow, I forgot how good this was."

"I'm sure it can't live up to some of those fancy brunch places in the city, but I do my best." A shadow briefly passed over Rhonda's face. "Business has been a bit slow lately."

Nora looked up at her mother, surprised. She had no idea that things had slowed down at the inn, and she felt a sharp stab of concern. The holiday season was usually one of the busiest. Evergreen Hollow had made itself into something of a Christmas destination, the perfect picturesque

Vermont town, and Nora had been expecting to come downstairs to a full table. But now that she thought about it, it had been odd that the living room had been so empty the night before too—no guests sitting by the fire and playing chess or checkers or reading, no one sipping cocoa or a glass of mulled wine.

She took another sip of her coffee, on the verge of asking how long things had been that way, when the back door opened and Nora saw her eldest sister kicking snow off of her boots.

The moment Caroline stepped into the kitchen and saw Nora, Nora could feel the tension starting to thicken in the air.

All of it came rushing back in an instant, tightening Nora's chest—all of the reasons for their estrangement and why she'd been so hesitant to come home and deal with her sister on top of the hurt from her breakup. It had been more than a decade since their falling-out, since Caroline had called Nora selfish and thoughtless for taking off for Boston with Rob instead of staying home and helping with the inn after their mother's surgery, but it still stung as if the argument had happened yesterday.

There had been times when Nora had wanted to

reach out. But *Caroline* never had, and Nora couldn't make herself be the first one to do so. Like so many other things dealing with 'back home', she'd told herself that she would deal with it later, put it off for another day. Days turned into weeks, months, and years—and now she was sitting at the small family table in the kitchen, looking at her sister's blue-eyed glare from across the room.

Caroline's gaze swept over Nora, and Nora felt her cheeks burn. It was exactly the look she'd been imagining when she got ready. Caroline looked the same as she always had, if a bit older—no nonsense, with her slightly graying brown hair pulled back in a low ponytail and not a speck of makeup highlighting her narrowed blue-gray eyes. She was the tallest in the family, nearly as tall as their father, and it made Nora feel even smaller than usual, even from a distance. She was wearing the same faded, worn jeans that she always had, a flannel with the sleeves rolled up to her elbows despite the cold, and a pair of duck boots that had hints of chicken feed still clinging to the laces.

She had always been the most casual of the sisters, but Nora felt the difference more glaringly than ever with that one sweeping look.

Caroline had never made any secret of what she

thought about Nora and her preferences, or the life she chose—but it had all come out more bluntly than ever in that final argument.

All you want is glamor and money. It's all superficial, and you can't even see it. Clothes that cost too much and hours spent on things that don't matter, a job throwing parties that could be done for a fraction of the cost with a lot more love. You're leaving people who love you for a soulless city, to work at the beck and call of people who don't care a thing about you. Here, at least your work is appreciated. Everything you do matters. It matters to your family most of all. But you don't care about that. You just care about looking like you walked out of one of those magazines you spent all your allowance on when we were kids.

Nora could still hear it all, ringing in her ears. Caroline had always thought she was silly and superficial. That the hard work that Caroline had done since they were teenagers, caring for the animals and learning how to do maintenance around the place from their father and always being the one to take responsibility meant that she was the one who knew what was right. That Nora running off to Boston meant that she was shirking her duty to her family—and that her eagerness to get away was a fundamental flaw.

They'd gotten into another fight, that one visit home. Nora had come back, in her designer clothes and with stories about her job in Boston, and Caroline had scoffed at all of it.

I work hard at my job. It's not my fault I like to look good while I do it. Nora had sniped at her sister, tired of being torn down. And Caroline had been just as quick to bite back.

It doesn't matter how much varnish you put on particle board, it's still not real wood. Nothing about your life is real. Everything here is.

Caroline let out a long breath, bringing Nora back to the here and now. "I'm surprised you came back to *lowly* Evergreen Hollow for the holidays," she said finally, the words flat and toneless. "Boston *must* be more exciting this time of year, right?"

A faint, pinched line appeared immediately between Rhonda's brows, a familiar sight that Nora was used to, when she and Caroline were in the same room. "Be kind to your sister, Caroline," Rhonda murmured gently. "Just enjoy having her back, all right? There's no need to be rude to each other. Plenty of time has passed."

Nora set her fork down, her appetite gone. She'd forgotten, ever so briefly, how difficult it was to be in the same room with her sister—and now she was kicking herself for having forgotten it at all. That twisting feeling in her stomach returned, making her wonder once again if this had all been a mistake.

Caroline let out a sharp breath. "I'm glad you're back here for the holidays with us, Nora." There was some genuineness in her words peeking through, but they were still stiff. Nora could tell that she was still biting back what she really wanted to say.

"I'm glad to be here." Nora poked at the quiche, but she couldn't bring herself to take another bite. A small part of her had hoped that Caroline would have forgotten about the divide between them, but it was still there, as wide as ever.

"See? That wasn't so difficult, girls." Rhonda smiled at both of her daughters. "Now, Caroline, what did you need?"

Caroline cleared her throat, glancing once more at Nora before turning to her mother. "I was looking for Dad. He has some of the tools I need to fix the water heater."

Despite herself, Nora couldn't help but be impressed. Caroline had always liked learning from their father, but it was clear she'd become even more handy in the years since Nora had left. She just wished that Caroline didn't have to be so smug about it, as if she were the one holding everything together, while Nora did nothing at all with her life.

Just because my life isn't what she would want doesn't mean it's worthless. Nora pushed the thought down, trying to stuff the resentment down along with it. She had never wanted to run the inn, and Caroline had always seemed to think that was a fault. That *not* wanting to own a bed and breakfast was somehow a character flaw.

"Go check out front," Rhonda said, still looking at her older daughter. "I think he might be on the porch." She glanced back at Nora as Caroline walked away. "*Try* to get along with your sister. I know she can be difficult, but she means well. She's just trying to look out for us all."

Nora let out a short, sharp breath. "I'll try. But I can't make any promises."

"That's all I ask." Rhonda got up, reaching for the plates, and Nora started to stand too.

"Is there anything I can help with?"

Rhonda shook her head, waving a hand at her daughter. "Don't worry about it. Go see Melanie at the coffee shop, why don't you? Get reacquainted with Evergreen Hollow a bit. It's been so long since you've been back."

"All right." Nora nodded, leaning in to give her

mother a hug and a kiss on the cheek. Whatever concerns she had about being home, she was glad to see her mother again.

She went to get her coat, drawing in a deep breath. It was time to make herself at home again. As much as she'd be able to anyway—considering the fact that she had no intention of staying.

Not past the holidays anyway.

CHAPTER SIX

There was no better place in town to grab a quick bite to eat than Rockridge Grill. It was good enough that it drew people from miles around, even outside of Evergreen Hollow.

Part of it was the atmosphere—a rustic, homey space with a knotted pine floor, wide booths and lacquered-wood tables, the windows topped with cheerful red-and-white valances. But more than anything else, it was the food. The lunch menu was written on the chalkboard above the pickup counter, along with the card-stock menus on every table, and Aiden glanced at it as he walked up. He'd ordered an elk burger with parmesan fries—a good, hearty lunch with cheese, onion, pickle, and the grill's special sauce on it. But the menu for the day had him considering coming back for dinner.

There was the usual homemade lasagna, a beef and vegetable stew, a pork belly BLT, and the special for the day: bacon wrapped venison with mashed potatoes and roasted root vegetables. He considered himself a decent enough cook, but it couldn't match up to that, especially that last item.

The bell over the door chimed as he waited for his order to come out from the back. He glanced over to see Leon's wife walking in—Bethany Woodrow—her black scrubs covered in pet hair. He smothered a smile at the sight. No matter what Bethany wore, it was *always* covered in fur. She ran Pets First, the pet shop and groomer in Evergreen Hollow, and the fur followed her like a cloud.

No one held it against her though. Bethany was one of the sweetest, friendliest people in town—and also good to know if you wanted any of the gossip. Even Aiden had to admit to being partial to hearing what was going on from time to time—Bethany knew everyone, and always seemed to know what was happening.

"Hey there." She smiled at him as she walked up to the counter, a huge tote bag slung over her shoulder.

"Hey. Picking up lunch?" Aiden returned the smile, leaning up against the wall. "Any problems with that door?"

"I thought I'd grab something and take it over to the store for Leon and me. And no, the door is perfect. What a relief." Bethany shifted the bag on her shoulder. "I thought the old one was going to drive me mad."

"That's what Leon said." Aiden's gaze shifted. "Hey, what's in the bag?"

Bethany grinned, a mischievous look crossing her face as she reached inside. He didn't know what he'd expected, exactly, but it wasn't what came out. He couldn't help but start to laugh.

It was a *huge* reindeer costume, and surprisingly realistic. He shook his head, still chuckling. It wasn't unusual for people in Evergreen Hollow to go all out for the festival, but this was over the top. Coming from Bethany, it didn't surprise him. She was always enthusiastic this time of year. Evergreen Hollow was full of cheer all around, but it was like an aura around her, from October straight through the New Year. She could power the whole town's Christmas spirit all on her own, if need be.

Aiden rubbed his hand over his chin. "That looks a little big for you."

Bethany grimaced, nodding as she looked at it. "I thought the same thing. I was hoping I could doctor it up so it'd fit." She peered at him, a glimmer of excitement flickering into her eyes. "It would be great for you, though! You should try it on."

Aiden put up his hands, shaking his head. "Oh, no. Not a chance. Besides, my food is going to be up any minute." He looked at the counter and around the corner, hoping it would show up so he could go. This hadn't exactly been in his plans for the day.

"Why not? It's a great idea. If it fits you, no need to take it in. You could be our Rudolph this year." Bethany thrust the costume at him, her face taking on an expression that he knew all too well. Once she got what she thought was a good idea in her head, it was hard to pry it out.

"Really, I'd rather not." *The food, any minute now.* "Besides, you need me out of costume at the festival, just in case something breaks. Your repairman has to be on call."

"Or, you could relax and have fun." Bethany shook the costume at him again. "At least try it on so I can see how it looks. Maybe I'll talk Leon into it if it's good."

"Fine." Aiden let out a long sigh. "I'll try it on."

He was glad the restaurant was all but empty.

Getting the suit on was no easy task. He tried it with his work boots on first, only to find he couldn't get his feet through, and had to disentangle himself long enough to take them off and try again. The food still hadn't come out, so there was no wiggling his way out of what he'd already agreed to, and Bethany had a delighted expression on her face that suggested this was making her whole day.

Finally, he managed to get the ridiculous thing on. "How do I look?" he asked resignedly, the answer already apparent from the sparkle in Bethany's eyes. Probably not *good*, but definitely hilarious.

"Perfect." She clapped her hands. "Now I just need you to agree to wear it at the festival!"

The bell over the door chimed again, and as he saw who walked in, Aiden felt his face flush red.

He'd talked himself out of thinking that he'd seen Nora on the porch of The Mistletoe Inn on his drive home. She hadn't been back for more than a decade; there was no reason to think she'd suddenly show up now. But here she was, in the flesh, walking into the grill with her friend Melanie at her side.

He quickly turned away, hurriedly trying to remove the suit without tripping over himself. His face was still flaming, and he wondered why—it shouldn't really matter to him if she saw him in the costume, no matter how ridiculous it was.

It felt like being back in high school all over again. As if he were once again standing just outside of her view and trying to get her attention by being "cool," or fretting over whether or not what he was doing was too "uncool" to make her notice him. It was an even more ridiculous feeling than the costume itself.

He was a grown man now, he told himself firmly, as he wrestled out of the reindeer costume. He shouldn't care about that—shouldn't even have the thought cross his mind. But just one glimpse of Nora, in that soft-looking hazelnut-colored sweater and dark jeans, brought back the feelings of that old crush as if they'd never left.

Jonathan, the owner and head chef at the grill, stepped up to the window just in time. "Here's your order, Aiden," he said, passing a bag across the counter to him. "Yours'll be up in just a minute, Bethany."

"Thanks," she said sweetly, taking the costume from Aiden as he handed it over. "No rush."

Aiden shoved his feet back into his work boots, glancing over at Nora and Melanie as they sat down in one of the booths. Nora had her back to him, and the two women were deep in conversation. Deep enough that Nora didn't even seem to notice that his name had been called.

Not that it would matter, he thought to himself, taking the bag and turning to go.

Even if she'd heard his name, it probably wouldn't ring a bell for her. They'd run in different circles in high school, and if she had ever noticed him enough to know his name back then, she certainly wouldn't remember it. It'd been too long.

He didn't like that he wished it *would* ring a bell.

Jonathan chuckled as Aiden took his order.

"You wear the reindeer look well," he said offhandedly, a slight smile on his face as he turned away to go back to the kitchen. Aiden laughed, more out of embarrassment than anything else. He was glad Nora hadn't seemed to see him trying on the ridiculous thing in the middle of the restaurant.

Nora and Melanie had tucked themselves into a booth on the far side of the restaurant, and he ducked his head as he walked toward the door, trying to stay out of her line of sight. He wanted to get out of there before she had a chance to say anything—he wasn't sure which would be worse, her remembering him and him having to act like it didn't matter one way or another, or her introducing herself as if they'd never met.

He definitely didn't want to find out.

Aiden strode back out to his truck, lunch in hand, thinking that he'd eat at the construction site and then finish his work for the day. After that, he thought he might go for a hike. The snow was thick enough to make for a nice trek through the woods, and he didn't want to risk seeing Nora again around town.

She made him feel odd, off-balance, like a moony teenager whenever he caught sight of her. It made him want to give her as wide a berth as possible.

Which was as silly as the feelings themselves, because Evergreen Hollow was a small place. Small enough that they were guaranteed to cross paths again before too long, regardless of whether or not he went out of his way to avoid it. But he could at least give himself a little time to come around to the idea of her being back in town.

Enough time that he could hopefully keep his cool, the next time he saw her.

CHAPTER SEVEN

It only took a couple of days after getting back to Evergreen Hollow for Nora to remember just how little there was to do in town. She'd stopped in at the grocery store and The Mellow Mug and the bookstore over the last few days, making the rounds as she tried not to be bored already, and all anyone could talk about was the festival. The ladies ahead of her in the grocery checkout line, a couple of girls looking through romance novels at the bookshop—even every single customer that stopped in at the Mug while Nora was having her coffee talked about it. She thought, wryly, that it was the most exciting thing in town. One event, once a year, and the whole place orbited around it.

She'd planned to go to the grocery store to pick up a few more things for her mother—Rhonda still wouldn't let her do much to help out around the inn, but she could at least do that—and figured she would make a stop at Sugar Maple general store to see about grabbing a scarf. There wasn't anything in the way of actual clothing stores in town, and the general store was her best bet. She'd forgotten how chilly it could get, walking around everywhere. In Boston she would have taken her car, but she didn't have any means of transportation staying in Evergreen Hollow. The only option would have been her dad's old truck, and there wasn't a chance she could drive that. For one thing, she'd long forgotten how to drive a stick shift, and even if she could remember, she didn't trust it in the snow.

There was a certain charm to Evergreen Hollow, she had to admit. Especially this time of year, all the rustic wooden buildings were covered with a frosting of snow, icicles hanging down off of some of the gables, the cobblestone paths cleared off neatly so that the remainder of the snow rose in drifts on either side. Without many cars in town, the snow stayed more pristine, so it didn't get filthy and slushy the way it quickly did downtown in Boston. The town center of Evergreen Hollow could have been plucked out of a postcard.

Nora tucked her gloved hands into her wool peacoat, trying to ignore the few glances she saw tossed her way here and there. Everyone knew and remembered her, so no one said anything rude to her face, but she felt that she knew what they were thinking. She stood out, like varnish on old wood, and she couldn't help it. Back home, her outfit would have been elegantly casual, but here it was blatantly overdone. Her clothes looked expensive, her hair too neat, and she knew she was out of place. It made her wonder every day if she should have just holed up in her apartment for the season.

Rob still hadn't called or texted. She'd given up checking every morning, first thing, to see if he had. There was no point in it, and it just made her feel bad, seeing how easily he'd cut her out of his life. *He* hadn't run back home with his tail tucked between his legs, seeking out some crumb of nostalgia to try and tape his heart back together. He was probably back from his work trip, and she winced as she walked into the Sugar Maple general store, trying not to wonder if Julie was there with him. *That* wasn't a line of thinking that would make any of it better.

She waved to Leon, the owner, as she walked in. He was behind the counter, a Styrofoam container with a slice of lasagna and a salad in front of him, and he held up a hand in return greeting as Nora walked to the back. There was a shelf with folded scarves on it, in between a counter with baskets of handmade soap and a display of makeup, and Nora looked through them, trying to find something she would like. They were all handmade, soft angora and wool, but most of them were brightly colored. Other than a few jewel-toned items, most of her wardrobe was neutrals, and she winced as she looked past a stack that was entirely oranges and yellows.

"See anything you like?"

Nora jumped as she heard Bethany's voice behind her, and quickly turned. "Bethany! I thought you'd be at work."

"I closed up a little early today—no clients scheduled, and I figured any walk-ins can wait until tomorrow. Thought Leon and I could have a late lunch." She stepped back, appraising Nora. "I'm so glad to see you! I'd heard you were back, but I hadn't seen you yet. Leon!" She turned, shouting toward where her husband was sitting. "Did you see Nora's back in town?"

"I waved to her when she came in." Leon waved again, and Nora couldn't help but smile. The homeliness of the town grated on her sometimes, but it was impossible not to like Leon and his wife.

"I'm headed over to Meg's house," Bethany continued. "Meg Lawrence. You remember her?"

Nora nodded. She remembered vaguely, and she figured that was good enough.

"That's the other reason I closed up early, other than grabbing a bite with my old man. There's a planning meeting tonight for the festival. Normally we'd have it at the event center, but the men are still working on getting it fixed up after that storm. Rhonda told you about that, right?"

Nora nodded again. Rhonda had mentioned it—a freak snowstorm that had swept through right after Thanksgiving. She vaguely remembered her mother leaving her a message, letting her know the inn had mostly been unscathed. She felt a flicker of guilt, remembering how long it had taken her to call back.

But she and Rob had just gotten back from visiting his family for Thanksgiving, and she'd had a pile of work, and...

She quickly shoved down the thought of Rob, and focused on what Bethany was saying.

"Anyway, those repairs should be done soon.

They've been making great progress. And we need to get started planning! So we're doing it at Meg's tonight." Bethany paused. "Want to come along?"

Nora wasn't sure if she did, but there wasn't anything else to do. Caroline had been particularly prickly earlier that day, and she thought that the two of them could still use some space from each other. Hanging around the inn would only invite more criticism—too much time alone in her room, too much time not engaging with the guests, or whatever else Caroline thought that she was doing wrong.

"Sure," Nora said, snagging a navy-blue angora scarf off of the shelf. "Why not?"

She went up to the counter, handing Leon her credit card as she wound the scarf around her neck and tucked it into the collar of her coat. It was soft and warm, and she thought that it would be nice to have after she went back to Boston. A little reminder of home.

Bethany's car was parked behind the store, and Nora breathed a sigh of relief as she followed Bethany out. She slipped into the passenger side, not at all surprised when Christmas music flooded the car as soon as Bethany started it up. She didn't object, watching the town slide by as Bethany drove.

It wasn't far to Meg's, which was a gabled two-story brick house with an attic and a porch wrapped around it. There were several other cars out front, and Bethany parked behind a big truck, getting a bag of takeout from the grill as Nora slipped out. She followed her up the stairs, dusting her boots off as she stepped inside.

Nora was pretty sure half the women from the town, if not more, were gathered in Meg's living room. It was a cozy spread—a bowl of spinach dip and crostini sitting on the coffee table side by side with a plate of meat and cheese, and another bowl of what looked like taco dip with tortilla chips next to it. She heard a few of the women exclaim happily when they saw that Bethany had brought takeout, and Nora stood back, shrugging off her coat and hanging it up as Bethany walked past her.

She felt a twist of anxiety in her stomach. Everyone would remember her, and she felt sure that they'd have opinions about her, where she'd been the last several years and what she did, even if they didn't voice them aloud. All the same, she went into the living room, thankfully spotting an unoccupied armchair that would let her sit on her own and listen while everyone else chatted over appetizers and wine.

"Nora!" Valerie, one of the women she

remembered, smiled brightly as Nora walked in. "It's so good to see you. I heard you were back in town."

I think everyone has, by now, Nora thought, but she smiled in return, hoping that everyone had the same bright view of her return. "I'm glad to be back. I just thought I'd make the trip for the holidays."

"Well, we're certainly glad you're here." Meg smiled at her as well, and there was a general murmur of assent around the room, everyone agreeing how glad they were to see her back. Nora hoped it was all genuine.

Bethany returned, an aluminum roasting pan full of takeout white chicken casserole in her hands, and she set it on the table with a spatula and paper plates. "Jonathan said this was the best one yet," she said, cutting herself a piece and adding some spinach dip to the plate as she sat down. "He added green chiles, said it gave it a little kick."

Nora's stomach grumbled, and she got up, going to get a little of the food as well. She was sure that she'd have to get new jeans from the general store if she wasn't careful—she hadn't eaten so much rich food for every meal in years—and the thought made her go easy on the casserole. All the food was so good though, and at least she no longer had to worry about picking out a wedding dress in the spring.

The thought didn't sting quite as much as it had before, and she hoped that meant she was coming to terms with the idea. She'd been excited about planning her own wedding. But surely it would be better, in the future, with a groom who was excited about it too.

Maybe that should go on my checklist, she thought as she sat back down. *A fiancé who actually cares about our wedding.*

"Who do we have for decorations?" one of the women asked, and Meg raised her hand.

"I still have some packed away from previous festivals, and Bethany does too. No reason to let them go to waste. But I know Valerie's daughter is looking to be a florist. Maybe she can make some of the arrangements. Blake can get us a fresh tree. We'll set that up in the middle of the event center, like always. And there are some garlands from the Winter Wonderland dance."

"We'll have the grill do the catering," Bethany added. "Jonathan is working on the menu. He's a little behind on it, with how busy things have been at the restaurant, but he'll pull it together marvelously. He always does."

"For music, the school band will play like they always do. It's such a nice opportunity for the kids,"

Meg added. "And as far as booths, we're looking through all the applications now."

Nora tried to keep the expression on her face blank, picking at her casserole. Her mind was already spinning, going through all the things that *she* would do if she were handling the event planning.

It was a nice idea to let Valerie's daughter practice floral arrangements, but if they didn't come out the way the others wanted, it would be too late to have a professional do it without an outrageous cost. Recycling decorations was a nice idea in theory, but she couldn't help thinking that it was a part of the reason the festival always seemed a little outdated and tacky, and the catering made her wince.

She'd only needed to go to the grill once to know that while it was a good place to eat, it didn't have the staff to handle an event of this size. Marie's would have been a better choice, since it didn't stay as busy as Rockridge Grill, but even they probably weren't as equipped as they should be. Getting an *actual* catering service would have made more sense to her, and been more efficient, with no chance of running out of items or missing anything for the big day.

There was a reason why there were professional services for this kind of thing, Nora thought. Yes, they were more expensive, and they didn't have the rustic touch of everyone in the town chipping in, but it made sure that everything ran smoothly, that everyone got exactly what they wanted, and the vision of the organizers was created flawlessly.

But this wasn't her festival, and she hadn't been put in charge. So she politely kept quiet instead, taking another bite of her casserole as she listened.

"Getting the grill to cater this year was *my* idea." Sabrina Burns spoke up then, pushing her glasses up her nose. Nora recognized her as the owner of the newspaper in town, the *Evergreen Hollow Gazette*. Nora remembered her as someone with a lot of opinions, and she usually didn't like having them argued with. She was nice enough, but Nora remembered that she also liked to pick things apart until they were to her liking.

Probably for the best, then, that she'd decided not to speak up.

"And recycling the decorations. Good for the planet, and all of that." Sabrina beamed. "I think we'll have the best festival yet. I intend to make sure of it."

Nora smiled as a couple of the women glanced her way, nodding along. No one had asked for her opinion, so she thought it was probably better if she didn't give it. But she saw Bethany glance over as well, her face brightening as if she'd suddenly remembered something.

"Nora works in event planning," Bethany said, sitting up a little straighter and leaning forward. "I imagine she must have some great ideas. What do you think of the planning so far, Nora?"

Oh no. I'm not getting dragged into this. She had thoughts, but they were all going to be stonewalled by the fact that a festival in Evergreen Hollow was never going to be like an event in Boston. She was here on vacation, not work, and especially not to work on something that would resist any kind of change.

"I think it's all great," she said, as gently and sincerely as she could manage. But from the looks that flickered over a few faces, she thought she might not have concealed her reservations as well as she thought she had.

Sabrina sniffed, looking slightly annoyed. "Are you sure?" She looked at Nora, raising an eyebrow. "Is it up to the Boston standard?"

It was clear that she was trying to sound playful, but Nora could hear the offense in her voice. Maybe it was because she heard it so often in Caroline's, but she knew she wasn't mistaking it. Sabrina had clearly come up with a lot of what was being planned, and she clearly didn't appreciate Nora not being as enthusiastic as the others.

It was easier to shrug off than Caroline's disapproval though. She didn't know Sabrina all that well, and it was easier not to take to heart. Nora just smiled, taking another bite of her casserole, and stayed quiet. It only took a moment for Sabrina to go back to the conversation, although her tone was still slightly peeved.

Nora stayed quiet for the rest of the meeting, trying to just enjoy being around the other women she used to know. She found herself relaxing a little, the friendly atmosphere reminding her of the parts of living here that she had liked. It could be suffocating sometimes, with everyone knowing each other and so much about everyone else's business, but there were good parts too.

She just didn't think she could ever do it again. She'd always felt on the outside, looking in, and nothing about that had changed.

Coming home for the holidays was one thing. Staying was entirely another. And by the time the meeting was finished and she went to get her coat, she was ready to retreat back to the inn.

The festival would go off exactly as the residents

of Evergreen Hollow planned it. And, since she was no longer one of those residents, Nora saw no reason to involve herself in the planning more than necessary.

It wasn't as if they really needed her anyway.

CHAPTER EIGHT

Aiden set his hammer down for a moment, cracking his knuckles as he looked around the nearly-finished roof. It was past eight on a Saturday, the town mostly quiet except for the sounds of a live band drifting over from Rockridge Grill, and he was still up on the roof. He reckoned he could have come in and finished up in the morning, instead of being out in the evening cold, but they were too close to being finished for him to reconcile it. Better to finish up that evening, since Blake had been willing to stay, and get a full day off tomorrow.

Blake shielded his eyes from the floodlights as he came around, carefully making his way across the roof toward Aiden. "The place looks great." He crouched down, fishing out a handful of nails to start on a few more of the shingles. "Really pulled this together in hardly any time at all."

"Couldn't have done it without such good help." Aiden grinned at his friend. Blake Monroe had been working with him since he'd returned to Evergreen Heights from Albany, and they'd picked back up as if no time had passed at all. It was good to have friends like that, he thought, as he started back in on the shingles as well. Friends who just picked up and carried on, and kept the closeness that you'd had before, regardless of how long you'd been gone. But Evergreen Hollow was good at that. The slow pace and tendency to hold onto the past was viewed as a bad thing by some, but he always saw it as a means to hold onto what mattered. A little time at the trade school in New York hadn't changed anything.

He'd been able to come right back home with no problem at all. Everything had effortlessly felt just like it always had, and there was a real comfort in that.

"I think you were right. We'll finish it up tonight and be good to go." Blake had a satisfied look on his face as he surveyed the rooftop. "Bethany will be happy about that."

"She will." Aiden rubbed a hand over his chin. "The ladies will be able to move all their loot for the festival planning inside in the next day or so. They'll really be able to get the ball rolling then."

Blake glanced at him. "Have you had a chance to make any plans for the festival? Any idea what you might get up to?"

Aiden shook his head, nailing down another shingle. "I never was much for all the festivities. It's a good thing for the town, and I'm no Grinch, but it's a bit crowded and loud for my taste. I usually take a spin around and then go tuck in by the fire, you know that."

"Why were you trying on that reindeer costume at the grill if you're not into all the festivities?" Blake gave him a sly look. "Sounded like you might have a little extra Christmas spirit in you this year."

"How on earth did you hear about that?" Aiden asked, exasperated. He set down the hammer, shaking his head. "I can't believe—"

Blake shrugged. "Word travels, man. You know that." The sly tilt was still on his face. He was clearly getting a kick out of it too.

Aiden just rolled his eyes, refocusing on the roof. He knew all too well how right that was, when it came to a small town. No one sneezed without someone else knowing about it. There was good and bad to that too—it meant everyone could rally for each other when times were hard without anyone having to ask for it, but sometimes it meant being in other people's business when someone didn't need to be. And sometimes it meant a single embarrassing moment could follow a person around.

He was still glad that Nora hadn't seen him in it. She might hear about it—likely, she *would* hear about it—but he told himself that didn't even matter. She wasn't going to remember him from their days in high school—there was almost no chance of that. And he didn't have any reason to care one way or another, he reminded himself.

Aiden shifted down, getting onto the ladder to work on the finishing touches for the edge of the roof. Just as he got himself settled, he heard the door below open, and the sound of feminine voices wafting through.

"Who's there?" Blake called out, and a laugh drifted up.

"Anybody home?" Melanie Carter's voice drifted up—Aiden recognized it. He stopped into her coffee shop now and again—usually he made his own at home, but a good cup that someone else had brewed didn't go amiss now and again. And she had some of the best coffeecake he'd ever tasted, so he treated himself every once in a while.

Blake laughed. "Just a couple of guys finishing up some work. You're welcome to stay and watch. Who you got there with you?"

"Oh, Nora's here." Melanie said it off-handedly, as if it wasn't of any real consequence, and to Blake it probably wasn't. But Aiden felt his foot slip as he jerked in place, nearly slipping in his surprise. He hadn't expected Nora to walk out of the building. It almost felt as if he'd summoned her, just by thinking about her.

Which, of course, was a foolish thing to think, just like every other thought he'd had about her since he'd spied her sitting on The Mistletoe Inn's porch.

In fact, *any* thought he had about her was foolish, because he was very certain she wasn't sparing a single thought for him, nor had she ever.

"You all right, Aiden?" There was real concern in Blake's voice—he must have seen Aiden almost slip—and Aiden waved a hand quickly to fend it off. He was fine, and he didn't want to draw any unnecessary attention to himself. Better to not have to deal with any conversation. He peered down at the shingles, pretending to be intensely focused on how they lined up along the edge of the building's gutter.

"They've put *so* much work into restoring this

place," Melanie enthused from below, talking to Nora. "That storm just really tore through the town. No one was prepared for it. My place had some damage to the gutters and the flower boxes, and the door was almost taken clean off the front of the general store! But this building really got the worst of it. Absolutely wrecked the roof."

"Well, you'd never know now," Nora murmured, and Aiden felt an unnecessary flash of pride. He really shouldn't care if Nora thought he was doing good work or not, but the idea that she'd noticed and approved sent a warmth through him.

"I can tell that they made some improvements too, while they were at it. Long overdue, really, but needing to repair the roof was as good an excuse as any. I bet that was your idea, wasn't it, Aiden?"

Aiden winced, hearing his name. *So much for staying hidden up here on the ladder.*

"Those shingles look different too. Sturdier than what was there before. And that scallop on the edging along the side of the roof—that's so charming. Was that your idea too? I can't imagine Blake came up with it."

Melanie's voice was sweetly teasing, but Aiden had to bite back a sigh. She clearly wasn't going to let his silence go, and it gave him no choice but to descend the ladder and join the conversation.

When his boots hit the snow, he saw that Nora's back was to him. She was looking around, Aiden noted, and she seemed a little disinterested in all of it. Her expression, when he caught sight of her profile, seemed bored.

He couldn't blame her, really. He remembered that Evergreen Hollow had always seemed to be too small and boring for her, back when they were growing up. She had always talked about going off to college and what city she'd move to, with bigger dreams and plans than a small town like this could contain. It would have been more surprising, really, if she'd *taken* an actual interest in any of this. Why would she care about the event center that hosted a festival that she couldn't care less about? He was sure she was just tagging along with Melanie and being polite.

"How quickly do you think we can get the materials for the festival moved in?" Melanie asked, shoving her hands down into her pockets. "Maybe tomorrow evening? Or is that too soon to start with finishing cleaning up in here?"

"Hmm." Aiden tried to think, but it was difficult to focus with Nora standing a foot or so away. He'd had a timeline for when the ladies could take the space back over in his head earlier, but it seemed to have flown away, and there was no getting it back. He scratched the back of his neck, brushing away some wood chips. "I think tomorrow night will probably be fine."

Nora tilted her head, giving the space another once-over. "Does anyone have an extra generator for all the lights?" she asked suddenly. "At the planning meeting, it sounded like they were planning to put up a ton of them. This place is kind of small. You wouldn't want to blow a fuse. That would really put a damper on things."

Melanie shrugged, glancing at Aiden. "Is there an extra generator?"

Aiden cleared his throat. Nora had turned to face him, and his thoughts felt a little muddied. "We do," he said finally. His gaze flicked down to the navy scarf wound around her neck, tucked into the collar of the expensive-looking peacoat she was wearing. He questioned how warm a coat like that actually was, but he couldn't deny that she looked cute in the scarf. It was a thicker, bulkier wool than the rest of her clothing, and it was tucked up beneath her chin, her dark hair spilling out over it.

She was always pretty, back in high school. He'd

noticed it then, for sure. But at some point between graduation and now, she'd gone from pretty to beautiful. It felt hard to take his eyes off of her.

Nora didn't appear to be having the same problem. She looked at him, and Aiden waited for her to say something, but there was no hint of recognition in her face or voice. No inclination that she remembered who he was.

He wasn't sure if that was a relief or a disappointment.

Aiden turned back to the ladder, intending to leave the rest of the talking up to Blake. Company or no, he intended to finish the roof tonight, and get some rest tomorrow. Whatever else they had to talk about, it wouldn't require his input.

He couldn't help listening though. Nora was asking about the size of the space, if there was room enough in the back for keeping food hot, or if someone would need to go back and forth from the grill throughout the day. She mentioned something about a hot cocoa bar, which sounded like a nice idea, but she was concerned with the space for outlets to once again—keep everything warm.

It surprised him that she was giving it any thought at all. She was clearly home for the holidays, sure, but that didn't mean that she needed to have any input about the festival. No one would have blamed her for just taking a back seat and showing up with her family on the appointed day—or maybe not showing up at all. The festival was really a resident and tourist thing, and Nora was neither of those.

He reminded himself, as Nora asked about decorations and whether or not they avoided anything fragile with so many children, that she worked at some fancy ballroom back in Boston. He didn't know much about what she did now, but he'd heard that through the grapevine at least. She probably couldn't help herself, thinking about the details at any venue she was in that happened to be hosting an event.

When Melanie said their goodbyes, the sounds of two sets of boots crunching off in the snow toward a waiting car, Aiden couldn't help but let out a sigh of relief. That had gone better than he'd thought, at least.

"That new girl seems to be a good businesswoman," Blake said thoughtfully, climbing down from his own ladder to put away some of the tools. He hadn't gone to high school in Evergreen Hollow, so he didn't recognize Nora. Aiden didn't particularly feel like catching him up. "Not a bad looking one either," he added wryly.

Aiden didn't say a word, focusing on putting the final touches on the roof, but inside he couldn't deny that Blake was right.

Nora Stoker had grown up to be a very fine-looking woman, indeed.

CHAPTER NINE

Nora was sitting wrapped up on the front porch of the inn, looking out over yet another fresh snowfall and drinking hot tea when her cell phone rang.

She set down her breakfast—a homemade banana muffin leftover from breakfast, soft and airy and still warm on the inside, with fresh butter from the local farm that tasted better than anything she'd had in a long time—and reached for it.

"Hello?" She reached for her tea, wanting the warmth of the mug in at least one hand.

"Nora! How's the small-town life treating you?" Her coworker Linda's voice chirped over the line, bright and cheery. "Have you turned into a snowman yet?"

"Not yet. But I'm sure they'll be rolling me up

into one any day now." Nora tried to sound upbeat, but she felt a flicker of self-consciousness. She knew Linda—and her other coworkers, probably—were expecting her to have more to report. They were probably expecting stories of pink-cheeked sledding days and handsome lumberjacks, bonfires, and plenty of town gossip. But Nora had never been a fan of sledding, bonfires weren't really a common pastime in Evergreen Hollow, and she avoided gossip like the plague. The propensity for it in a small town was, in fact, one of the reasons she'd been glad to escape.

There were few things she liked less than people knowing all of her business, all of the time.

As far as lumberjacks went, Evergreen Hollow still seemed to be in short supply, although there had been that pair of carpenters working on the roof. But one of them had seemed to have eyes for Melanie, and the other had been the strong and silent type.

So... not *her* type.

"Earth to Nora!" Linda giggled on the other end of the line. "Come on, spill the tea. What's it like being home?"

"It's nice," Nora hedged. She truly didn't know what to say. It wasn't as if she'd been helping out much at the inn—her mother seemed insistent that

Nora was on vacation, and Melanie said the same whenever Nora offered help at the coffee shop. Caroline determinedly did whatever she could to keep Nora from sticking her nose *anywhere* near the inn's business. So she'd spent the past days just puttering around town, and everything moved so much *slower* in Evergreen Hollow. Like maple syrup through snow, really, and she couldn't measure her days by her productiveness the way she could back in Boston. There was no hustling out here, and that was really all she knew how to do.

She'd become very good at hustling, and standing still felt a bit like she might vibrate out of her skin at any moment.

"How are things there?" she asked, pivoting quickly to a more comfortable topic. "Nothing has exploded since I left, right?"

"Not at all," Linda assured her. "It's all running just fine. Not so much as a hiccup."

Nora knew Linda meant to be reassuring, but the response made her a little sad. She'd always worked so hard to be *good* at her job, irreplaceable, really— and she knew she was good at it. But it was clear that they didn't actually need her there. It wasn't that she wanted things to fall apart in her absence, obviously, but she found herself wishing that Linda had said things weren't the same without her—or *something* along those lines.

Rob clearly didn't need or want her either. There really was no one in Boston who *depended* on her. No one who noticed her absence acutely, and needed her to come back as soon as possible.

"Don't even worry about it," Linda continued, driving the knife in deeper. "You enjoy your vacation for as long as you want. Goodness knows you've earned it."

"Absolutely." Nora tried to sound cheery, hoping Linda couldn't hear the small crack in her voice.

"Tell me more about this Evergreen Hollow! You never really talked about home. What's it like there?"

Nora leaned back in the rocking chair, tucking her feet in their fluffy Ugg slippers underneath herself. "This time of year, everything really centers around this festival. The 'Evergreen Snowman Festival'. It's this huge event, and people come out of town for it. There's booths and costume contests and everyone goes completely over the top—but at the same time it's really rustic? They're reusing decorations from the school's winter dance, for goodness' sake."

Linda laughed. "It sounds very quaint and fun.

A little haphazard, maybe, but unique. Really sounds like it has that small-town charm."

"It does have that." Nora took another sip of her tea. "It's an every year thing, so they really just have it on autopilot at this point, I think. Although it does sound like there are some new ideas being pitched this year. I've mostly stayed out of it."

"Stayed out of it?" Linda snorted. "Really, you should be the one putting it together, with all your experience. I bet they've never seen a *real* event planner before. I'm joking, obviously," she added in a hurry, as if worried that Nora might take offense.

Nora didn't though. If anything, the comment struck her, taking her aback for a moment. She knew Linda hadn't meant it as a challenge, but she couldn't help having the same thought that had sprung into her head at the meeting—she could spruce up the festival, if she wanted to. It definitely *needed* sprucing up, just like the event center that Melanie had said that handsome carpenter had made improvements to, but everyone seemed perfectly happy to keep doing things the same old way. If anything, they were making it *more* homey and rustic. What it really needed was a facelift, and Nora knew she could do exactly that. *If* she wanted to, of course.

She might not have any interest in staying in Evergreen Hollow in the long term, but she was a professional event planner. She could make *any* event successful, if she wanted to.

"That's an interesting idea." She found that it perked her up a bit, oddly enough, saying it out loud.

Linda laughed, more loudly this time. "I *knew* you wouldn't be able to sit still for long out there. You're too much of a go-getter for that place."

"It does feel like there are forty-eight hours in the day here, instead of the usual twenty-four." Nora bit her lip, picking off another piece of the banana muffin. "I should probably go. My tea is getting cold out here."

"You're sitting *outside*?" The shiver in her voice was palpable. "They really have gotten to you already."

"Just getting a little of that color in my cheeks is all. I'll catch you up later," Nora promised.

Just as she was hanging up the phone and tucking it back into the pocket of her cardigan, she saw Bethany's car pulling into the driveway. Bethany got out a moment later, as Nora was standing up with her plate and tea, retrieving a box of decorations from the trunk.

"Oh, Nora!" She flashed her a smile as she came

up the stairs. "I was going to see what Rhonda's thoughts on these were. Sabrina left some at the store this morning, and I thought we might go through them."

"I'm sure she'd like that." Nora opened the door, letting Bethany and her armful of decorations walk in first. "She's in the living room, going over some things."

Nora tried to hide her expression as Bethany walked past. The decorations themselves weren't even out of the box yet, but Nora could see that they were mismatched, and a little rough around the edges. Definitely not what she would have chosen.

She carried her plate and mug into the kitchen, rinsing them off, and by the time she came back out to the living room, she saw that Bethany had started unpacking them. Rhonda was making small approving noises, but it was clear from the look on her face that she didn't really like them any more than Nora did.

Nora winced, sitting down across from her mother. She didn't want to say anything, but the decorations looked tacky to her. Popcorn garlands, a wreath done up with fake holly covered in gold and silver glitter, and faux mistletoe that would look like plastic even from yards away. That didn't begin to cover the strings of Christmas ball ornaments, or the miniature reindeer that didn't have the best paint job.

"These are—nice," Rhonda said, looking at the string of ornaments. "Where are we thinking of putting these, exactly?"

The question at the end of the sentence was clearly enough to break Bethany. She let out a sigh, sitting back in her chair. "I *know* they're awful." She shook her head, looking between Nora and Rhonda, clearly as aware as the other two women that they all knew the decorations were bad. "But Sabrina is in charge of decorations. And she's so busy with getting the articles together *about* the event for the newspaper that she's not going to have time to replace them with all new decorations. You know how on top of that place she always feels like she needs to be. Really, she'd have to be in three places at once, and you know she can't do that."

Linda's words from earlier echoed in Nora's head. She'd sat back so far and watched, but it was *painful* to see people making such rookie mistakes, when she knew she could step in and easily put it all to rights. They were stumbling around in the dark, and she could clearly see the path forward.

But she knew that wasn't all there was to it.

Linda was right. She was a go-getter, someone who liked to keep busy. She needed a project to focus on while she was in town, or she'd go crazy. She'd tried to give herself one by helping Melanie out with her staffing issues at The Mellow Mug, but Melanie had remained so steadfast in her insistence that Nora couldn't lift a single finger on her vacation that it had come to nothing.

"I'll help," Nora said quickly, and she didn't miss the surprised look that her mother shot her. "I can see about some different decorations. It's easy enough for me to figure it out—I've got tons of experience sourcing this kind of thing. Really, it's no trouble at all," she added, before Bethany could argue.

Bethany didn't seem all that inclined *to* argue. "That's amazing, Nora. Really. You're a lifesaver. If you don't mind, could you stop by the *Gazette* to give Sabrina the good news? Let her know that you're happy to take something off of her plate. And I hear the event center is basically good to go, so if you want to stop in there, you could look around and get some ideas for what you want to do."

The beaming smile on her face felt like a balm to Nora. *This* was what she enjoyed, taking someone's vision and turning it into the best possible version of that.

She returned Bethany's smile. The festival might not have been *exactly* what she had had in mind, when she came back to Evergreen Hollow for the holidays, but she was glad to have something to focus on.

It would make the days pass, at the very least.

CHAPTER TEN

That morning, Aiden had slept in a little past his alarm, and he decided it was one of those days when maybe he should stop in to The Mellow Mug for a coffee and breakfast instead of making it himself. He threw on his usual jeans, sweater, work boots, and heavy Carhartt coat, and went out to the truck, considering the possibility of something sweet. Most mornings he had eggs and sausage, but a pastry sounded nice. A treat, since he'd gotten the work on the event center done ahead of schedule, and could now focus on his other projects for the town.

The coffee shop was quiet when he walked in, empty other than Melanie standing behind the counter, and smelled of roasting beans and sweet, yeasty baking. He walked up to the counter, giving

Melanie an affable smile as he looked up at the menu. There were several holiday drink specials available, and as usual, Melanie had named the signature Christmas drinks after beloved Evergreen Hollow residents.

"Hey there, Aiden," she greeted him. "Is there something I can get for you?"

"An Americano and a cinnamon roll will do it, I think."

The cinnamon rolls looked fresh out of the oven, as big as his hand and dripping with thick white icing. Better than anything that came out of a can, that was certain.

"Coming right up." Melanie scooped a cinnamon roll out, slipping it into a takeout container and handing it to him before going to prep the coffee.

The bell above the door chimed just as Aiden went to stand at the end of the counter, and he glanced over to see Nora walking in.

In any other place, it would have seemed like too much of a coincidence that she kept popping up where he was. But in a town this small, it was just the way things were. He wasn't going to be able to avoid her as long as she was in town, even if he wanted to, which meant he was just going to have to get used to the odd feeling in his chest whenever she showed up. She made him feel off-balance, something he couldn't recall feeling since he was a teenager, and that unsettled him. But it was only temporary, so he could deal with it.

"Hi there." Nora greeted him politely as she walked past, clearly seeing that he was looking at her, but once again there was no real recognition in her expression. She walked toward where Melanie was standing, and he saw her glance back at him briefly, her brow slightly furrowed as if she were trying to place him. Maybe trying to remember if she knew him from before, or not.

He could have said something, but he didn't. It seemed worse, somehow, to remind her that they went to high school together—to point out that he remembered her when she clearly couldn't recall him. He didn't want to embarrass her or be embarrassed himself, so it seemed better to just let it lie.

"Can I get a French vanilla latte? And one of those cinnamon rolls looks good." Nora pursed her lips. "I'm just going to hang out here for a little while, I think. I need to brainstorm some ideas to go over with Bethany about the decorations for the festival."

"Yeah?" Melanie sounded surprised as she scooped out another of the pastries for Nora, putting it on a plate this time. "You and Bethany are knocking around ideas for it?"

"Well..." Nora hedged a little, reaching for the plate. "I might have volunteered to help with them. I guess Sabrina Burns was in charge of it, but she seems to have a lot going on with the newspaper, so I said I'd help. They really are in need of some sprucing up, and it really shouldn't take that much time."

"Really." Melanie raised an eyebrow. "You really can't *not* work for a month, can you?" Her tone was sweetly teasing, but it was clear to Aiden that she was thoroughly surprised by Nora's volunteering.

Truthfully, he was surprised too. Nora was always kind in high school—not snobbish or mean—and she was popular with everyone whose orbit she entered, but it had always been clear that she was chomping at the bit to get out of Evergreen Hollow. She hadn't even made it through the summer before leaving for college—he vaguely remembered that she'd taken off on some charity trip, really just an excuse to get away.

It had meant that even though he had wanted her to like him, in the way any teenage boy does with a girl he has a crush on, he'd always really known it was hopeless. He was a small-town boy through and through, devoted to Evergreen Hollow and its residents, and if he was ever lucky enough to have a family, he'd want to raise his kids in Evergreen Hollow and give them the same kind of life he'd always had.

He'd always felt as if he was never going to measure up in Nora's eyes. She wanted out, and he wanted to stay, and that was a gulf between them that there was no means of bridging. He'd never had the courage to go up and talk to her himself of his own volition, and she'd never noticed him. She'd always been way out of his league—with too many others competing for her attention for him to ever have a chance.

"Well, if anyone can spruce it up, you can," Melanie said cheerily as she finished fixing Aiden's Americano. "And you'll have the brand-new event center to decorate too! It's like the start to a whole new festival."

"Don't say that too loudly," Nora said dryly, taking her cinnamon roll and notebook and putting them on one of the tables. "If you say the word *new* too loudly, someone might burst into flames."

That's the charm of this place, Aiden thought, but he bit his tongue.

He took his coffee and his cinnamon roll,

thinking that he needed to get to work, and he would leave the ladies to their planning. He glanced once more at Nora as he gathered his things, and a flash of memory came back to him unbidden—a memory so old that he hadn't thought of it in a long time.

There had been a spring fling-type event at the high school, one of those where the marching band had a little performance and the cheerleaders showed off the moves they'd been practicing and it was all finished up with a pep rally in the auditorium before the football game that night.

It had started to rain mid-afternoon, one of those out-of-nowhere spring storms that blew in before anyone really had a chance to notice that it was on its way. There had been a bunch of picnic tables stacked up out of the way to make room for the band and the cheerleaders, far away from the building, and somehow he and Nora had both ended up using them for shelter.

He still didn't know what she'd been doing out there when the rain had blown in, but he'd been taking a little time away from all the noise, and when the storm had sprung up he'd figured he would just wait for it to blow over before he went inside.

She had grinned at him, he remembered, as she'd slipped under the precarious shelter. The grass had been damp, but she'd sat down next to him anyway, and even though she clearly hadn't had any idea who he was, she'd been nice to him all the same. *Not unlike now,* he thought wryly, as he remembered it.

It had been their junior year, and she'd asked him if he'd had the meeting with the guidance counselor that they'd all been individually dragged to, asking about their plans. They'd been sitting there, watching the rain, and he remembered thinking that his answer probably wasn't going to be what she wanted to hear. But he'd always been nothing if not honest.

"Probably find something I can work at around here," he'd said. "Maybe a teacher, but I really like working with my hands better. I just know I like it here. I don't really want to leave."

"You could teach shop class," Nora had joked, but her laugh had fallen a little flat when she'd seen he was serious. "Or... I don't know. There's not really many options here, are there?'

"I suppose not." He could feel her agitation, shimmering off of her like heat on asphalt. Even now, she couldn't seem to just sit still. "What about you?"

She shrugged, biting her lip. "I want to go somewhere else. A city. Maybe New York, or Boston, or Chicago, even. I want to see more than just this place. But no one else really seems to get that. You'd think my parents would be proud of me for that, but they really just seem disappointed that I don't want to stick around and help run the inn. At least that's what it seems like to me anyway. So who knows. Maybe I'll just stay."

He hadn't known how to feel about that. He couldn't deny that his heart gave a little leap when she mentioned staying, but the dejected tone of her voice told him that wasn't the right feeling. Staying in Evergreen Hollow clearly wasn't going to make Nora Stoker happy. And he felt, oddly enough, that it really mattered if she was happy.

"You only get one life," he said, looking at her, and he remembered thinking she had the biggest, prettiest blue eyes he'd ever seen. He could have looked at them forever, sitting there listening to the patter of the raindrops on the wooden table. "You should live it on your terms."

He'd meant it too. And it seemed like they both had. He'd learned a trade and come back with the skills to keep Evergreen Hollow exactly that— evergreen—and Nora had gone off to the big city and made an accomplished woman of herself. Now she was back here, but she certainly wasn't going to stay around for long.

The memory flooded his chest with warmth, but it was short-lived. Nora had gone back to her chat with Melanie, clearly assuming he was just another customer. She didn't remember him at all.

That afternoon in the rain had been a special memory for him, but maybe it hadn't meant much to her at all. They'd never hung out apart from that anyway, so it made sense that she wouldn't remember it—or him.

A lot of time had passed since then. A lot of water under the bridge. And some really didn't need to be crossed again.

He shrugged off the thought, trying to shake off that lingering feeling of his old crush along with it. Caffeine and breakfast in hand, Aiden headed out the door, going on to his workday ahead.

Hopefully, without any more memories of Nora.

* * *

Fortified with pastry and caffeine, Nora made her way to the *Evergreen Hollow Gazette* after breakfast. She'd made notes of what she thought might suit the event and how they could best arrange them, and she felt more than prepared to broach those suggestions with Sabrina. Really, as busy as the woman was, she felt sure that Sabrina would probably be glad for the respite. Running a newspaper probably took up most of her time.

The *Gazette* was in the same building Nora remembered, a wood-slat building with stonework in the front and the ubiquitous gabled roof, made of dark wood dusted with snow. The path leading up to the dark, green painted front door was made of neatly fitted stones of varying sizes, meticulously cleared off after the last snowfall, holly bushes near the steps. A large wreath hung on the door, with a knocker in the center, but Nora opened it and walked in. It was a business, so the knocker was really just there for show.

It reminded her of most of the businesses in Evergreen Hollow. Decidedly small-town, but neat and respectable.

A tall, auburn-haired receptionist was sitting at the front desk, flipping through a magazine with one hand and typing with the other. She glanced up as Nora walked in, a bored smile on her face. "Can I help you?"

"I'm just looking for Sabrina Burns, if I can snag a minute with her," Nora said politely.

"You can go to her office. Last door on the left." The receptionist pointed, and Nora followed the direction of her finger. It wasn't a large building anyway, so it was hard to get lost.

Sabrina's office door was cracked open, and Nora knocked lightly. "Come in." She heard from inside, and she nudged it open, walking in.

The office was decently large, with a hardwood floor and two tall white-birch bookshelves along one wall. Sabrina's desk was maple, with a black leather seat behind it and two blue velvet chairs on the other side, and an unused fireplace along the opposite wall. Nora noticed there were harvest decorations piled in the space on the iron rack instead of wood—the fireplace clearly never used for its actual purpose— and candles scattered along the mantel along with Christmas cards.

Sabrina looked up, her eyes immediately narrowing when she saw Nora. She gestured brusquely to one of the chairs, pushing her cat's eye glasses up on her nose as she set down her pen. "Is there something I can do for you?" she asked primly, and Nora let out a breath, sitting down.

What on earth did I do to make this woman so prickly around me?

She really couldn't imagine. She'd tried to keep her opinions to herself during that first meeting, and she hadn't even said anything yet to Sabrina about helping out with the festival. Sabrina just seemed on edge around her, and she truly didn't know why.

"Bethany came by the inn, and she was discussing some of the decorations with my mom," Nora began, careful not to bulldoze her way into this too quickly. "They were looking them over, and I thought I might be able to help with some of the decor planning. I offered, since Bethany mentioned you're very busy here, especially this time of year."

"There was nothing wrong with the decorations I had in mind." Sabrina's tone was instantly defensive, and her shoulders stiffened. "They were perfectly well-thought-out and I chose them myself."

"Of course there's nothing wrong," Nora said tactfully. "They were absolutely fine. I just thought I could lend a hand and help out. I'm happy to do it, really," she added quickly. "So many of the others are juggling the planning *and* work, and I'm currently on vacation with a lot of time on my hands. There's no reason I can't pick up the slack."

Sabrina gave her a suspicious look, and Nora charged forward, hurrying to explain further.

"I have a lot of experience with event planning." She chose her words carefully, not wanting to put Sabrina even more on the defensive than she already was. "This time of year is always very busy for us too.

There are plenty of over-the-top wintry decorations, like ice sculptures, or themed trees, or light displays, but it's also really easy to do things both beautifully and economically." Nora could feel herself slipping into a pitch, but it was hard not to. This was her element. What she was good at. She felt a little of the confidence that she'd lost since Rob had dumped her curbside coming back.

"A pinecone centerpiece, for example. Not expensive at all, but with some neutral linens on tables, a little bit of a gold accent, and those pinecones? Rustic chic, right there. And you can't go wrong with greenery, maybe with a bit of berry accents here and there. Simple, but with small festive touches. Red and green plaid bows on the back of wooden Chiavari chairs. Chiavari can run a tab up, so there are less expensive options too. We could definitely do this in a way that wouldn't be excessively costly, but still pretty and seasonal."

Nora could see, throughout her entire spiel, that Sabrina was listening grudgingly at best. Her red-lipsticked mouth was pressed thinly together, her arms crossed over her cream-colored ribbed sweater, but she *did* listen, at least.

"Fine." Sabrina let out a sharp breath. "I'm slammed here. These articles all need proofreading, and our typographer went and sprained her wrist skiing last weekend. As if anyone has time for a vacation right before Christmas. So if it will give you something to do, go ahead and fiddle with the decorations. I'm sure some of your ideas will be just fine."

Nora didn't miss the small dig about her vacation, but she let it slide. It was clear that Sabrina was still on the defensive, but she was on board at least, and that was all Nora really needed. As long as Sabrina didn't stand in her way, she could move forward.

She let it all roll off her back, as she said her goodbyes and headed back out into the chilly Vermont afternoon. It was impossible to live and work in a city like Boston without developing something of a toughness, and she was more than able to handle Sabrina's coolness toward her. She certainly wasn't going to let it mess up her work.

She was determined to make sure the venue looked fantastic.

CHAPTER ELEVEN

Aiden hummed lightly to himself—*God Rest Ye Merry Gentlemen*—as he worked on sweeping up the floor of the event space. The roof was entirely re-shingled, new and improved, and cleaning up the bits of sawdust and leftover detritus was the last task before the job was officially done.

He discarded it all into a black garbage bag that held the rest of the wood shavings and leftover trash, and headed into the front room to get his tools and ladder. He'd load them into the truck, take the bag to the dumpster, and then turn in early for the day. Maybe take another of those hikes, since that recent one had done a lot to clear his head.

Humming the last few bars of the song, he strode into the front room—only to stop short.

Someone was *on* his ladder, almost all the way to the ceiling. His heart stopped for a second before he even saw who it was. It certainly wasn't safe to be up there, unless the person knew what they were doing, and from the look of the heeled boots they were wearing...

"What on earth are you doing?" His heart thudded again as he took another look at those boots, and the shiny fall of dark brown hair, and realized it was Nora. "You shouldn't be up there."

Nora turned sharply to look at him, startled, and the ladder rocked precariously.

"Be careful!" He lunged toward her without thinking, instinct kicking in. He quickly assessed the situation as he moved, looking for where the ladder might tilt if it fell, and how he might be able to catch her without injury.

Nora clung to the ladder, her face going a little pale, but her lips were twitching in a smirk. "*You're* the one who yelled and startled me," she pointed out wryly, as she gingerly started to feel her way for a means to get down.

Any other time, he'd have been quick to banter back, but he couldn't think of a single thing to say. He was too worried. His mind was blank except for thoughts of what might happen if Nora slipped, or if that ladder came down, and his chest tightened all over again. "Get down from there," he said, a little more harshly than he intended, stepping forward. Nora started to climb down as he said it, and he reached for her waist without thinking, intending to lift her down the last little bit.

Nora swatted at his hands immediately, and he noticed her fingernails were done with light pink polish, rounded off in a way that was definitely artificial. Another thing that made her stand out. No one here could make fake nails last a day.

"I'm perfectly capable of safely descending a ladder," she said, making her point as she pushed him away and climbed the last few rungs down. "So long as people aren't *scaring* me and making me lose focus, that is."

She was far too close for comfort. Aiden breathed in, seeking out the relaxing scent of fresh wood and clean floors, and instead got a deep whiff of her perfume. It smelled like vanilla and sandalwood, and he winced inwardly, trying not to think about how good it smelled. He stood a step back, releasing the light grip he still had on her waist, and trying to ignore the allure of her big blue eyes. They seemed, unfortunately, to have the same effect on him that they always had.

He'd always wanted to lose himself in them. It seemed twelve years didn't really make a difference, when it came to that.

"What on earth were you doing so high up?" he asked, trying to distract himself from all of that. And really, it was his business to know what someone might be doing, scaling his ladders when his back was turned.

"Getting ideas for decorations." Nora put her hands on her hips, turning around to look at the space. He noticed she was wearing a red and black checkered shirt—very festive, but as always, it stood out. Anyone in Evergreen Hollow would have been wearing real flannel—thick and not all that flattering to a feminine shape. Nora's shirt was flimsy as tissue paper and looked just as soft, clinging to her over the black tank top she was wearing beneath it, every bit as inappropriate for her surroundings as the high-heeled boots she was wearing. "I thought I should take a look up there to see what kind of hooks I might need to purchase."

Aiden folded his arms over his chest. Nora had been the one on the verge of sliding off the ladder a moment ago, but he felt as off-balance as ever. Face-to-face with her, alone in the event center, it was hard to think straight. He'd thought he was well on his way to brushing off his old crush, reminding himself just this morning of how far apart the two of them were in everything they wanted, but it seemed that only lasted until she physically showed up again. Now he was back to feeling like there wasn't quite enough air in the room when she was standing in front of him.

"So, what I'm hearing is that you want to drill holes in the ceiling I just repaired." He tried to inject some dry humor into his voice, but he wasn't sure if it quite got there. He thought he just sounded a little strangled, and she was likely to misinterpret that.

Nora arched one perfectly-groomed eyebrow. "I know how to make sure the ceiling isn't damaged. I'm a professional event planner. In Boston. I'm familiar with keeping venues pristine."

"If you're so successful doing this in Boston, what are you doing organizing the 'Evergreen Snowman Festival?'"

He regretted the words the moment they came out of his mouth. He'd said it without thinking—because he couldn't seem *to* think around her—and he knew as soon as he said it that it was the wrong thing. But he hadn't expected the sudden hurt that flashed across her face.

He hadn't meant to be rude. But he'd always

thought she was disinterested in the small-town stuff, and he'd never heard or seen anything to suggest he was wrong. It felt like a bit of whiplash, to suddenly see her climbing ladders in pursuit of crafting the perfect festival.

Before he had time to say any of that, Nora seemed to recover from her shock. "I'm just doing this as a favor." There was a crisp tautness to her voice that hadn't been there before. "Now, do I have permission to look around the rest of the place?"

He didn't miss the faint sarcasm that tinged the crisp, businesslike tone. He wanted to go back to a moment before, when she'd been lightly joking and his hands had been on her waist. That felt better than the sudden chilly distance between them, in the wake of his ill-advised comment.

Aiden cleared his throat, stepping back and nodding. Better not to say anything else, he figured, than stick his foot in his mouth again. "You can go anywhere you want, so long as you don't go climbing up on things again." He winced inwardly as he said it, hoping that she didn't take that the wrong way too. He wasn't trying to tell her what to do, exactly; he was just worried about her.

Nora walked past him without a word. She cast her gaze around the space again, standing there thoughtfully, and then turned back to look at him. He saw, with surprise, that there was a softer look on her face than before.

"You look extremely familiar." She cocked her head slightly, looking at him in an appraising way that made him go warm all over, despite the chill in the room. "Do we know each other?"

Aiden's heart lurched into his throat. From the moment he'd driven past The Mistletoe Inn and thought he saw her sitting on the front porch, he'd been waiting to hear her say those words. Every encounter, he'd been poised for her to recognize him, to ask exactly that, at the very least.

He was tempted to tell her yes. To explain to her that they'd passed each other now and again in high school, even had a conversation once. But that would mean admitting that he remembered things she'd obviously long since forgotten. That he'd remembered her since she'd shown back up in town, and even before, whereas she was looking him right in the face and still wasn't sure.

Aiden cleared his throat again instead, blaming it on the wood dust. "It's been a long time," he said, as casually as he could. "I'm not surprised you don't remember."

A look of clear confusion crossed Nora's face,

and she opened her mouth as if to say something. But before she could, Aiden strode past her, heading for that black bag, his tools and the truck, and his way out of here.

All the way out, he could feel Nora's eyes on his back, staring after him.

CHAPTER TWELVE

Later that night, Nora sat by the fireplace, flipping through some old photo albums as Melanie curled up on the other side of the couch. She'd come over for dinner at Rhonda's request, and Rhonda had made one of Nora's favorite meals: roasted chicken stuffed with mushrooms and spinach and lemon, with roasted asparagus and carrots on the side. She'd even made quinoa tossed in balsamic vinegar and the leftover roasting juices for Nora, instead of potatoes.

Now, there was a plate of shortbread cookies and homemade hot cocoa with those big, fluffy marshmallows on the table in front of them, and Nora scooted a little closer to Melanie, looking through the pictures.

"Do you remember this?" Nora pointed to a

series of photos taken after one of the school plays. "You were so excited for us to be in this together."

"I do!" Melanie leaned over, peering at them. "You're always right up front in all of them too. Always in the spotlight, ready to take over the world. We should have always known you'd do exactly that."

Just like the conversation with Linda, Nora knew it was a comment meant to be uplifting. But she felt her heart sink a little. She *had* accomplished so much, but it felt as if everything she'd worked for had begun to fall apart. Her perfect fiancé had deserted her, her job clearly didn't value her as much as she'd always hoped, and there was nothing really waiting for her when she got back home.

Her apartment would be there, perfectly curated as always, but she didn't feel the same warmth that she always had before when she thought of going back to it. She didn't have a lot of close friends, because she'd spent so much time working or with Rob that she had never really had time.

And now, it felt like Boston was a more lonely place than it had been before. Her job had been the center of her universe, but it was clear that she was just a blip to them. Just one person, whose absence was missed but not panicked over.

Rhonda walked in just then, as Nora tried to keep her mood from slipping too far, grinning at her daughter and Melanie. She had a stack of thin hardback books in her hand, and when Nora focused on the bindings, she saw that they were school yearbooks. "Look what I found in the attic," Rhonda said mischievously, coming to sit on the other side of Nora.

Nora chuckled, eyeing the books. "Photo albums are one thing. High school yearbooks might be taking it a bit too far."

Rhonda started to reply, but just at that moment Caroline walked in, and it was as if Nora could *feel* the room cool by a couple of degrees.

Caroline was always busy, never taking time to rest, never sitting down. It made Nora feel like she was doing something wrong whenever *she* was relaxing, even in times like these—late in the evening, post-dinner, when she couldn't imagine what anyone should be doing other than exactly that.

She found it ironic that despite her 'go-getter' attitude, it felt like Caroline was far more type-A than Nora herself was. Nora, at least, knew how to sit down with a cup of cocoa and a walk down memory lane.

She'd always dreamed of getting out of

Evergreen Hollow, it was true, and even the cozy memories didn't change that, but she'd also always been a people person. Just because she didn't want the small hometown life didn't mean she was *rude* to the people who did, or unfriendly with anyone in town.

She'd always had fun with friends, thrown herself into school events, and joined in on everything that there was to do in Evergreen Hollow. She hadn't kept herself apart, as if she thought she was better than anyone else. She just hadn't wanted to *stay*, and she didn't know why Caroline seemed to view that as some sort of crime.

Caroline, on the other hand, seemed to think that staying made her a saint. But even with the people she was supposed to care about, she was stern and serious and rigid. Nora thought that was much worse than just wanting a bigger life.

Melanie leaned over Nora, interrupting her thoughts as she grabbed one of the yearbooks from the stack on Rhonda's lap. "Come sit with us!" she urged, gesturing at Caroline. "You were on the yearbook staff, right? Let's look at those accomplishments. I bet these are all *great*."

Caroline chuckled, and for a brief moment, she seemed to warm a bit at the memory. And then, just as quickly, Nora saw her sister's tension return. "I was," Caroline said briefly. "But that was a long time ago. There's not really any point in dwelling on days gone by, now is there? There's too much to do now."

She turned on her heel, walking out of the room, and Nora couldn't help letting out a sigh. The barbs in her sister's voice were clear as day, and she simply couldn't understand why. What was the harm in reminiscing a little? It wasn't as if she harbored any great fondness for Evergreen Hollow, and even she was enjoying it. She didn't know why Caroline wouldn't like going over memories of a place she was so attached to.

"Have the two of you gotten a chance to talk at all?" Melanie opened the yearbook, flipping to the first page, covered in signatures of varying colors and scrawls. "I know you had a little bit of a falling out, last time you left." She glanced at Nora cautiously.

"I don't think she wants to talk." Nora shrugged, wanting to leave it at that. She didn't really want to discuss Caroline. Not much about her sister made sense to her, and she was beginning to think that nothing ever would. She didn't know if she wanted to expend any more energy on it.

Melanie nudged closer, continuing to flip through the yearbook.

"Hah, look at this," she said, clearly trying to distract Nora from the momentary gloom of Caroline's entrance and exit. "Remember that week that they had us all come in in different costumes throughout the week? Look at the eighties day. Aren't we absolutely *ridiculous*? And look, here's the superhero day. You were so obsessed with Wonder Woman."

"And now she's actually Wonder Woman." Rhonda chuckled. "The eighties day was so much fun to dress you for."

"I think you liked coming up with the costumes more than we did, sometimes." Nora laughed, and Melanie kept flipping through the pages. She turned to a shot of several students standing in front of a new wing of the high school, and Nora gasped.

"Wait." She put her hand on Melanie's wrist, stopping her from turning the page again. She narrowed her eyes, looking closer. And then she realized why the handsome man from the event center had looked so familiar.

It was Aiden Masters. Grown up. He was taller and more muscular, and definitely more confident than she remembered him, but she *did* finally remember him. They'd gone to high school together. She recalled him being sweet but painfully shy—and then another memory came back to her, as she looked at the page.

They'd had a moment, one day. The only time she could really ever remember talking to him. They'd gotten caught out in a rainstorm, and hidden under some picnic benches. She'd thought she had gotten the feeling that he'd liked her—maybe that he had for some time, and just hadn't had the nerve to say anything—and she'd almost thought he might ask her out after that. She'd thought he might, at least, seek her out to talk to her again.

But he never really had, and even though she'd thought he was cute and enjoyed that brief conversation, she'd always thought that maybe she'd misread things.

She couldn't believe that she hadn't recognized the man at the event center—the man who she'd seen in a number of places around town, actually, she realized now—as Aiden. But to be fair, he'd grown up and changed so much, from a shy, bookish kind of boy to an incredibly rugged and handsome man. He'd been stick-thin back then, but now he was taller and broad-shouldered, someone that she supposed she couldn't blame herself for having been confused by.

"I ran into him earlier today." Nora tapped her

nail against the photo. "Aiden Masters. He was there that night we were poking around too, wasn't he? You were talking to him. And he stopped by the coffee shop. I really didn't put two and two together." She laughed softly. "He didn't expect to run into me either, today. He got so freaked out seeing me up on his ladder that he yelled and almost made me fall off."

"To be fair, no one would expect to see you up on a ladder," Melanie said wryly.

"To be *fair*, I usually have people to do that." Nora tucked a strand of hair behind her ear, glancing back at the photo once more. "What has he been up to since school anyway? I remember he wanted to do something around here. I guess he really did stick to that."

"He went to a trade school in Albany, to study carpentry." Melanie shrugged. "And then he came back here. That's why he was there with Blake at the event center that night—they and some of the other guys have been repairing it since the storm. But Aiden does all that kind of work around town. He takes some other projects too, for places outside of Evergreen Hollow. I think he'd have to, in order to make enough of a profit. It doesn't help that he undercharges pretty much every resident here, I think," Melanie added wryly.

"I just don't understand why he would want to come back here," Nora murmured, her gaze returning to the picture. Her brow furrowed as she studied it, remembering what little she knew of him. He'd been smart. Quiet, but definitely intelligent. He could have done a lot more than come back to Evergreen Hollow and patch up the buildings in his hometown for a pittance.

"I mean..." Melanie let out a small sigh. "A person might come back to their hometown for any number of reasons." Her voice was gentle, but there was a slight pointedness to it as she continued. "I still live here too. And I love it. I don't want to be anywhere else, even if I could make a lot more money running a coffee shop in a bigger city, or do anything else. I know small-town life isn't for everyone, but it is for some of us. And for those who like it, this place feels like... like an oasis. A calm, quiet place away from all of the chaos, where we've made our lives exactly how we want them."

Something about the sincerity in her friend's voice struck Nora. She still didn't understand the feeling, but it was clear that Melanie did, and Aiden must too. She might not understand the particular charm of Evergreen Hollow, but it was clear that they believed in it. It held a clear allure for the people who lived there, and even if Nora thought they were a bit deluded, Melanie was clearly happy. Aiden had seemed happy too.

Maybe she *had* been a touch too judgmental. Just a little.

Melanie reached for her cup of cocoa, taking a sip as she continued flipping through the yearbook. Nora looked at the photos, her gaze roaming over the pep rally pictures and the cheerleaders with the football team and the parades, the science fairs, and the end-of-year awards. As she did, she thought of all her ambitions, all those years.

She had always been so laser-focused on what she had wanted for herself, on what she was going to *achieve* in the future. Her life had centered around plotting her escape from Evergreen Hollow, and she hadn't bothered with anything other than fully detaching herself from those roots once she was gone.

She'd kept in touch with Melanie, as best as she had felt she could manage, but no one else. None of the classmates she'd once considered friends, or even those she'd known in passing, like Aiden. They'd vanished from her thoughts once she'd managed to flee Evergreen Hollow, and she hadn't looked back.

She felt a little guilty for not recognizing him. She wondered, as Melanie picked up their junior yearbook, why he hadn't brought it up when they'd met again at the event center. He could have mentioned that they'd gone to school together once he'd realized she didn't recognize him, but he hadn't, and she wasn't sure why. If anything, he'd seemed a little guarded around her. Like he wasn't entirely sure what to say.

"I have an idea," Melanie said suddenly, cutting through Nora's thoughts and startling her a little. Her voice had that bright, enthusiastic ring that Nora knew meant she was excited for something that she'd just thought of. "While you're here, I'm going to show you a different side of Evergreen Hollow—all the things to do that we have fun with." Her eyes sparkled, and there was a determined set to her jaw. "I want to show you there's more going on here than you think."

"That's a fantastic idea!" Rhonda spoke up immediately from Nora's other side, and Nora knew instantly that she was outnumbered. Her mother sounded as thrilled about Melanie's idea as Melanie herself was. "You could go ice skating!"

"There's a weekly cooking class at the event center too. It's themed. I think next week's is French cooking. From that Julia Child cookbook," Melanie added. "Or the shelter always needs people to volunteer to walk the dogs, and there are such gorgeous hiking trails here, even in the winter."

Nora laughed, shaking her head. As hesitant as she was to immerse herself any further in Evergreen Hollow, she had to admit that it did sound like fun.

"Slow down," she said, still chuckling. "I've already committed to helping with the festival, so I'm not going to have *too* much free time on my hands. I'll start with one thing and go from there. How does that sound?"

Melanie and Rhonda glanced at each other, and Nora saw a look pass between them that she couldn't figure out, almost as if they'd thought of the same secret at the same time. She couldn't imagine what it could be. In a town where everyone knew everything about everyone else, she didn't think there were that many secrets to be shared.

"You should try a ballroom dancing class," Melanie said decisively. "There's a little place at the edge of town called the Crescendo Dance Studio. It's really fun, and the teacher is very patient. I think you should start with that."

She couldn't come up with an objection. She thought it was as good an option as any. Ice skating seemed more likely to end in a broken ankle, and she'd always been so bad at cooking that the idea of *that* class made her think it was only going to result in embarrassment.

As for the shelter idea, she didn't mind dogs, but she was already walking around outside in the cold far too much for her own comfort. She had experience with dance, at least, although the fact that neither Melanie nor her mother realized that reminded her uncomfortably of the distance that had grown over the years.

"Ballroom dancing it is," she agreed, and frowned as Rhonda and Melanie exchanged another of those knowing glances. "But the festival takes priority."

"Of course!" Both women on either side of her agreed in tandem, and Nora let out a breath.

It was decided, then. But there was no rush.

She'd get around to it eventually.

CHAPTER THIRTEEN

By the following afternoon, Nora had printed out pictures of all the new materials that she had ordered for decorations, with excited plans to go to the *Gazette* and share them with Sabrina. The woman had been a bit prickly when she'd been there last, but Nora felt sure that once she saw what had been chosen, she'd share in Nora's excitement. After all, it was one less thing for her to worry about to ensure that the festival went off without a hitch.

She'd printed off the photos in the small office at the inn, tucking them into a manila envelope and sliding them into her big leather tote purse. She bundled up, opting today for a cheery red angora sweater that matched the festive town mood, slim black jeans, and her Hunter boots with her cashmere wool peacoat and the navy scarf she'd bought over it all. She needed to make a stop at the general store today as well, since she needed a handful of odds and ends for securing the decorations once they arrived. Thumb tacks, hooks, and twine, all things that she could get easily at Sugar Maple.

Leon was behind the counter as always when Nora arrived, a cup of coffee in front of him as he went over something in a notebook. He had a friendly smile and a wave for her as she walked in, and she raised a hand in response, making her way around the store as she picked up the few things she needed. She couldn't help but notice that there was a more relaxed pace to her errands these days. In Boston, she would have been running around frantically if she needed to make a stop for something like this, probably on a call while answering a text on her Apple watch at the same time. There was no need for any of that here. No one was rushing her to get this done, and she hadn't even brought her watch with her.

Similarly, her phone had remained markedly silent for days. She'd been mildly hurt by it at first. That her boss and coworkers weren't frantic to ask her questions about things that needed to be done, and that Rob hadn't regretted his choice within a day or two and started to blow up her phone. But now, she was starting to find that she enjoyed the peace, just as she was enjoying sipping the latte she had gotten from Melanie while browsing the shelves at the general store.

After a few minutes, she took her purchases up to the counter. Leon grinned at her as he rang them up, reaching for a paper bag.

"I can't tell you how thrilled we are to have an expert like yourself helping with the festival this year," he said, and she could hear the mixture of fatherly teasing and sincerity in his voice. "Between the new and improved event center, and your hands in the planning, this one is going to be one for the books I think."

She felt an unexpected flush of pride at that, and she returned the smile, reaching for her bag. She'd thought of helping out as a way to fit in a little better while she was here, while also keeping her hands and mind busy, but she found that she liked the idea of Evergreen Hollow's residents being glad that she was a part of it. She wouldn't have thought she'd find much satisfaction in planning a small-town festival, but it was becoming more rewarding than she'd imagined.

I should stop in and say hello to Bethany too, she thought as she stepped out of the store, tucking the paper bag into her tote. The Pets First pet store and grooming salon that Bethany ran was on the way to the *Gazette*—most things were on the way to one another here, as small as the town was, truthfully, but she thought that Bethany might like to see the photos she had as well. Besides, while Nora couldn't imagine ever actually having time for a pet of her own, she liked stopping in and seeing the cats and dogs there.

Bethany was clipping a small Pomeranian's nails when Nora walked in, and she glanced up quickly, smiling at Nora before returning to her task. "What are you doing today?"

"Oh, just a few errands, and then I'm going to take Sabrina some examples of what I ordered for the festival decorations." Nora leaned up against the counter on the other side of the space where Bethany was working. "I can show you if you like, once you have a break."

"You might be here for a while. I have a pretty full morning. Actually—oh, wait! There she is. You won't need to go to the *Gazette* after all."

Bethany waved as Nora turned, seeing Sabrina walk in the front door. She was holding a white poodle, her attention fully on the squirming dog in her arms.

"I'm here for Pookie's appointment!" she announced, walking past Nora and up to the counter. "I'm a little early, so I'll wait."

"I should be done with Taffy here in just a minute." Bethany swiftly finished the back paw she was holding, reaching for the left front as the Pomeranian let out a small but slightly menacing growl.

"Actually, while you're waiting..." Nora reached into her purse for the manila envelope. "I was coming by the *Gazette* anyway. I wanted to show you the decoration materials I ordered. They should be here fairly quickly."

"I don't see the point in you sharing what you've chosen, since you're clearly taking over all the planning anyway." Sabrina's voice cut through the air between them, as stiff as her posture. She held the dog closer to her, her nose tipping up as she looked at Nora through her cat's eye glasses.

Nora could feel the air between them thicken. Bethany glanced between them awkwardly, clearly at a loss for what to say, and even the grumbling Pomeranian had quieted down. No one in the room seemed to know quite how to respond.

Carefully, Nora slipped the folder back into her tote bag. "I'm just lending a hand," she said carefully. "I want the festival to be successful—it's so important to everyone, my mother and best friend included. I thought my experience might be useful. Everyone seemed happy to have my help."

"Well." Sabrina sniffed. "I could have made it successful on my own too." Her lips thinned, her irritation clearly rising.

Nora let out a slow breath, opening her mouth to reassure Sabrina that she wanted her feedback, that it was valuable. But before she could say a word, Sabrina turned on her heel, storming out of the salon.

On the other side of the counter, Bethany let out a sigh. "Don't take it to heart," she said quietly. "Sabrina can be very passionate about things she's set her mind to. And—oh, I don't know, maybe she was more attached to her role in the festival than we realized. We were trying to lighten up her workload, but..." Bethany set the nail clippers down, rolling her shoulders to ease some of the tension. "It does seem to have backfired a little."

Nora nodded. Sabrina had left Pookie waiting for the appointment, and the small dog was sitting patiently on the grooming table where she had set her down, head turning back and forth between the two women. The dog seemed very sweet, and she couldn't help thinking how at odds that was with her owner's cool demeanor. Nora wasn't sure she understood it.

It was clear that Sabrina hadn't really had the time to devote to the planning. The *Gazette* was her baby, that was plain enough, and she had her hands full running it. Nora couldn't see why having some help was a bad thing. She certainly had enough people to delegate to when she planned an event in Boston. Just decorations alone would require at least one other person to help her.

But it wasn't her job to manage anyone else's emotions—just the part of the festival that she'd been asked to handle. Nora reached out resignedly, scratching the poodle once between the ears before bidding Bethany goodbye, with plans to pick up lunch from Rockridge Grill before going back to the inn.

She would just keep doing what she was doing, she decided. And she would keep making the effort to include Sabrina, even if the woman was prickly as a cactus.

It would be on Sabrina, then, to warm up to her.

Or not.

* * *

It was nearly five when Aiden finished repairing the last of Jonathan Keller's stairs on the front porch of his home—another victim of the surprise Thanksgiving storm. Blake was working on adding the last coat of paint to the boards of the porch that they'd refinished while they were at it, complete with a weatherproof varnish.

Jonathan emerged from the other side of the house, dusting off his hands on his jeans. He had a small greenhouse in the back, and he'd been working in there on his day off while Blake and Aiden tackled the front porch. "Thanks for the great work," he said, surveying the results in front of him. "I'm handy in the kitchen, but house repairs are beyond me."

"My pleasure." Aiden straightened, setting his hammer down in his toolbox. "Just keep those venison burgers on the menu at the grill, and I won't have a complaint in the world."

"I second that." Blake rolled the last of the varnish over the porch, and Jonathan chuckled.

"I'll certainly keep that in mind. And speaking of food..." He nodded to the house. "I have some to-go bags in there for you that I brought back this afternoon, when I stopped in at the grill to check on things. Dinner is the least I can do, when you've gotten this handled so quickly."

"I certainly appreciate it." Aiden gave him an appreciative nod, starting to pack up as he and Blake waited for Jonathan to come back out with the food. His eyes widened when the other man returned with two large bags, one for him and one for Blake. "There's more than just a burger in there."

"Ah, I might've thrown in some lasagna and maybe a little of the apple pie we were serving. Just in case." Jonathan shrugged. "Can never go wrong with extra leftovers, hm?"

"Not at all," Aiden assured him. "I appreciate it."

Blake nodded, echoing the sentiment. "We both do."

"I need to head out though." Aiden glanced at his watch, tucking the bag of food under one arm as he reached for his toolbox with the other. "Can you finish cleaning up the last of this, Blake?"

Blake chuckled, a smirk at the corner of his mouth. "Oh, yeah, it is Thursday. Time for you to bring out that alter ego of yours. The *Lady Killer*, right?" He said it with a dramatic flourish, and Aiden rolled his eyes.

"I'm just glad I don't have to think about cooking. See you around, fellas."

He headed for the truck before Blake could rib him any further. He'd eat on the drive over—Thursdays were always hectic with his schedule, going straight from one job to the other. But the savings made it worth it, and he did like both jobs. That was more than plenty of folks could say about even one.

He'd go home, clean up, and then head right back out again. And truthfully, he really didn't mind it.

It was good to stay busy. And Thursday nights were always entertaining, in their own way.

CHAPTER FOURTEEN

Originally, Nora had planned to wait a little while before taking Melanie and her mother up on the ballroom dancing suggestion. She figured she had plenty of time—there was no reason to rush into anything. And she *was* busy with the festival planning.

But then, she'd gotten back to the inn, and Rhonda had pointedly mentioned that they were having a mulled wine tasting that night, and the inn would probably be busy—but the dance studio was having one of their classes that night. Nora could take a hint—she had nothing to lose, and after the unpleasant interaction with Sabrina, she'd found that she wasn't as enthused about spending the evening planning for the festival. Truthfully, she could use a night off from it.

Going to the ballroom dancing lesson seemed better than mingling with Evergreen Hollow residents in a small space over mulled wine, so she'd found a pair of low heels that would work as dance shoes—her actual dance shoes had been left back in Boston—and picked out one of the two 'party' dresses she'd brought with her. She hadn't honestly expected to wear either one, but it was good to have options.

She'd chosen the dark purple dress. It was knee length, with a flirty scalloped hem and elbow-length sleeves, and a modestly scooped neckline. Nothing that she had to worry about misstepping and flashing someone in, as rusty as she was at dancing, but still fun and pretty enough that the lesson felt like a special occasion. A little treat for herself, something indulgent to do simply for the sake of doing it.

It had occurred to her, as she was getting ready, that she rarely did things like that back in Boston. She usually felt like her time needed to be accounted for, and used efficiently. Even relaxing, she tried to make sure she was accomplishing something with it. Finishing a reading challenge. Watching a show that was also educational in some way. She rarely did anything just for sheer pleasure, without there being a *reason* to. She had no real reason to take a ballroom class, other than it had sounded fun when Melanie and her mother suggested it.

So here she was.

The glow from the windows on the chilly night and the lilt of a waltz spilling out from inside was soothing. She tugged her peacoat around herself, her boots crunching through the snow as she walked up the pathway to the wooden door. Like a lot of the businesses in Evergreen Hollow, it resembled a residential house more than a commercial building, hollowed out and redesigned inside to fit the needs of the business.

There was an older woman with short, snowy hair in tight curls sitting at the front desk, and Nora handed her the drop-in fee in cash, smiling at her. Now inside the dance studio, she felt the warm glow of familiarity, soothing her further. She recognized the music, a song she'd waltzed to often, and it was nice to hear the sound of the dancers moving across the floor. It felt like a bridge between Evergreen Hollow and her life in Boston, something that she had in both places.

She'd taken a fair few dance classes in Boston, partially just for fun, and partially to have a bit of a challenge. It came in handy to be familiar with ballroom dance as a part of her work, since it so often came up in the events she planned, which had factored into her decision.

And there it was again, of course. Practicality and efficiency, even in her fun. But here, there was no reason for it other than it was a comforting and enjoyable way to spend an evening, and she was looking forward to losing herself in it.

"Thank you," she said, as the woman finished taking her drop-in fee and directed her to the small room just outside the classroom to change her shoes. She sat down on a bench, taking off her boots and slipping on the low heels, and glanced up as a young woman sat down next to her.

"Are you new in town?" The young woman had a short brown bob, slightly curled at the edges, and bright blue eyes. "I haven't seen you here before."

"I grew up here." Nora slipped on her other shoe and sat up. "I'm just visiting for the holidays. I didn't even know this studio was here, honestly."

"Oh! Well, I'm Callie." She held out her hand. "The instructor here is wonderful. You're going to love him."

"I'm sure I will. I've danced a little before—I've

been lucky to always get good teachers. I'm sure this won't be any different. I'm Nora, by the way," she added quickly. "I'll be in town through the New Year, so I might come back more than once."

"I hope you do!" Callie stood, gesturing. "Let's go on in. The instructor will be here any minute."

Nora followed, a little bemused by how quickly everyone tended to make friends here, smoothing out her skirt. There were a handful of others in the main studio room, a mixture of men and women of varying ages, and she was just about to say something else to Callie when the teacher walked in.

"Sorry I'm a few minutes late," he said, stopping in the middle of the floor. "But we'll go ahead and get started with the waltz class."

Everyone else started milling about, getting into place, but for a moment Nora couldn't move. She stood there, speechless—and utterly shocked.

The ballroom dance instructor was none other than Aiden Masters.

He was dressed differently than any of the other times she'd run into him in town, in soft-looking joggers and a t-shirt that clung attractively to his muscled torso. She knew she was gaping as she looked at him, her shock written clearly across her face, but she couldn't stop staring. She felt incapable of closing her mouth—which she was all too aware was hanging a little bit open.

Aiden's gaze swept over the assembled students, landing finally on her, and Nora saw the surprise flicker over his face. He lingered for just a moment, looking at her, but he managed to keep his composure far better than she had.

"Let's get started," he said smoothly, and the music began.

Nora knew all the steps. Out of all the classes she'd taken, she had waltzed most often. She liked the simplicity of it—once she learned the rhythm, it became much easier to work on grace and cadence, and she liked the ability to focus on refining one skill in dance, rather than learning a wide variety. She'd occasionally dropped into a foxtrot class or two, and once even a tango, but she preferred the waltz.

It was good, she thought as they began going through the beginning steps, that she happened to be as familiar with it as she was. If not, the lesson would have been a disaster. She couldn't focus, moving through the steps and rotating partners feeling as if she were sleepwalking, entirely taken aback by the shock of the instructor being *Aiden*. She remembered the glance between Melanie and her mother and felt faintly betrayed. They'd clearly both had a mischievous hand in this when they'd made the suggestion.

Then, as if things couldn't get any more complicated, she heard Aiden call out, "Rotate!" The next thing she knew, she found herself face-to-face with the man himself.

He was very close, and he smelled like sandalwood and juniper. Her mind blanked out momentarily, and she looked up at him, reminded suddenly of his hands on her waist as he'd tried to help her down from the ladder.

"I think I'm in less danger of falling tonight." She was trying for a joke, but the words came out stilted, and she couldn't tell from the expression on his face if he was amused or not.

"I would hope so." He turned her, the two of them moving in perfect rhythm, but Nora could feel how tense she was.

"I didn't know you could dance," Nora said lamely, and Aiden raised an eyebrow.

"Of course not. Why would you?"

"We went to school together." Nora only just refrained from biting her lip. The man was making her act like an idiot, and she had no idea why. Their history was years ago—there was no reason for him to make her trip over her words and dance like she had a board taped to her spine.

Aiden gave her a look she couldn't quite read as they turned again.

"Did you just realize that?" His voice was dry, humorless, and Nora winced internally.

"I didn't at first," she admitted. "But once it clicked... I remember you clearly now. Why—"

She was about to ask him why he hadn't said anything on any of the occasions when they'd run into each other after she'd arrived in town. But before she could, the music hit a high note, and Aiden stepped back, flawlessly spinning her in a circle to execute a twirl and bring her back in.

Or at least, his side of it was flawless.

She was a decent dancer. She applied herself to anything she attempted, and she'd been to a good number of classes in Boston. Ordinarily, something like that should have been easy. Simple. But her mind was spinning, confused, and flustered by her reaction to Aiden, and she was more distracted than she could recall having been in a very long time.

Which meant, that as he spun her and brought her back in, she turned too far—and her elbow smacked him directly in the cheekbone. As if to add insult to injury, she felt her heel come down on his toe as she attempted to jump back, bringing it all to a grinding halt as he let out a sharp, pained sound.

Nora felt her face flame red instantly. "Oh my goodness," she gasped, one hand coming up to cover her mouth. "I'm so sorry. I'm usually better than this."

"It's all right," Aiden reassured her, taking a step back. "It happens. Rotate!"

And then he was gone, paired off with another partner as a stodgy elderly gentleman with two left feet took his place with Nora.

She couldn't leave fast enough. She finished the class, because it would have been too mortifying to flee immediately, but the second the music stopped and Aiden dismissed them, she made a beeline for the door. She didn't even bother to change her shoes, flinging on her coat and grabbing her boots as she hurried out, wincing as she tried to cross the icy, snowy parking lot in the heels she was wearing.

This was a terrible idea.

She had intended to focus on the festival, and that was what she should have done. The evening should have been spent up in her room, with a glass of mulled wine and her planner. Her gut instinct not to allow herself to be distracted by Evergreen

Hollow's 'charms' that her mother and Melanie wanted her to experience had been the right one all along.

Nora let out an audible sound of frustration as she reached her car, digging into her purse, and realized that she'd forgotten her keys inside. Now she'd have to trudge back and get them. *That* was really adding insult to the literal injury she'd given Aiden.

She sighed, turning and stepping carefully as she walked back into the building. And she let out another as she walked in and saw that, naturally, it was Aiden at the front desk as the others left. The older woman must have gone home before the lesson was over.

He held out her keys, a bemused smile on his face. "Are you looking for these?"

Nora nodded sheepishly. "Thank you." She took the keys, wincing when she saw the ice pack in his hand. Her cheeks flushed, embarrassment sweeping through her all over again.

"I'm sorry," she said, feeling like the apology was clumsy at best. "I don't know what happened."

"Don't worry about it," Aiden said smoothly, his voice calm and brusque.

Nora got the distinct impression that he was

being polite. That he didn't really want to continue the conversation. And how could she blame him? She felt like a jerk for not having recognized him at first, and then on top of that, for elbowing him in the face once they'd finally gotten a chance to talk about it.

She felt a strange pull to stand there and catch up with him after all those years, to speak to the kind boy that she'd talked to that day under the shelter. But even though she felt that tug, that desire to pass the time with him and find out what had happened in the years in between, it felt clear that he didn't feel the same.

"The class was great," she said finally, letting out a breath. "You're a really good dancer."

His expression didn't change, and Nora left it at that, heading back out to her car.

Her thoughts were in a whirl the entire drive back to the inn. She thought again of the looks between Melanie and her mother, and huffed out a dry laugh, feeling certain that she'd been set up. They'd planned it on purpose, to send her to a class Aiden was teaching after she'd recognized him in the yearbook, and she didn't know whether to be frustrated or amused that they'd so easily messed with her.

So much for this being a relaxing evening out. She couldn't pinpoint why, exactly, but her heart was racing.

And it didn't slow, all the way back to The Mistletoe Inn.

CHAPTER FIFTEEN

That Saturday morning, Aiden decided to head to The Mellow Mug to get his usual Americano and sit and read for a little while. He had the day off, and while he'd usually spend it at home, he felt oddly restless. He'd felt that way since he got up, with the whole day stretching out in front of him, and his solution to that was to go and do something. The coffee shop was just as nice a place to sit and read his book, and the change of scenery would be pleasant.

Of course, just as he walked in, he saw Nora sitting at a table, her phone at her ear. He overheard something about *getting back to the city*, and realized she must be talking to someone at her work in Boston.

She was fully engrossed in the conversation,

not even noticing him as he walked up to the counter and gave Melanie his order. It was more out of habit than anything else, since he always got the same thing, and Melanie knew it as well as he did.

"—order extra flowers," Nora was in the middle of saying. "No, I know, but we've worked with this client before, and she always wants more. The last two times we've had to rush them last minute, and she gets more upset when there's a rush charge. No, of course that's normal. But she doesn't see it that way. They'll approve the expense, I'm sure of it, but you can say I agreed if there's trouble."

Aiden knew he probably shouldn't be listening in to her work call, but he couldn't help it. She was right there, and he also couldn't help thinking how professional she sounded. Competent and confident. She was clearly very good at her work, just based on that small snippet of conversation that he'd gotten, and it was clear that she was well versed in event planning. Despite himself, he had to admit he was impressed.

He stepped back as Melanie went to make his drink, going to the end of the counter with his book in hand, and as he walked over he saw Nora look up and notice him. She hung up the phone a moment later, setting it down and giving him a slightly sheepish smile.

"Hey there," she said, her cheeks turning the slightest bit pink. She was probably recalling the incident at the dance class—his cheek was still a little sore from that—but his heart raced a little anyway at the sight of her smile.

Don't let your old crush get carried away, he reminded himself, as he reached for his coffee. She might have finally remembered him, but it didn't change anything. She was still the big city girl that she'd fashioned herself into, and they were still complete opposites in every way. There was nothing to suggest that she didn't see him as a country bumpkin, someone who had passed up opportunities to stay in his uninteresting hometown and do the same thing that he'd done before, every day for the rest of his life.

Except that he didn't see it that way. And a part of him wished there was something that could make her look at it differently too.

"Hey." He glanced at her phone, planner, and the magazine spread open in front of her. "You look busy."

Nora shrugged, taking a sip from the mug in front of her. "Oh, you know," she said breezily. "Just checking in on things back home. Work doesn't stop, even though I'm out of town. They've been getting along fine without me, for the most part, but I told them to call me if they needed me even though I was on vacation. One of my coworkers had some questions about an event I passed on to her so I could take the time off."

"You're also helping with coordinating the Snowman festival," he remarked, leaning up against the counter. "You really don't stop working, do you?"

Nora shook her head, her fingers drumming anxiously in front of her. "I offered, and I've tried to help, but I'm not sure Sabrina really wants it. She hasn't been thrilled with my ideas so far."

There was a glimmer of hurt in her eyes, Aiden thought. It surprised him. He'd always seen her as the popular one when they were in school, exuding confidence. He wouldn't have thought she'd be hurt by someone's rejection. He would have imagined she'd just brush it off, leaving it in the dust behind her.

She had always seemed a little larger than life to him, but she was more human in that moment, changed a little by the sudden vulnerability. He always envisioned her as someone who breezed through life, uninhibited and unhampered, but it was clear she had some of the same insecurities that he did. That anyone did, for that matter.

It made him want to ease them, just a little. If he could.

"They're lucky to have your help. Even if Sabrina isn't totally on board yet."

Her expression brightened just a little, and he felt a flush of warmth in his chest. He'd just taken a sip of his Americano, and he told himself it was that—the heat of the coffee. Nora couldn't continue to affect him in this way. They were two entirely different people, and just now, she'd been on the phone with her job in Boston. Her *current* job.

She was staying for the holidays, and then she was leaving again. Evergreen Hollow was a novelty to her, but it was home to him. There was no point in indulging the crush.

He realized that the silence had started to turn awkward just as Nora spoke up.

"How's your—uh—face?" She gestured toward his cheek, and he shrugged.

"It's fine," he assured her. "You really don't need to worry about it."

Another beat of silence. Nora gestured toward the seat next to her. "Sit down," she suggested.

"Unless you were planning to head out once you had your coffee?"

It would have been easy to say yes, and put an end to the conversation. Or it should have been easy. He hesitated, but he found himself sinking down into the seat, drawn to her as always. He felt a little awkward, sitting down to have a conversation with her, considering how things had been between them. But as he settled in, he found that it was nice. It had been such a long time since they'd actually talked.

Since that afternoon in the rain, really.

"So you're a carpenter *and* a dance instructor?" Nora teased lightly, closing her planner and setting it aside. He was surprised that she was putting up her work to talk to him. "That's a very diverse skill set."

"Ah, well, steady feet on the dance floor helps with ladder safety." He saw Nora's eyebrows go up and chuckled. "Not to suggest you need help with either, obviously."

Aiden thought he saw her cheeks flush again, just a little. He realized too late that the statement sounded a little flirtatious, and he would have sworn he hadn't meant it that way. But he also liked seeing that pink tint in her face.

"You're really good at dance. I was surprised to

see you teaching it, honestly. I wouldn't have guessed. Did you learn that at trade school too?" Her tone was still teasing, and his heart tripped a little in his chest.

She'd been asking about him—or she'd at least mentioned him enough for someone to go volunteering information, if she knew about carpentry school.

"I like it *because* it's so different from carpentry, honestly." He reached for his coffee, taking a hasty sip. "It's something I picked up for fun. It's just a bonus that I can make a little extra, getting paid to teach it. I like having a hobby that has nothing to do with my job."

Nora smiled, and he thought privately that the expression that crossed her face then could almost be described as dreamy. "I don't know what that would be like," she admitted. "I've been *so* focused on building my career, ever since college. It's all I think about, really. What steps to take, how to best use my time, the most advantageous ways to keep progressing. Even most of my leisure activities have something to do with it back at home." Nora laughed a little, but Aiden thought he heard a hint of chagrin in it. "I learned ballroom dance, in Boston, so I could be a better event planner. It all comes back to that, eventually."

That's no way to live.

It was the first thought that popped into his head, but he didn't say it out loud. He couldn't.

"That makes sense," he said instead, and it did. For Nora, of course it did. He knew her well enough to know that, even if they hadn't talked much in school. "You were always so ambitious, back then. Always set on doing big things. And it appears you have—which is impressive. Not everyone pulls off their goals so flawlessly."

It was meant as a compliment. He truly had meant it sincerely. But to his surprise, Nora's face fell a little as he spoke.

"I thought so, too, about a month ago," she said quietly. She reached for her mug, taking a long sip, her expression going from vaguely sad to contemplative. "I'm really not so sure now though. Honestly, it feels like every part of my life is on uneven ground right now."

Nora set her mug back down, glancing over at him. "I was engaged. Right up until the day before I decided to come back here."

He knew he didn't have any right to feel a stab of... some emotion that he couldn't name. It wasn't quite jealousy, but it was definitely close. He hadn't spoken to Nora since high school. Since before they'd even been *out* of high school. He didn't have any actual reason to hear that someone had put a ring on her finger, and feel his chest go a little tight.

Or a feeling of relief, once it sank in that she was talking about it in the past tense.

"My ex? He broke it off like that." Nora snapped her fingers. "Easy. Like he'd been thinking about it for a long time. I thought he was surprising me, coming to grab a goodbye kiss before he left for a work trip, and instead he was dumping me while we stood on a curb after I'd just finished up a wedding. Ironic, really."

She bit her lip. "Melanie convinced me to come back here for the holidays. A change of scenery. But it's not all syrup and jolliness here either. Things have always been strained between me and Caroline —my older sister—but it feels like it's even more tense now. She doesn't even want to be in the same room with me, it feels like. I was hoping that helping to plan the festival would get my mind off of everything, but it really hasn't."

She paused as he watched her, visibly wincing as she seemed to realize how much she'd just said.

"I didn't mean to unload on you like that," she murmured. "Sorry."

Her voice was chagrined, and she licked her lips

nervously, tapping her fingers on the side of her mug. A tell, he thought, for when she was anxious.

"It's just a rough patch," Aiden said gently. "That doesn't mean you haven't been successful. Those are always going to happen, from time to time."

Nora gave him a small, watery smile. "That's true." She bit her lip, turning her coffee mug around in her hands. "It's been hard. But I'll find my way back to steadier footing, I'm sure." She laughed softly, looking up to meet his gaze. "After all, a wise person once told me that you only get one life. It should be lived on your own terms."

The words hit him directly in the chest, making him feel briefly as if he'd forgotten how to breathe. It was a shock to hear those words come from her lips.

"You—you remember our conversation?" He could hear himself stammering out the question, but he couldn't quite bring himself to care. He remembered it clearly, and even if he did make a fool out of himself, he wanted to know.

"Of course." Nora's smile brightened a little more at the shared memory. "I thought you were really nice that day," she admitted almost conspiratorially, leaning forward over her coffee mug. "I thought maybe we'd hang out more after that, honestly. Or that maybe you'd ask me out. But I wasn't sure if you really liked me or not, or if we'd just happened to get stuck together that day, and you tolerated me for a little while."

Aiden nearly burst out with a shocked laugh at that, stopping it just in time.

She didn't think I liked her? When I had such a massive crush on her?

The idea seemed preposterous. Impossible. But he looked at her face, calmly remembering the moment, and he tried to think of it objectively.

He never *had* tried too hard to actually talk to her, he supposed. He'd just assumed she wouldn't want to talk to him, honestly. She was so popular, so bright, someone who everyone wanted to orbit around. He'd had her on a pedestal, and he realized in retrospect that she'd stayed there, all of these years. It had gotten in the way of seeing her as a person.

Nora was still looking at him, and he cleared his throat. "No," Aiden managed quietly. "I did like you."

A moment of awkward silence stretched between them, and he could feel an unspoken tension hovering in the air. Much like the moment in the event hall, when he'd thought she was going to fall off the ladder and grabbed her, or when she'd walked into his dance studio without knowing he'd be there. But it was even more charged now, with his admission.

He'd gone far enough for today, he decided. Maybe far enough, for good.

"I should get going." He started to stand up, thinking he'd read his book at home after all. But before he could push his chair back, Nora interrupted him.

"Do you maybe want to go to dinner? With me." She flushed the tiniest bit, probably realizing how silly the last part sounded. "I want to catch up with you," she added. "Find out a little more about what you've been up to. It would be nice, don't you think?"

Nice. That was one word for it.

"Besides," Nora added quickly, as if she were worried he was about to turn her down. "I owe you a meal, I think, after doing you bodily harm in class."

The teasing lilt was back in her voice. She'd clearly moved on past the charged moment, but he was still there, shocked that this was happening. All these years later. He couldn't quite believe it.

"Sure," he managed. "I'll pick you up at six tomorrow. How's that sound?"

Nora flashed him a truly stunning grin. "I'll see

you then," she said, reaching for her coffee and planner, and he nodded, retreating to the door of the coffee shop.

It was just a dinner. Just a little catching up between old acquaintances.

But if that was all, he wondered as he walked to his truck, then why couldn't he stop his heart from racing?

CHAPTER SIXTEEN

Nora sank down into the chair by the small kitchen nook table as Rhonda opened the oven, taking a tray of snickerdoodles out. She would have known which cookie it was even if she couldn't see them—the sudden burst of warm air was filled with the scents of sugar and cinnamon, and she could practically taste the soft, pillowy cookie melting in her mouth already.

She'd come down to the kitchen because that seemed like exactly what she needed—a cookie and maybe some of her mother's hot cocoa. She hadn't gotten much more planning done at The Mellow Mug earlier—she'd been too distracted after her run-in with Aiden.

They were going on a date. *Not a date. A dinner*

to catch up. But no matter how she tried to turn it around in her head or look at it differently, it *felt* like a date.

She'd said that back in high school, she'd thought that he might ask her out. He'd reassured her that he *had* actually liked her back then. And then she'd asked him to dinner.

It definitely felt like it fit the requirements of a date.

The thought made nerves swirl around in her stomach like snowflakes in a globe. It had been *years* since she'd been out on a first date. She'd been with Rob for so long that she'd forgotten what it felt like to go out with someone for the first time, even someone who she already knew. She'd even forgotten what it really felt like to go on a date—her and Rob's nights out, which had been few and far between, had lost the spark of romance over the last few months. They had started to feel more like debriefings, catching each other up on all of the things they hadn't had time to talk about because they'd both been so overwhelmed with work.

She'd told herself, all the times she was disappointed, that things would calm down. That it was a rough patch, and once the wedding was over and they lived together, date nights would feel special again. Romantic. Less like a conference.

Now, she wasn't so sure that would have turned out to be the case. And clearly Rob hadn't been sure either, since he'd broken things off.

She wasn't sure if it was just the excitement of dinner with Aiden, but she didn't feel the same pang that she had before when she thought about Rob. It hadn't hurt so much either, telling Aiden about the broken engagement today. She'd felt more frustration than anything else—frustration that she'd been so busy and preoccupied that she'd missed all the signals that her relationship wasn't working... and there *must* have been signals. There always were. She just hadn't had time to pay attention. Her life had been a whirlwind, a rush of work and efficiency and focusing on her career, and she had thought Rob had liked that about her. That they were both so driven.

But maybe it would have been good for them to both slow down a little.

She didn't mourn the end of the relationship as much as she'd thought, she realized, as she watched her mother scoop cookies onto a plate and pour hot cocoa. If they'd really been right for each other, Rob would have talked to her about his misgivings, instead of letting them build until he unilaterally decided to dump her. Maybe she'd missed the signs, but he should have told her how he felt.

"How's the event planning going?" Rhonda carried the plate of cookies and the cocoa to the table, and Nora frowned, remembering her reason for coming down here in the first place. She'd been upstairs trying to work on what she hadn't managed to get done this morning, but her thoughts had drifted to Aiden, and then to how frustrated she was with Sabrina, and then to wondering if she should be doing this at all. Around and around, until she'd decided that coming downstairs and seeing what was being baked was probably her best choice.

A good choice, Nora decided, when she took a bite of cookie. It was exactly as good as she remembered, soft and buttery, sweet and spiced in exactly the right measure. Paired with the thick, rich cocoa, it was even better. She would miss this when she went home.

But maybe she didn't have to stay away for quite so long this time.

"Sabrina clearly doesn't want my help." Nora took another bite of cookie, letting the cinnamon sugar soothe away the sting of remembering Sabrina's reaction. "I went to show her some of what

I picked out, and she said she didn't see the point in bothering to share it with her, since I was going to do it all anyway." Another bite of cookie. The hostility still felt bad, even with the time that had passed since then. She'd done all of this as a gesture of goodwill—peace on earth, and all of that—and Sabrina seemed intent on interpreting it in the worst way possible.

"Just keep doing what you're doing." Rhonda sat back, taking a bite of her own cookie as she looked at her daughter. "We're lucky to have your expertise. If Sabrina doesn't realize that, it's on her. And she'll come around, I'm sure."

Like Caroline? Nora bit the words back. Her mother didn't want friction between her daughters, of course—so of course she'd tried to reassure Nora that her sister would come around. But Caroline hadn't, so far, and Nora didn't feel confident that Sabrina would either.

So long as everyone else remained happy with what she was doing, she reassured herself, it would be fine. Sabrina was one cranky voice. She shouldn't let it get to her.

Speaking of voices—Nora craned her neck, looking out toward the living room. She could hear the crackle of the fireplace from there, but not much else. "It's so quiet," she observed, reaching for a second cookie. "*Really* quiet."

Rhonda sighed. For a moment, Nora got the distinct impression that she'd touched on something that her mother really didn't want to talk about—had been avoiding talking about, maybe. "There's only one guest," she said finally, and Nora's brows rose.

Concern pricked at her instantly. She thought of the tense look on Caroline's face, and her mother's attempts to do more holiday events, and the pieces started to come together. "How long have things been this slow?"

That hesitant look passed over Rhonda's face again. "A while," she admitted. "But I'm sure it's really nothing to worry over. Caroline gets stressed about it, but I'm hopeful that things will pick back up if we just give it a little time. There's always ups and downs, rough patches."

It wasn't dissimilar to what Aiden had said that morning. Nora's mind was already ticking away, thinking of what could be done to give the business a boost. She didn't say anything—she knew her mother had already been reticent to talk about it. She didn't want to make her feel worse.

But she could think of some things to do. Packages—maybe ones appealing to couples away on a romantic Vermont holiday or friends having a girls' weekend. Add-ons—a guided fishing trip, or a maple syrup tour. The inn offered rustic, charming rooms and delicious breakfasts and a cozy place to relax, with a few small in-house events here and there like the mulled wine tasting—but Nora saw places to expand.

She was sure that Caroline would have an aneurysm if she heard Nora thinking about changing anything around the inn.

"How was the dance class?" Rhonda asked, abruptly changing the subject. "Did you enjoy it?"

Nora gave her a pointed look. "I know what you and Melanie did. You could have warned me, at least, that Aiden would be teaching the class."

"Would you have gone?" her mother countered, and Nora sighed.

"Probably not."

"So? How was it?" Rhonda's eyes twinkled, and she reached for her cocoa. Nora knew her mother had been waiting for the moment to get her to spill the details. She wondered how long Rhonda and Melanie had conspired over this. She doubted it had been a spur of the moment thought.

"I was caught completely off guard. I stepped on his toes and elbowed him in the face when we ended up dancing together." Nora let out a dramatic sigh. "But we ended up talking today at the Mug, actually. He was there while I was working. Obviously, I had to apologize again for almost taking him out."

"Obviously," Rhonda murmured.

"And then offer to *actually* take him out to dinner." Nora bit her lips nervously. "Sort of... kind of a date. Tomorrow night."

"Oh?" Her mother's eyebrows rose. "A date? With Aiden? Your vacation home is getting interesting. Maybe I should send some mistletoe with you."

"Easy there." Nora laughed. "I can't exactly classify it as a date. We didn't say it was that." She felt the flutter of nerves again, wondering if she was being ridiculous by even thinking of it in the same terms as a date. He'd said he liked her—but he could have meant that he just liked talking to her. Chatting companionably. He hadn't said he wanted to *date* her, and she hadn't been specific about it. In fact, even when referencing the old days of high school, she'd said she had thought he might have wanted to hang out again *or* ask her out.

He could have been referencing either, really.

"Do you want it to be a date?" Her mother looked thoroughly intrigued. It made Nora wonder what she'd thought of Rob. Clearly, Rhonda had no compunctions about Nora getting over him. But then again, for all the years that she'd been with him, he'd barely met her family. She was sure her mother had thoughts about that, that she'd kept to herself.

"Maybe." Nora reached for her cocoa, taking solace in the rich chocolate. "He really did grow up to be impressively good-looking. And he's charming, and funny when he wants to be. He's hard to ignore. Even if I wanted to." *And I'm not sure I want to.*

"He had a thing for you back in high school," Rhonda observed, and Nora laughed softly.

"I thought the opposite. I thought he wasn't interested. But maybe I was wrong about that. And… I don't know. I don't know what to think. It's not going to go anywhere, but I get a little bit of butterflies thinking about it being a date."

Nora was surprised to hear herself admit it out loud, and to her mother. They'd never really talked about boys. Nora had been too focused in high school to date much, not seeing the purpose when she intended to flee Evergreen Hollow as soon as possible, and they'd never talked about who she was seeing in college.

She'd told her mother about Rob, and they'd met briefly, and of course she would have sent an invite to the wedding. But it had never been like *this*, mother and daughter sitting in the kitchen with cookies and cocoa, talking about Nora's love life.

It felt nice. Like home, if she was being honest. And she didn't really know what to do with that feeling either.

Rhonda gave her a gentle look, reaching over to pat her daughter's hand. "Have fun, Nora. You deserve it."

It still felt like an alien concept to her, just having *fun*. Not worrying about where it might go, or if it was silly to go on a date with a man who was never leaving Evergreen Hollow when she had every intention of leaving again. Normally, she would have said it was pointless. That all of these thoughts and feelings were foolish, when they couldn't *become* something.

But maybe her mother had a point, just like Aiden had a point earlier when he talked about just having a hobby.

Maybe a date could just be that. A date because it gave her butterflies and sounded fun, and she wanted to go. Maybe some things could just be because she wanted to, and not because they had a purpose, or would help her career, or would lead to an eventual marriage.

Maybe not everything had to check off a box on a list.

"Thanks." Nora stood up, bending to give her mother a kiss on the cheek. "For everything," she added, as she took her mug to the sink.

She wasn't sure what the dinner out with Aiden would be like.

But she was excited to find out.

CHAPTER SEVENTEEN

Aiden felt like a nervous schoolboy as he drove up to The Mistletoe Inn, parking his truck in the driveway as he slid out to go knock on the door and pick Nora up for their dinner out. Their *date*, he nearly thought—but what it really was, he reminded himself, was a dinner between old acquaintances to catch up. Thinking of it as a date wouldn't do anything except get his hopes up for something that he had no concrete reason to think of it as.

The door opened almost as soon as he knocked, and he saw Nora's mother, Rhonda, standing there.

"Come in!" She stepped back, holding the door open for him. "It's cold out. Nora should be down soon—Nora!" Rhonda turned toward the stairs, calling her daughter's name, and Aiden stifled a smile as he knocked the snow off of his boots and stepped into the warm entryway.

The whole thing had a tinge of nostalgia to it—a little like they were getting a high-school do-over, he thought. Like he was coming to pick her up at her parents' house and take her out.

"I'm coming!" Nora's voice drifted down from the upper floor, and Aiden felt a small tingle of excitement. Whether the dinner turned out to really be a date or not, this was something he'd wanted for a long time, and the anticipation of seeing her tightened his chest. It felt a little like a dream, if he was being honest.

"Where are the two of you going?" Rhonda asked politely, and Aiden smiled.

"Nora said she got a reservation at Marie's. I don't have an occasion to go there often, so I'm looking forward to it."

"That's a nice place to catch up." There was a small, amused twitch at the corners of Rhonda's mouth that made Aiden think she had some opinions about what kind of dinner it was too. He got the feeling that she was hoping it was a date too.

The sound of heels against the wood floor made Aiden turn, and his jaw nearly dropped. Date or not, Nora had made an effort for their dinner out—

she always looked beautiful and put together, but just then he thought that she looked especially stunning. She was wearing a charcoal gray knit sweater dress with a shawl collar, tall black velvet high heeled boots, and she'd added a red lip to her usual light makeup. He noticed she was wearing a pretty gold necklace with a pearl dangling from it, and matching earrings, her hair lightly curled so it swept around her shoulders. It was hard not to stare.

"Hi, Aiden." Nora smiled, and he felt a similar smile spread across his own face.

"Hey there." He couldn't quite think of anything else to say, momentarily frozen in place by just how beautiful he thought she looked—and the only thing that saved him from Nora realizing he'd gone speechless was the sound of the front door opening heavily again.

He recognized Caroline as she walked by, striding past their small group with barely a glance. He didn't see her often around town, but he remembered her. She had the same vaguely irritated expression on her face that it seemed she always wore, and she was dressed for work in faded jeans, a heavy flannel, and outdoor boots with a Carhartt jacket over it all. She paused as she passed Nora, seemingly taking in her sister's appearance, and then glanced back.

"Oh. Hey, Aiden. Long time no see." She pressed her lips together, looking between him and Nora. "What are you up to?"

Rhonda spoke up before either he or Nora had a chance to respond. "They're headed out on a date." There was a hint of glee in her voice that confirmed what he'd been thinking at the start—she was thrilled that he and Nora were reconnecting. It gave him a small boost of confidence. He'd reminded himself often since Nora's invitation not to get his hopes up that it might go somewhere—at the end of the day, Nora was still just visiting. But having family in his corner mattered to him when it came to this sort of thing, and just in case, he was glad that it seemed Rhonda approved.

Caroline smiled, but it looked stiff, not quite meeting her eyes. "Well, have a good time, you two." She gave her sister another cursory glance, and then swept from the room.

Nora's eyebrows rose ever so slightly, but her face was otherwise blank. "Well then." She smiled at Aiden. "Should we go?"

"Have fun!" Rhonda called as they walked out, Aiden holding the door for Nora and walking a bit ahead of her so that he could open the side door to the truck. She gave him a small, almost amused smile, but pulled herself up into the passenger side without a word.

"Very chivalrous of you," she said once he was inside, starting the engine so the cab could begin to warm up. She still had that small smile on her face, but he could see she was tense. He had a feeling it had something to do with Caroline's reaction—that it had bothered her. She'd been perfectly relaxed until her sister had walked in.

"How are things between you and Caroline?" he asked carefully, putting the truck in gear. "She still has that look like her shirtsleeves are a little too tight."

Nora's sudden laugh came out almost as a snort, and she put a hand over her mouth, stifling the sound. The sound of it, and the sideways look she gave him, made him chuckle too. *A good start*, he couldn't help but think—the two of them already making each other laugh.

"Things have been—strained, with us," she admitted after a moment. "I mean, they have been for a while. Years, really. Mom had that hip replacement right when I was moving to Boston, and Caroline had some pretty clear opinions about it.

She thought I should be moving back home and helping with the inn, not heading off to start a career in the big city. I didn't see why I should give up everything when she clearly was more than happy to be in charge, and I thought I could still be a part of the family from a distance. I had all of these goals and dreams, and coming back to Evergreen Hollow to help run Mistletoe wasn't part of that. It felt like Caroline thought I wasn't doing enough to help—that I haven't been, over the years. I always felt guilty about it." Nora twisted her hands together in her lap, and Aiden saw her look out of the window at the town passing by. "I don't think she'd believe that I felt guilty, but I really did. And I feel even more guilty now, since I'm back home and Caroline can give me all of those looks in person."

He felt a pang of sympathy. It was clear it weighed on her—he could hear it in her voice. And it felt obvious to him that she *did* care—that she always had, even if she'd gone on to Boston instead of coming back home. If she hadn't cared, she wouldn't have given all of it a second thought, or felt as guilty as it was clear to him that she did. "Personally," he said, turning the truck down the main street toward Marie's, "I think it's amazing that you stuck to your goals and achieved everything that you planned to.

Plenty of people have dreams and goals, and they just think about them and don't ever put it into action. You did exactly what you set your mind to, and that's pretty impressive in my opinion."

"Thank you." Nora gave him a small, grateful smile, and he tried not to think about the way it made his heart race.

"We're here." He turned the truck into Marie's parking lot. A warm glow was coming from the large, black-framed windows set in the cream stone building, lighting up the snowdrifts and welcoming them in. Aiden walked around to open Nora's door for her, getting another of those tiny smiles, and he returned it as they walked to the large black door at the front of the restaurant, flanked by two old-fashioned light fixtures.

He hadn't been to Marie's in so long that he'd forgotten what a romantic atmosphere it had. They were led by the hostess into the main dining room, to one of the white-cloth covered tables near the lit fireplace. That fireplace and the candles on the tables and set along the windowsills were the only source of light in the room, giving it a soft glow that felt close and cozy. There was a garland hung on the mantel of the fireplace, with small silver and gold ornaments catching the flickering light, and as he pulled out Nora's seat for her he couldn't help thinking that this *definitely* felt like a date.

It didn't feel like the sort of dinner where acquaintances just sat down to catch up, that was for sure.

"I haven't been here in so long," Nora murmured as she picked up the wine list, echoing his thoughts from earlier. He wondered, briefly, what she would think of the selection—if she'd be disappointed. She'd probably been to plenty of restaurants in Boston fancier than this. But she seemed to spot a wine that she liked immediately, glancing at Aiden. "Do you like red or white?"

He shrugged. "I don't drink often. I'm happy to drink whatever you pick."

Nora laughed softly. "There's that whole thing about red with meat and white with seafood, but I really just prefer red with anything, honestly. It's very gauche of me, I think, but that's what I like."

"Get that, then." Aiden grinned, and she gave him a mischievous smile, as if she were doing something she shouldn't.

"A bottle of—this Malbec, please," she said when the waitress came to their table, tapping her nail against the list. "And a water? We'll need a minute for appetizers, I think."

"Water for me," Aiden added. There was something very self-possessed and elegant about her, as he watched her order, and he could see why anyone would think she was out of place back here in Evergreen Hollow. But he thought there was a little of both in her still—the small-town girl and the big city go-getter, and he privately thought that he didn't see why they couldn't coexist, if she wanted them to.

As the waitress left to get their drink order, Nora looked sideways at him, glancing between him and the menu in front of her. It was cream-colored stock, with fine black script listing the menu items, and he wasn't at all sure what he might want. When he wasn't getting takeout from Rockridge Grill, he usually cycled through the same three or four easy dinners at home.

"Have you ever gotten pushback from your family about your career choices?" The question might have seemed blunt, but he knew she was circling back to what they'd talked about on the drive over, about her own sister's opinions.

Aiden sat back a little, considering. "A little, yeah. Most people seemed to think I should have moved to a city after I finished trade school. Better money, better opportunities, all of that. I've heard it from Leon before, for sure—that I'm too good at my job to spend it all here in Evergreen Hollow, even though he says it in terms of how lucky the town is to have me here."

He shrugged. "But I wanted to come back home. My family is here, my roots are here. How you felt about going to Boston despite what everyone else might think about that choice, that you knew it was the right thing for you—that's how I felt about coming back home. I love this town, and I want to make sure it keeps thriving. That can only happen if people pour their hearts into it."

"You really care about Evergreen Hollow, don't you?" Nora had stopped looking at the menu, and was just looking at him. "You feel like it matters."

"I know it matters. It's a place where everyone counts on each other. Where they'll put aside their grievances and try to understand each other, even if they're at odds sometimes. Most of the world—no one leans on anyone else anymore. Independence is a good thing up to a point, but having people you know you can rely on in a pinch, who won't keep a ledger of debts owed after the fact—that matters a lot. And feeling a connection to something—that matters too, I think."

He broke off as the waitress returned, setting down the bottle of red wine and two glasses as she poured for them both. "Do you want an appetizer?" she asked, and Nora glanced at Aiden.

"The brie with pears and maple sounds good. What do you think?"

Aiden wasn't sure he'd ever eaten brie, but he nodded. "I'll try whatever you're having," he said with a grin, and Nora flashed him a return smile.

"We'll have that, then. And then maybe a little more time before we order our meal."

It was clear she wasn't in any hurry to rush the dinner along, and that made him feel good. He wasn't in any hurry either—he was enjoying her company, and it was good to see that she seemed to feel the same. She reached for the wine, nodding a little as she took a sip.

"It's really good."

Aiden took a sip of his. "I don't think I have much of a refined palate for wine," he said with a small laugh. "But it tastes good to me."

"It is nice, being back in Evergreen Hollow," Nora admitted. "Everything is a lot slower. I forgot how much. I thought it would drive me crazy, but it's honestly been relaxing, once I got past feeling guilty for liking it." She let out a small laugh. "And it's been a little bit of a blow to the ego, finding out everything didn't collapse without me in Boston—but it's also given me a little freedom to let myself enjoy being home."

Aiden felt a small flare of hope, as Nora paused, thanking the waitress as she brought the appetizer. He could tell that the conversation was encouraging Nora to stop and think differently about Evergreen Hollow—about the things that made it important, small as it is. The smile on her face was genuine, and she looked relaxed and happy, spreading a bit of the melting cheese on a toast point with the fruit and syrup. He could picture her here easily, again. He could picture this being a more usual thing for them both.

Would she ever consider moving back here? He reached for a bit of the appetizer for himself, putting it on the small China plate in front of him. The thought fled as soon as it slipped into his mind, as he watched her take another sip of her wine.

Nora was a driven, big-city girl to her core. She had been as long as he'd known her, before she'd even had a chance to actually go and carve out a place in Boston. She might be enjoying a breather while she was home for a little while, but that didn't mean she was going to upend her whole life.

She'd get over her breakup, and then she'd want to leave. He knew it was true, but it didn't stop the pang he felt as she turned to him with a smile, nodding at the bite of food on his plate.

"What do you think?"

He popped the bit of cheese and pears on toast into his mouth, considering. It was creamy and rich, the earthy flavor of the cheese mingling with the sweetness of the baked fruit and maple syrup. On its own, it was fantastic—paired with the wine, it was even better. "You really know how to choose food and wine," he said with a small laugh, and a pleased flush spread over Nora's cheekbones.

"Catering is one of my favorite parts of being an event planner," she admitted. "Helping people choose menus for events is always so much fun. Sometimes they want my advice and sometimes they don't—sometimes they just go directly to the caterer, but when I get to sit in on those planning meetings, I always enjoy it."

"Maybe you should have your own catering company, then."

Nora laughed, shaking her head. "I like *all* the aspects of event planning. Not just that. I'd miss the other parts too. All of it is part of one big whole—taking someone's ideas and vision and the things that are important to them and making a day that they'll remember. But the food is a really fun part of it."

After a few minutes, the waitress returned, and they put in their order for dinner. Nora picked a lobster risotto, and he chose the lamb chops with roasted vegetables and garlic mashed potatoes. The fire crackled next to them, the sound of soft piano humming through the air as Nora refilled their wine, and he felt that he didn't want the evening to end. It had barely begun, but he was already anticipating whether or not he might get to see her again. Not just in passing—but spending time with her like this, just the two of them.

Nora took another bite of the brie and pears, sipping her wine. "Thank you for giving me another chance to hang out with you," she said with a smile, setting her glass back down. "And for forgiving me for hurting your eye."

She reached out as she said it, touching the corner of his eye. He knew she'd done it without thinking from the way she froze an instant after she touched him, her fingertip lingering for a brief second before she pulled back. She'd never touched him before, and the intimacy of the gesture made his heart beat hard in his chest. Her fingertips were soft, and he smelled a whiff of her burnt vanilla perfume.

He felt a flip in his stomach as she pulled her hand back, her cheeks flushing a little deeper. She reached for her wine quickly, her gaze flicking away, and he hurried to alleviate what could turn into awkwardness.

"I'm more than okay," he said quickly. "I've gotten hit harder than that bumping into a door at work. Not that you don't have a good right hook on you, I'm sure." He grinned, and Nora smiled into her glass, that flush of red still high on her cheeks.

"Carpentry is dangerous, then?" She laughed, and the moment eased, the relaxation between the two of them returning.

"I've bruised all ten of my fingers more than once, that's for sure." He paused as the waitress brought their dinners, setting the lamb in front of him and the risotto in front of Nora. "Can't say I was ever all that fond of heights either. But it's one of those things I just have to get over, for the parts of the job I do like."

"What are those? Besides building and preserving the town." Nora took a delicate bite of her risotto, and he cut a small piece off of one of his lamb chops. It was perfectly cooked, the meat melting on his tongue, spiced in a way that brought out the rich flavor of the meal.

"I like feeling useful. And there's a feeling of

completion that comes with having repaired a door, or fixed a windowsill, or put a new roof on. It's tangible. I've touched it, built it, I can see the results of that hard work every day. And I suppose I like taking care of the people that matter to me. Something happens in town—like that storm—and they know they have someone they can turn to that will make it right."

Something softened in Nora's face as he spoke, her gaze fixed on his, and his heart did that somersault in his chest again. "What about you?" he asked, clearing his throat as he scooped up a bit of garlicky mashed potato. "What are the hazards of event planning?"

Nora laughed, taking another bite of the lobster on top of her dish. "Bossy mothers-in-law, mixed-up dates, broken zippers on dresses, and the wrong color of flowers being delivered. Not nearly as dangerous as a smashed thumb, but it definitely requires thinking on your feet. Any of those things can ruin a day, if they're not fixed quickly."

"So we both fix things." Aiden looked at her, considering. "We both make something come into being, and we repair it when it goes wrong."

Nora gave him a small, tentative smile. "Mine only lasts for a day."

"A day that clearly means a lot to the people you create it for."

She sat back a little, reaching for her wine glass. "It means a lot to me too. I always feel like Caroline, for instance, thinks it's so shallow. That people spend so much money on an event that only lasts for a little while."

"The memories last though."

Nora brightened instantly. "Exactly. Memories, photos, even bits of things that get saved, like a bouquet. It all matters. I'm not just creating an event, I'm creating memories. Happiness. And it feels good, every time—even when things don't go quite according to plan."

She was passionate about her job, he could see it. As passionate as he'd always been about using his carpentry skills to keep Evergreen Hollow thriving.

He found himself wishing that he'd been brave enough back in high school to approach her. He'd made up a story back then in his head, he realized, about who Nora was and how she couldn't possibly be interested in him. He saw now that wasn't necessarily true.

There was no way to know what would happen now. Back then, he knew, nothing would probably have come of it either. He had always intended to learn a trade and come back home, and Nora had always been dead-set on leaving. One of them would have had to give, to make things work, and if they'd done that then one of them would have been unhappy. But as they shared a crème brûlée and finished the bottle of wine, he found himself hoping that there might be a second chance.

He stood up as Nora did, retrieving her credit card from the leather folio with the bill in it—she'd insisted on paying, since she'd invited him, and he'd let her. She wouldn't have let him pay, and there was a feeling that if one of them did, it really did make it a date.

"Ready to head back?" he asked, feeling a small sinking in his stomach at the knowledge that the night was almost over, and the way Nora looked at him as she nodded settled his resolve.

He didn't know where this could go, but he wasn't going to let fear hold him back again. If it didn't work out, things would be exactly as they were already—except he would know for sure. And he didn't want to let her go again without knowing.

That thought lingered in his head all the way back to The Mistletoe Inn, through their casual conversation about the dinner and their plans for tomorrow. He got out to open her door for her again, and as her boots hit the snow, she said what was on his mind at the exact same moment that the question spilled from his lips.

"I'd like to do that again," Nora said, right as he spoke.

"Can I take you out again?"

She laughed, the sound bright in the still, cold air, and he had the urge to lean down and kiss her. She looked up at him, her eyes sparkling, and he chuckled softly.

For a moment, everything seemed to slow. Nora was still looking up at him, and he wondered if she wanted him to kiss her. He wondered for a second too long, because she smiled, closing the door behind her as she turned to go up the stairs to the inn. "Let me know when you want that second date, Aiden Masters," she said with a cheeky laugh, and then she was headed up to the porch, disappearing inside.

He climbed back into his truck, watching the door close behind her. And he wondered, to himself, how it was going to feel when she left again.

But she hadn't left yet.

CHAPTER EIGHTEEN

It took Nora a moment to realize that she was humming to herself as she made her coffee the next morning. She felt more light-hearted than she had in a long time, flitting between the coffeepot and the refrigerator for the creamer, her planner and notes spread out on the small kitchen table. She was so caught up in her own thoughts that she didn't even hear her mother walk in at first.

"You're certainly cheerful this morning," Rhonda remarked as she walked to the basket of muffins on the counter. "The date must have gone well."

"It did," Nora admitted, reaching for a banana nut muffin and retreating to the table with her coffee. "I really didn't expect to go out on a date with anyone so soon after Rob and I broke up, honestly. I wasn't sure if I should even really think of it as a date, but it definitely was."

"Oh?" There was a small smile on Rhonda's face as she sank down in the chair across from her daughter. "Tell me more."

"I like him a lot." Nora twirled her pen, reaching for her coffee with her other hand. "We're going to go on another date. We pretty much asked each other at the same time when he dropped me off." She felt her face flush slightly at the memory. She had really thought he was going to kiss her, for just a second. Part of her was glad that he hadn't yet, since it would have complicated her feelings even more, but the other part of her felt giddy at the idea of a first kiss with Aiden.

"Well, that all sounds like good things." Rhonda tore off a small piece of her muffin. "Aiden is a good boy. He definitely always liked you."

"I'm really trying not to get caught up in the what-ifs." Nora took a sip of her coffee. "I want to just enjoy the moment, even if it doesn't go anywhere. I always look ahead to the next thing, the next step."

She let out a slow breath, glancing out of the

window for a moment at the snow-covered yard beyond the kitchen window. It was hard to admit how she felt out loud, even to her mother. The things she'd talked about with Aiden had been things she hadn't really admitted even to herself yet, but it had felt freeing. And he'd been understanding of it all.

"I've started to wonder if being so caught up in my ambitions for my life made me miss important things over the years." Nora looked down at her planner, tapping her fingernails against her to-do list. "There were things about Rob that should have told me he wasn't the right one for me a long time before he broke off our engagement. But I didn't see them, because I was so focused. My job, my apartment, hitting all the right milestones in our relationship. I just kept looking forward to the next thing, the next box to check, and everything else kind of got glossed over, I guess."

Rhonda looked at her for a long moment. "You shouldn't be hard on yourself," she said finally. "But if there are lessons you can learn from moving at a slower pace for a little while, then you should embrace them."

She reached out, putting her hand gently over Nora's. It was warm and delicate, exactly as Nora remembered when she was a child—that hand on her forehead when she was sick, or holding hers when they crossed a street. She'd pulled away from her family so much while she'd been gone, but they were happy to let her come back home. She felt a small ache in her chest, a pang of that feeling that she'd missed more than she realized, and she curled her fingers around her mother's hand.

"I'm going to do my best to just let things be, for now," Nora said firmly. "And just let everything play out without thinking too far ahead. Right now, I have a festival to plan."

"You do." Rhonda smiled, getting up from the table to go and pour herself another cup of coffee. "And the festival is going to be better for it, I'm sure."

Nora felt a renewed vigor when she headed out for the day, a feeling of confidence. She had no idea why Sabrina felt it necessary to make things difficult, but she was determined to plan the event anyway, exactly as she and the other women had discussed. If Sabrina didn't want to talk about what was bothering her, Nora couldn't make her.

That feeling ebbed, just a little, as soon as she walked into the event center for the planned meeting and saw that Sabrina was there, sitting next to Bethany with a list in her lap. Everyone had been so adamant that Sabrina had too much to handle with the newspaper, and Bethany had said not to expect to see her at any more of the meetings. But she was there, her cat-eye glasses perched on her nose, and a frown on her face.

As Nora got closer, sinking into one of the chairs in the circle that had been set up, she saw that the list in Sabrina's lap was the catering menu Nora had put together and finalized last night, after she'd gotten back from her date with Aiden. She'd been even more excited about it, after their conversation at the restaurant. His suggestions that she should lean in to how much she had always enjoyed working on catering menus had made her want to put her all into the choices for the festival, and she felt a tight knot of apprehension in her stomach as she looked at the red pen in Sabrina's fingers.

There were a number of slashes through items on the menu, notes made next to them. Nora bit her lip, frowning.

"What's wrong with the choices on the menu?" Nora tried to keep her voice even. She didn't want to be the cause of any more friction with Sabrina, but she felt a wave of disappointment, seeing the menu being butchered. "I put a lot of thought into that."

"Well." Sabrina looked up, her expression

pinched. "I'm sure this menu is fine in *Boston*, but here we like things a little more down to earth. Shrimp and crème fraiche on crostini? Duck pastrami and blueberry thyme jam with goat cheese? And down here, deconstructed chicken bites with maple glaze. I've never heard of so much fancy nonsense."

"Some of this we don't even have to cater outside of town. Marie's said they can accommodate over half this list, and then—"

"I know you're not familiar with the kinds of things we like," Sabrina continued, as if Nora hadn't even spoken, her tone slightly patronizing. "But I'd prefer if we just stick to smaller-portioned sizes of foods we already eat regularly. Maybe lasagna bites from Rockridge Grill? Deep-fried. And the maple is a nice touch, but mini pancakes instead, with syrup and local butter. We could do that with a hot cocoa bar."

Nora bit her lip, trying to fight back the instant emotional response. She'd worked so hard, and been so proud of it, but maybe she'd gone overboard. She let out a slow breath, nodding. "Some of these things I think would still be really nice to try. The duck pastrami, and the boar sausage, the deer salami?

Those things I thought would be a nice nod to the hunting that's so popular here. Elevated versions of popular game meat..." She trailed off, seeing Sabrina's eyes narrow. "But the bite-sized pancakes are a fun idea," she finished lamely. "And I love hot cocoa bars."

"Well, that decides it." Sabrina crossed something else out, turning to murmur something to Bethany, who caught Nora's eye. *Just go with it,* her expression seemed to say, and Nora let out a sigh.

She was sure some of it could be salvaged. Sabrina probably wouldn't be putting in the catering orders, after all. She wanted to keep the peace—but she couldn't help but feel confused as to why on earth this woman was so put off by her involvement. It felt almost petty, some of the changes. Like she was so determined to undermine Nora that she found any excuse to find fault.

Nora found it hard to concentrate for the rest of the meeting. Afterward, she cornered Melanie as they helped clean up, eager to tell her about the date with Aiden.

"It was really nice," she confided, as they cleared leftover cups and plates off the long table that had held snacks for the meeting. "I remembered him being sweet and friendly in high school, but he's really grown up. And he loves Evergreen Hollow so much, it was really heartwarming to hear. It's clear he's put a lot of work into trying to take care of it."

"So it was a good date?" Melanie gave her a mischievous smile, and Nora laughed, shaking her head.

"I'm not getting my hopes up," she said firmly. "But it was fun to go on a date with someone who was so smart, and sweet, and funny. It made me realize how stale my relationship with Rob was. If nothing else, it really made me see that the end of that relationship was a blessing in disguise. Whatever happens next, I know I'll make sure to look for someone who has more in common with me than just ambition. Someone who I can laugh with, and who really gets excited to hear about the things I'm interested in."

"You deserve that." Melanie pushed a piece of hair behind her ear, carrying a bag of trash to the back door. "I'm glad you're finally starting to see it."

Nora bit her lip. "We have a second date planned," she confided, unable to keep a small quiver of excitement out of her voice. Melanie's face lit up, and she felt a smile spread across her lips.

"I knew it." Melanie grinned. "One date, and you'd want to see each other again."

"Don't get ahead of yourself," Nora warned. "It's just a second date. It's nothing serious. Just us enjoying each other's company. But I *am* excited." She glanced around, making sure that it was just the two of them. "I've been brainstorming ideas too. Not just for making the festival a success, but to increase business at the inn."

"The inn?" Melanie frowned. "I didn't know it needed help."

Nora let out a slow breath. "It's been slow lately. My mom doesn't want to say much about it, and I know Caroline would never admit it, but it's been difficult, I think. I want to try to help."

"Of course you do. I noticed Rhonda had been a bit more quiet lately. But I thought it was just the usual holiday busyness. I can understand how stressful it gets, running a business."

"Oh, I know. You do such an amazing job with The Mellow Mug too."

"And I love it. But it's definitely not easy."

Nora mulled that over as she and Melanie finished up, thinking that maybe she could understand a little more why Caroline always seemed so sharp and intense. She was under a lot of pressure. It couldn't be easy, feeling responsible for helping their mother keep things afloat. Maybe she could try to take some of that pressure off, if she came up with some ideas for the inn.

At least, she thought, her family would be more receptive to her ideas than it seemed Sabrina had been.

CHAPTER NINETEEN

Two days after their date, Aiden found himself still thinking about Nora as he sat in the cab of his truck, eating a sandwich on his lunch break.

Truthfully, he hadn't been able to *stop* thinking about her since then. Every time he thought about the date, he felt a grin spread over his face, making him feel like a schoolboy all over again. And it had gone better than expected, all things considered. He still felt a little nervous around her, but he'd been nowhere near as tongue-tied as he had a tendency to sometimes get.

He'd felt as if he were getting to know the real her, not just the perception of her that he'd always had from the outside. And he'd found that he liked that real version even better.

He took another bite of his sandwich, glancing at his phone on the dash. He could text her, he thought, see what she might want to do for that second date. He wanted to suggest something different—something more unique than just another dinner out or a movie.

Nothing ventured, nothing gained. He finished his sandwich, reaching for his phone and finding her number.

AIDEN: What do you think about a hike for our next date? Sound fun to you?

A tapping sound against his window made him jump, and he looked over to see Blake standing there. "Should we get back to work?" he called through the glass, and Aiden nodded, opening the door and sliding out of the cab, his boots crunching on the snow.

"Sorry about that," he said, a little sheepishly. "Lost track of time."

"No worries, man." Blake looked at him curiously, a hint of mischief in his eyes. "What's on your mind? You're not usually so distracted."

Aiden glanced at him, considering brushing it off and keeping things to himself. But deep down, he wanted to talk about Nora. He'd felt like he was bursting for the last two days, wanting to tell someone about the date.

"I took Nora out Saturday night," he said, scratching the back of his neck as they started to walk back to the shed they were working on repairing. "Dinner at Marie's."

Blake whistled. "That's a fancy night out," he said with a grin, and Aiden shook his head.

"She was worth it. I've been wanting that date for a long time. Wasn't sure how it would go, exactly, but it was better than I could've expected. And we're going to see each other again, so..." Aiden lifted one shoulder in a half-shrug.

Blake grinned. "That's fantastic, man!" His voice brimmed with enthusiasm, and as casual as Aiden had tried to be about it, he could tell that Blake could see how excited he really was. "You've been waiting a long time to find a lady you really click with."

"Well, we'll see how it goes." Aiden rubbed a hand over his mouth. "Nothing serious right now. She's just visiting anyway. But it's nice to get out and spend some time with someone whose company I like."

"You're a great catch," Blake said, pushing open the door to the shed. "Any woman would be lucky to have your attention. If it's not her, it'll be someone else who sees it."

Aiden grinned. "Thanks, man. I appreciate it." He did too. It felt good to have his friend's encouragement. Blake had always had his back.

His phone buzzed in his pocket, just as he was about to set it down and get back to work. He glanced at the screen and saw Nora's name, his heart doing a little flip in his chest as he realized she'd responded to his message.

NORA: Hiking sounds fun! It's been a while since I've gone, so I hope you don't mind if we take an easy trail. There's not a lot of hiking in Boston.

Aiden grinned, typing out a quick response.

AIDEN: Easy sounds just fine. Just looking forward to hanging out again. You an early bird?

NORA: Always. What's early for you?

AIDEN: Six a.m.? I can meet you at the inn, pick you up.

NORA: Sounds like a plan!

Aiden set his phone down, feeling a flush of elation that warmed him through and through, despite the chill in the shed. He'd wondered how she'd take the suggestion, but it was clear she was excited about it. And he was too. More than anything, he was excited to show her something that she couldn't get in Boston.

Something that she could only do with him here, in Evergreen Hollow.

* * *

Nora felt a thrill of excitement as she came downstairs, the graying early morning light just starting to come through the windows as she poured herself a thermos of hot coffee and tugged her boots on. She hadn't been hiking in a long time, and she was a little worried about her ability to keep up, but she felt confident Aiden wouldn't mind. She was looking forward to spending time with him doing something different.

She'd been telling the truth when she said she was an early riser, but usually she was still tired, getting up *this* early. This morning though, she felt as if she were buzzing even without the coffee, eager to see Aiden and head out on the trail. She felt as if she had more energy than she'd had in a long time.

The sound of truck tires over snow and gravel came from outside, and she sprang up out of her chair, grabbing the thermos and going to the front door. Aiden was idling outside, waiting for her, and she headed over to the passenger side and jumped in.

"I brought all the gear we might need," Aiden said conversationally, as he backed out of the driveway and turned onto the road. "There's a pretty easy trail that goes up to a hill at the edge of the woods. It's a nice place to see the sun rise."

"I like the sound of that." Nora flashed him a smile. "I haven't taken the time to enjoy that sort of thing as much as I should have, I think."

"Well, if there's anything worth getting up this early on a day off for, it's seeing a sunrise over Evergreen Hollow." Aiden grinned. "I've always been an early riser, but this is a bit more than even I'm accustomed to."

"Me too," Nora admitted, laughing. "But I'm glad we decided to do this. It'll be a fun experience."

She glanced over at him as he pulled onto the main road, enjoying the light banter. It amazed her how well and how easily they got along, when they hadn't really known each other all that well before. It made her wonder what might have been different, if she'd approached him in high school instead of waiting for him to approach her, if something might have happened with them then. She could have skipped all the drama with Rob, not wasted years on a relationship that in the end, she'd found out had never meant as much to him as it had to her.

But then I wouldn't have left Evergreen Hollow, she thought, looking back out at the highway with a confused feeling in her stomach. So much of her life and her identity was tied up in that moment—the one where she'd stuck to her plans and left, no matter what anyone else had to say about it. When she'd taken charge of her life and *made* it what she wanted it to be. Aiden had even said he was impressed with that, with her ability to stick to her goals and insist on her life being what she'd dreamed of.

Where would she be, if she'd stayed instead of going to Boston with Rob? Would she have been happy if she hadn't left Evergreen Hollow?

The question swirled in her mind as they drove, and she still hadn't settled on an answer to it by the time they reached the trailhead and Aiden parked, killing the engine and coming around to open her door.

It was beautiful, every bit as much as she'd expected it to be—and more. The snowy vista stretched out in front of them, pristine and smooth, their boots sinking in the thick drifts as they started off. The trees were shadowy in the early dawn light, the cold sharp and biting, but she found that she didn't mind. The entire world felt quiet around them, narrowed down to just her and Aiden, and she felt her mind go quiet too. It felt easier than usual to leave her worries back with the truck, all the things crowding her thoughts, and just enjoy the moment.

Aiden reached for her hand, helping her over a patch where several branches had fallen into the path, and her heart leapt in her chest. She could feel the warmth of his palm through her glove, his hand broad and solid around hers, and she felt safe. Her pulse beat quickly in her throat, even after he let go, and when he did it again, she felt the same rush.

"This hike is one of my favorites for clearing my head," Aiden said as they walked, looking ahead to the trees in front of them. "Not too tough, but still requires enough focus that you need to leave all that other stuff behind. And it's so quiet out here, especially in early morning. Winter is my favorite time for it, believe it or not."

"You really have to like the cold to enjoy this," Nora said, laughing, and Aiden nodded.

"Nothing clears the mind like a brisk winter walk." He glanced over at her. "What about you? What do you do to relax? Back in Boston, I mean."

"Oh, I don't know. I'm not great at relaxing," Nora admitted. "But I do like being at home. Curling up with some tea and a bad tv show is always a favorite. Or a day at the spa. A good massage makes a lot of things better."

Aiden chuckled. "No spa out here. But I hear there's a nice hot spring a couple hours' drive away. I haven't been there myself, but I've heard it's a nice place to relax."

"That does sound nice." Nora paused, letting him help her over another rough patch, the path starting to turn a little steep as they got closer to the hill. "I was just thinking that, though—that this is really good for getting a break from all the stress. It's so beautiful and peaceful out here. I never hiked much when I lived here before, but this starts to make me wish I had."

"Why not?" Aiden glanced at her, and Nora shrugged.

"I have a really bad sense of direction," she admitted, and they both laughed.

For a little while, they fell into companionable silence as they walked. Nora looked around as they went further into the trees, seeing it with new eyes. She'd never really appreciated it before, feeling hemmed in by how rural it all was, how far away from 'civilization.' But after spending so long in the city, she found that she could appreciate the quiet better. The beauty of it seemed fresh and new, like she was seeing it all for the first time.

In a way, she supposed that she really was.

She looked over, about to say something to Aiden, and her heart nearly stopped when she saw that he wasn't next to her. She turned around, pulse beating for an entirely different reason, and she saw that some several yards back the path had forked. Lost in thought, she must have fallen back a little and veered off.

Quickly, she turned around, retracing her steps. She was sure he would come back too, once he realized they'd gotten separated, but she didn't see him. It *must* have been this fork where they'd lost track of each other, but when she went left instead of right, assuming she'd catch up to him quickly, she didn't see any sign of him. Not even boot prints, to suggest that he'd come this way.

She felt a spark of panic, blooming in her chest. *This was a mistake,* she thought. *The hike. Coming back. All of it.* She knew it was an overreaction, but turned around in the woods, it almost felt like a sign. Like a reminder that she didn't belong here in Evergreen Hollow.

Nora turned around, her heart hammering in her

chest—and then she heard Aiden's voice calling through the trees.

"Nora?"

"I'm here!" She lifted her hand, waving it, although she couldn't see him to tell if he could see her. "I'm over here!"

"I hear you! Just stay there!"

A moment later, she saw him coming through the trees, and she felt a little weak with relief. He caught up to her, concern on his face, and Nora felt herself flush a little.

"It all looks the same to me out here," she admitted, feeling a little embarrassed. "Just snow-covered landscape. I got turned around."

"Your lack of direction really is appalling," he said gravely, but she could see the corners of his mouth twitching. "At least one of us can find our way."

"Thank goodness for that." She could see the humor in his eyes, that he wasn't annoyed, and it eased her anxiety. She laughed, glancing ahead. "Want to help me find my way back to where we're supposed to be?"

"Gladly."

Aiden guided her back to the trail, and they hiked up the hill in companionable silence once more, Nora being more careful not to get separated. "This way," he said, pointing to the peak of the hill. "The best spot to watch the sun rise."

She followed him up, a little out of breath, but as they stood side by side she could see the sky starting to flood with color, the first rays of dawn breaking. It was stunningly beautiful, and it made her breath catch a little, seeing it.

"I'm sorry for the heartbreak you've been through recently." Aiden's voice startled her a little, low and quiet. "But I'm grateful it brought you back to Evergreen Hollow."

Nora turned, surprised. His face was serious, his eyes meeting hers, and she felt the quick leap of her heart in her chest. "I am too," she said softly, looking up at him, and she saw his lips curve in a soft smile.

His hand reached up, gloved fingers touching her jaw as he leaned in, and her heart raced. It had been a long time since someone had kissed her for the first time.

And when his mouth touched hers, there on the snowy hillside as the sun came up around them, she was glad it was him.

CHAPTER TWENTY

After the hike, Nora came home feeling the most rejuvenated that she had since she'd been home. Even the early hour that she'd gotten up and the physical exertion hadn't worn her out, and she came back to the inn eager to dive back in to planning for the festival. The inn had been quiet when she came back, but she'd grabbed a couple of banana muffins and another mug of coffee, and hours had passed before she'd looked up from her notebook and realized it was past lunch.

Her high spirits extended into the evening. She knew that part of it was because of the kiss with Aiden—a kiss that she had to admit a small part of her had been hoping for, but that she hadn't been sure would really happen.

She knew too, that she was starting to have feelings for him. It felt impossible not to. The easy way they were able to talk to one another, the way she felt so comfortable around him, the clear respect he had for her and her accomplishments even though her life had been so different from his—and it didn't hurt that he'd grown up to be an incredibly handsome man. She could feel the casual interest starting to grow into something more. Surprisingly, it didn't frighten her as much as she had thought it might.

Everything with him felt so different from how it had with Rob—night and day, so different that it felt impossible to compare, even if she had really wanted to. Which she didn't, because for the first time in a long time, everything about her romantic life felt so *good*.

It felt right. It made her feel as if she were finally on the right path, while simultaneously making her realize that she hadn't been before. Rob had never been right for her. She just hadn't been able to admit it, because it would have felt like failure. She hated failure.

She would have rather been trapped than admit a mistake. But now, she saw it all more clearly.

Her mother came in just then, her father just

behind Rhonda, and Nora's excitement crested. She'd been waiting all day to share her ideas with them, and she waved excitedly at her parents, gesturing at the chairs next to the fire.

"Can you sit down for a minute? I want to tell you something I've been thinking about."

"Of course," her father said affably, sinking into the chair. Rhonda sat down next to him, a curious expression on her face.

"What's going on, Nora? You look like you're about to explode at the seams."

"I have an idea." Nora turned to face them, trying to speak carefully through her excitement. "You told me a few days ago that things have been slow at the inn. Fewer guests than usual, this time of year."

Her mother's expression shuttered a little. "Well, yes, but—"

"I think I have something that will help it pick back up." Nora pressed her lips together, her enthusiasm nearly bubbling over. "The festival is coming up, right? We could offer a special promotion for the inn during the week of the festival." She tugged the sheet out from underneath her planner where she had written all of it down, handing it to her mother. "Anyone who stays here for three or more days during that week will get a discount on a stay of the same length during the following six months. They'll have an incentive to come back."

"Is that *really* a good idea?" Caroline's dry voice came from the doorway, and Nora's head shot up, along with Donovan and Rhonda's. None of them had realized Caroline was standing there listening, she realized. She'd just snuck up on the conversation, *as she often did,* Nora thought a little bitterly.

She was taking an interest in the inn for once, and she would have thought Caroline would be pleased by that, but of course she wasn't.

"I think it is," Nora said firmly, gathering her courage. "It could book out the inn months in advance. You need the guaranteed business, and it would incentivize people to give you exactly that. Guests you can plan for. You can even court more repeat business by making them feel special for returning. Maybe an extra add-on—"

"Why are you doing all of this?" Caroline interrupted again. "You've always made it very clear that you think the festival is silly and beneath you. That you don't have any interest in how this place runs. You've ignored it all this time, and now you've decided that since you have some spare time, you're going to stick your nose in? Because you know better?"

The tension in the room thickened, and Nora felt a cold sensation in the pit of her stomach. She bit her lip, unsure of what to say.

"Caroline." Rhonda spoke up. "There's no need for this."

"You never cared about the inn," Caroline snapped. "This is all just to make you feel good about yourself. You're bored, or... I don't know. When I said we needed you, you had better places to be. But now—"

Tears filled Nora's eyes before she could stop them, burning behind her eyelids. "Just because I didn't dedicate my *whole* life to the inn doesn't mean I don't care about its success," she protested, her voice cracking as she tried not to let the tears spill over.

She'd been so excited, so hopeful, and she could feel the idea falling flat, turning into something that she hadn't meant for it to be. An argument, when she'd truly just wanted to help.

"I *do* care about it," she insisted, looking at Caroline's impassive face. "And the festival. Would I really be putting so much work into helping it get publicity if I didn't?"

"Oh, for goodness' sake." Caroline shook her head, turning on her heel. She left in a huff as quickly as she'd come, and Nora stared after her, feeling bereft.

"Your sister doesn't mean to be so harsh," Rhonda started to say, leaning forward, and Nora turned, giving her mother a small smile.

"It's all right," she managed, trying to brush off the hurt feelings. "I get it."

And she *did*, a little better than she had before. These problems had clearly cropped up before Nora had become aware of them, and Caroline had been dealing with them for longer than Nora had realized. She couldn't entirely fault her sister for being so stressed and rigid, when so much was on her shoulders.

But at the same time, Caroline's words—and her dismissal of Nora's idea—had still hurt. She wasn't entirely sure how to reconcile the two feelings.

"I'm just going to keep working on it," Nora said quietly. "The festival, and ideas for the inn."

"I think it might be a good idea," Rhonda said, glancing at Donovan. "We'll have to run some numbers, and look at what that would mean for us, but it's certainly a starting place."

"It is," Donovan agreed, smiling at his daughter. "And I'm glad to hear your ideas."

Nora returned the smile, tapping her pen against the table.

If I keep trying, she thought to herself, *Caroline will see my actions mean something. It won't just be words.*

She had to hope so anyway. She didn't want to leave again with things so cold and tense between the two of them. She wanted Caroline to see that she really did care.

There was only one way to accomplish that though.

And she'd always been nothing if not determined.

CHAPTER TWENTY-ONE

Aiden stood at the counter of the Sugar Maple general store, waiting while Leon put the final touches on gift-wrapping the present he'd just purchased. He watched, thinking to himself that he was always surprised at what a deft hand Leon was at wrapping presents. It's not something he would have ever expected, but Leon had really perfected it over the years.

"You made an excellent selection here," Leon commented, taping down the last corner of the dark-green paper printed with silver and gold trees. "Who's it for?" He had a gleam in his eye as he looked at Aiden, his mouth curling up on one side, and Aiden knew he was caught.

"It's for Nora," Aiden admitted, unable to stop

the smile that spread over his face too. Just thinking about her had that effect on him, especially after the kiss they'd shared while watching the sunrise. He was eager to see her again and give her a gift that he hoped would tell her exactly how much he'd paid attention. How much he wanted to show her that he cared.

"You're both wonderful young folks," Leon said noncommittally, as if he were talking about the weather. "I could see the two of you being happy together, you know."

Aiden raised an eyebrow. "She has a whole separate life in the city." He said it flatly, as if he hadn't wondered since their first date whether or not Nora might change her mind about moving back. As if he hadn't imagined her deciding to take a different direction with her life, after coming home and experiencing Evergreen Hollow with fresh eyes. Now that things had changed between them—

He shook off the thought. He wouldn't move to Boston for her, give up the life that mattered to him here to go somewhere that he knew he wouldn't be happy, so why would he imagine that she would do the same in reverse? Their time together was limited, but he had been doing his best to simply enjoy it for what it was.

Leon seemed to read something in his expression. "Don't write off the possibility of things working out," he advised, tying a gold ribbon around the small package. "If the two of you want a relationship, there's always a chance it might go the way you hope it will. You never know."

"I'll try to keep that in mind. Thanks for this." Aiden picked up the package, nodding at Leon, and headed back out to his truck.

He'd been planning to save the gift until he saw Nora next, but as he drove past The Mellow Mug, he caught a glimpse of her familiar peacoat and navy scarf as she ducked into the coffee shop. On impulse he turned around, pulling into the parking lot and following her inside.

Nora looked up as the small bell above the door rang, and her face lit up when she saw him. He felt a flush of pleasure at that—at how happy she looked to see him. As if it had brightened her whole day.

She walked over to where he was standing as she waited for her coffee, smiling. "Come sit with me over there?" she asked, pointing to a corner table where Aiden saw that she'd set her things down. "Unless you need to be somewhere else."

"Nah, I can take a break for a little while. Perks of being my own boss." He grinned, and Nora laughed, a light musical sound that he thought he could easily get used to hearing. Leon's words echoed in his head. It was a long shot, but maybe he didn't have to entirely give up on the possibility of something working out between them.

They both grabbed their coffees, Aiden putting in an order for a macchiato after Melanie made Nora's, and Nora carried her drink and a plate with one of Melanie's buttery cinnamon rolls over to the table. They sat down next to each other, and Nora nudged her planner and magazines out of the way so there was room for their coffees and the pastry between them.

"Did you just stop by to get some midday caffeine?" she asked teasingly, and Aiden laughed.

"Actually, I was on my way to the grill to get some takeout. But I saw you coming in here, and I thought I'd stop because... well, I wanted to give you this." He reached into his pocket, taking out the gift that Leon had just finished wrapping. "Merry Christmas."

Nora's eyes widened as she took it from him. "Oh, Aiden, you didn't have to! I haven't gotten you anything! I actually haven't done any shopping," she added sheepishly. "I've gotten so caught up in festival planning I forgot I might need to get Christmas gifts for everyone."

He waved a hand. "You don't need to get me anything. I thought you would like this, that's all."

Nora carefully undid the wrapping paper, setting it aside as she lifted the lid off the small black box. She let out a small gasp when she saw what was inside.

It was a small golden compass on a fine gold chain, able to be opened up. There was a tiny diamond at the top, where the northern arrow would be. She stared at it for a long moment, and then back up at Aiden, her expression stunned.

"It's beautiful," she whispered, her eyes misting slightly, and he rubbed a hand over the back of his neck.

"Protection from getting lost again," he explained, smiling a little as he felt his face pinken. "Since you're so bad with directions and all."

Nora laughed, reaching for the necklace and immediately clasping it around her neck. She sniffed, touching it gently as it fell against the front of her sweater.

"I love it," she said, and leaned forward, her hand on Aiden's arm as she tilted her chin up to give him a soft kiss. The kiss lingered for just a moment, his hand covering hers, until he heard Melanie clear her throat from the counter.

"You know I can see you two, right?" Melanie teased from where she was standing, and Aiden felt his cheeks flush.

He chuckled sheepishly as he pulled back, and Nora laughed too, her eyes shining.

"What are your plans for the rest of the day?" Aiden asked, peering at the stack of magazines and the checklist stacked next to Nora's planner.

"I have a few orders to finalize for the festival." She gestured at her laptop. "Just some busy work is all, and then I'm going to brainstorm some more ideas for the inn."

Aiden took a long sip of his coffee, straightening. "Well, I don't want to keep you from it," he said, starting to get up, but Nora put a hand on his arm.

"You're welcome to stay while I finish up," she said, smiling, and the look on her face put him at ease. "After all, I can't finish this whole cinnamon roll by myself. And I like the company."

"I never turn down a good pastry." He grinned at her, relaxing back in his seat. He was happy that she'd extended the invitation. In all honesty, he thought as he picked at the cinnamon roll and sipped coffee while Nora opened her laptop and started looking over her list, he was enjoying just watching her work. He always thought she was beautiful, but there was something special about seeing her in her element, that focused expression on her face as she ticked away at items. He loved how he could see her mind racing as she scanned through ideas—it was obvious to him just how good she was at her job.

Leon always told him how lucky the town was to have him there, working to keep it in good shape, but he thought they were lucky to have Nora back too. Having her touch on the festival would make it an extra-special event this year, he was sure, and he was excited to see what she had in store. They hadn't talked much about the details of it, with too many other things to catch up on, and he was looking forward to the surprise.

He glanced up from his coffee a few minutes later, and saw Nora looking confusedly at her screen, her brow furrowed. "What's wrong?" he asked curiously, and Nora let out a breath, shaking her head.

"I have a Google doc for my inventory for the festival. I'm supposed to be the only one who has access to it, but I can see that Sabrina is active in it." She pursed her lips. "She's changing things I planned on ordering! I hadn't kept a backup list because this was supposed to only be available to me."

She turned the laptop around in an attempt to show him, frustration clearly written across her face, but Sabrina's icon had already disappeared.

"I don't see it," Aiden said apologetically, and Nora glanced back at the screen.

"She must have seen my icon in the document and logged off, knowing I'd notice." Nora's jaw tightened. "I don't understand why on earth she's so set on changing my plans for the festival. She's not even *talking* to me about it, she's just bulldozing in and doing things her own way." She let out a sharp breath. "I don't get it. I'm just trying to help."

Aiden ran a hand through his hair. "I wish I had an answer for you," he said quietly. He really did. He could tell the situation was frustrating her, and he wanted to do something to help. He just wasn't sure what that might be.

He couldn't solve the problem that was bothering her right then, that much he knew. But he wanted to do something to try and cheer her up. He ran a hand through his hair, offering her a smile.

"I'm going to be working late tonight. But maybe we could go for a walk tomorrow evening? Take your mind off things a little. And now you can't get lost."

He gestured at the dainty compass resting against the neckline of her blue sweater, winking at her teasingly.

Nora brightened instantly, and he felt a warm glow in his chest. "I like the sound of that," she said, agreeing instantly. "I think you're turning me into an outdoorsy girl after all, despite all that time in the city."

He grinned, cheered with the idea of how much the plan seemed to please her. She seemed genuinely enthusiastic, and Leon's words came back to him once more, generating a warm spark of hope in his chest.

Maybe she wasn't as eager to go back to Boston as he'd thought.

CHAPTER TWENTY-TWO

Saturday morning, Nora arrived at the event center with the planner and lists in hand, eager to get back to planning with the event committee. She'd made a backup document with her planned orders and inventory, locked so that Sabrina couldn't sneak into it, and she'd spent the night before telling herself that it didn't matter if one person was determined to get under her skin. Everyone else was on her side, and happy to have her helping out, and that was what mattered. At the end of the day, the festival would come together and be a success, and Sabrina would see that Nora's help had been worthwhile.

She set out the boxes of decorations that she'd already bought, a stack of custom signs sitting next to them, feeling her spirits rising again. She had a date tonight with Aiden to look forward to, and while her optimism had taken a bit of a blow, she'd always been good at bouncing back. That was part of what made her such an invaluable event planner in Boston—no matter who else was melting down about plans not going the way they should or something turning up missing, she was always able to keep a cool head.

The festival was getting closer, and she needed to focus on that, and what *was* coming together. She looked up from organizing the table, seeing Melanie, Bethany, and some of the other women starting to filter in, and she felt the spark of excitement return.

They all started unpacking what she'd brought, setting out garlands, velvet bows, and strings of light, laying out the custom signs.

"So what do you have planned for all of this?" Melanie asked, and Nora flashed her an excited smile.

"The decorations are going to have a theme for every area of the festival. Colors, lights, ribbons, everything with a theme and a color as you move from place to place. I had all of these ordered for the booths and each station." She gestured to the signs. "And then I have new tablecloths coming that match the themed tree for the main room for the buffet. There will be food stations throughout the festival too, with their own themes for each area, and I have a list of outside caterers I want to use. They're all highly rated. A few of the items that need to be fresh the day of I'll have Marie's handle, but the other caterers will bring in the menu items the day before."

"You've really planned out every inch of this." Bethany sounded faintly impressed, and Nora's excitement turned into a warm glow at the praise.

"I wanted to really make it something grand," she enthused. "It's had a little bit of a makeshift vibe in the past, and I wanted to make it more elegant, really showcase what it could be."

"That's exactly the problem." Sabrina's sharp voice cut through the air, and Nora and everyone else turned to see her striding in, her cat-eye glasses perched on her nose as she walked quickly to where the others were standing. "'Grand' is exactly what we don't want here. All of your 'grand' plans are going to ruin a festival that means so much to this town. Look at all of this." She swept her hand out, indicating the shipped items laid across the table. "There's no heart to any of this. None of it supports the locals in Evergreen Hollow. None of it is handmade by us, or cherished, or passed down, or has *anything* to do with who we are and what we want guests at the festival to see."

She crossed her arms over her chest, glaring at Nora. "The festival is supposed to be about *community*. And you've just turned it into some cold corporate affair."

Nora felt her stomach sink to her toes, Sabrina's words crashing into her like an icy wave. She looked at Bethany and Melanie for help, but Melanie was biting her lip, and Bethany seemed to be considering what Sabrina was saying. Some of the other women were nodding and murmuring, as if swayed by Sabrina's argument. Or maybe they'd just been thinking that all along, and had needed someone to say it out loud so they could agree.

Tears burned at the back of her eyes, an echo of a few nights ago when she'd broached her ideas for the inn. She felt crushed, defeated. She'd put so much work into the planning, creating an elaborate vision that she'd been so excited to see come to life.

But now, it felt as if no one had really wanted her to work on the event at all. That maybe they'd just felt sorry for her—running back home with her tail tucked between her legs after a breakup—and had thought they'd give her some busy work to take her mind off of it. Maybe they'd wanted her to fail, so that she could see once and for all that this wasn't the place for her.

So that she'd go back to where she belonged.

She bit her lip to hold back the tears, not wanting to cry in front of Sabrina. "I'm—I'm just going to go," she managed, hurrying toward the door. She wanted out of the event center before she fell apart.

Nora thought she heard Melanie call after her, but she ignored it. She needed to be alone.

They could figure it out. After all, it felt very clear that they didn't need her, after all.

* * *

Aiden pulled into the driveway of The Mistletoe Inn, pleased to see that Nora was already hurrying out of the front door, clearly eager for their walk. He opened the car door for her so that she could hop into the passenger seat, then backed out of the driveway and headed toward a quieter part of town past Main Street.

Many things were closed down for the day—including the antiques store, the post office, and a few other small shops—but the trees along the sidewalk were strung with fairy lights, and the snow had a warm and cozy glow as they parked and got out of the car.

Nora had bundled up in a soft, plush-looking

black jacket over leggings and boots, the navy scarf wound around her neck and tucked up under her chin, a thick black beanie pulled down over her dark hair. He thought she looked adorable all bundled up against the chill, but she had a slightly sad look on her face—not at all what he'd expected, considering how excited she'd been for their casual date.

"Is something going on?" he asked as they walked, not wanting to pry but worried about her. He linked his gloved fingers with hers, and Nora looked up at him, biting her lip.

"Sabrina and I had it out a little, at the planning meeting today. I had a bunch of the decorations ready and explained my ideas, and she just burst in and said it was all too grand!"

Nora's voice rose, more animated and cracking a little as she continued. It was clear that Sabrina had hurt her feelings badly.

"She said I've—that I've ruined everything that makes the festival special to Evergreen Hollow, that none of it supports or has anything to do with the people who live here, and that it's all just cold and corporate now." She sniffed, and Aiden thought it might not entirely be because of the cold. "I worked so hard on it, and it feels like it's all for nothing."

Aiden was quiet for a long moment as they

continued to walk, and he could feel Nora looking at him.

"What are you thinking?" she asked softly, and he sighed.

"You're not going to like hearing it."

He rubbed his other hand over his mouth, feeling the light scratch of stubble under his glove. He hadn't bothered shaving before they came out for their walk, in too much of a hurry to get Nora after he'd finished up work. Besides, he thought she might like it.

"I understand where Sabrina is coming from," he admitted, glancing at Nora to weigh her reaction. "The spirit of the festival is all about keeping things local. Outsourcing any of it takes away from that. It takes away from what it's always been meant to be about. It's not about how pretty or fancy it is, it's about showcasing what's here, right here in Evergreen Hollow."

Nora swallowed hard, audibly, and he felt her tug her fingers away. The color was high in her cheeks when he looked at her again, and he could tell that she was upset. It hurt his heart to see it. He hadn't wanted to upset her. But he also wanted to be honest with her. If they were going to have any kind of relationship, they had to be able to be honest with each other.

"Some of the other women felt that way too," Nora said quietly, shoving her hands into her pockets. "They were on board until Sabrina said her piece, and I could see they'd been having some of those same thoughts. Even Bethany and Melanie weren't completely on my side anymore." She bit her lip. "I just don't think I fit in here. I'm clearly not a good match with the people here. We don't think the same. We don't see things the same way."

She looked at Aiden, her expression dulled, the earlier happiness he'd seen in her drained away.

"In Boston, I was a successful event planner. One of the top ones in my field. People loved the events I put on. They came back and asked for me again. I did graduations and weddings, bridal and baby showers, all for the same people. There's a sense of community in that too, isn't there? But they loved what I did. Everyone here thinks it's soulless."

Aiden let out a breath. He wasn't sure exactly what to say, and he didn't want to make things worse. "Just because the people here want to keep the event more local," he said slowly, "doesn't mean they don't like you, Nora. It doesn't mean that you're not fitting in here."

She looked up at him, tears glittering in her eyes. "What else would you call it?" she demanded, her voice rising slightly. He could hear the crack in it, and it made his own chest ache. "I've started to see the beauty in Evergreen Hollow, but what does that matter if no one here wants anything I can bring to the table?"

Nora swallowed hard, looking away as she clearly tried to get her emotions back under control.

"At the end of the day," she said, her voice low and edged with frustration. "The people here just can't look beyond the confines of their small town. Not even to think a little bit outside the box."

Silence hung in the air for a long moment. "You're a great example of that," she said finally, her voice still quiet as she turned to look at him. "You have a great education as a carpenter. You went to a good trade school. You have everything going for you —talent, drive, recommendations—and yet instead of using it on a bigger scale, where your abilities could have really shone, you came back to Evergreen Hollow."

He recoiled slightly, the words stinging. He took a step back, slightly, feeling as if she'd reached in and poked a nerve that she in particular knew how to find. It hurt, to have his confidences used against him like that.

"And all you ever cared about was climbing the ladder," he retorted, his voice still quiet and even, but no less sharp. "There's more to life than that, Nora! All this knowledge you have about how to put together an event and what goes with what and how to attract visitors."

He waved his hands in frustration, letting out a breath as he tried to find the right words through his anger and hers.

"What *matters*, ultimately, is the personal touch. The thoughtfulness that goes into something. All these grand plans you have for the festival are perfect examples of *that*. These people don't want impersonal and fancy. They don't want perfectly catered menus and custom signs that someone who's never been to Evergreen Hollow or cared about it made."

He let out a heavy sigh, feeling a distance between them that hadn't been there before.

"They just want to have a good time with their neighbors, and celebrate with them," Aiden said finally. "Even if it comes off as a little tacky in the execution."

Nora swallowed hard, nodding. He thought he'd

never seen her look so sad, and his chest ached, knowing he'd contributed to it. But he couldn't have lied to her. He couldn't have said he felt differently than he did, and he hoped she wouldn't have wanted him to.

"I should've just let the planning committee handle it themselves." Nora turned away, starting to walk back toward where he'd parked the truck. "I should never have tried to help."

"That wouldn't have been necessary," he started to say, but she shook her head, walking a little faster.

"I'm tired." Her shoulders hunched forward, her head ducked down. "I should go home."

The drive back was silent, the truck filled with all the things he wished he could say and all the things she seemed to wish she hadn't. She got out of the truck before he could come around to open her door, without saying goodbye. There was a heavy feeling as she stepped out, and he wondered if he'd see her again.

They hadn't parted ways like this before. He didn't like it.

But he didn't know what to do to fix it either... or if he even should.

CHAPTER TWENTY-THREE

Nora sat in the otherwise empty living room of The Mistletoe Inn, on the couch closest to the fire, flipping idly through the photo albums. She had to look at something, do something with her hands, or she would burst into tears. The fight with Aiden, how much Sabrina hated her plans for the festival—it all left her feeling empty and sad, as if everything she thought she'd found here had just been a mirage.

She'd been right to plan to keep it all at arm's length when she first came, she thought to herself. Not to get involved, to spend time with her parents and Melanie, and leave the rest the way it had always been. None of it had anything to do with her, and the town didn't want her to have anything to do with it.

Tears brimmed on her lashes, and she sniffed

them back. She was just about to pick up another album when she heard footsteps, and looked up to see Caroline walking in. She stiffened a little, expecting a comment from Caroline about her being too soft, or asking what had upset her this time.

Instead, Caroline frowned, crossing the room to perch on the sofa next to Nora. "I can tell you're upset," she said, a little awkwardly. "Do you want to tell me what's going on?"

Nora swallowed hard. "I'm sure you have something else you need to be doing."

"Well, yes." Caroline let out a breath. "But it can wait for a minute. What happened?"

"It's nothing." Nora shook her head, unable to imagine explaining everything that had gone on that day to Caroline. She wouldn't understand. She'd certainly take Sabrina's side.

"We might have grown apart a good bit, Nora, but we're still sisters." Caroline narrowed her eyes at Nora. "I know that's not true. Come on. Out with it."

What's the worst that can happen? Another speech like the one Aiden had given her, maybe, but she expected it from Caroline, at least. She turned to her sister, setting the photo album aside, and began to explain.

She explained everything in a rush, the words

coming out in a tumble once she started to talk. The conversation with her coworker that had set it all off, her decision to help to give herself something to take her mind off of Rob, the way she'd really started to enjoy sprucing up the festival and adding to it. Her excitement over all the plans, and how she'd thought everyone was equally excited, only to see their doubt when Sabrina tore it apart. Sabrina's interference throughout the whole thing, and finally her conversation with Aiden, and how terribly that had gone.

To Nora's surprise, Caroline sat and listened to all of it, without interruption. "Maybe you were right," Nora finished, biting her lip. "Maybe I just don't have the right touch to plan a small-town event or help the inn. This just isn't what I'm good at."

Caroline let out a slow breath.

"It's not that," she said finally, and Nora's head snapped up, surprised. "You're on to some things. It's just that what Aiden and Sabrina are trying to explain is that you need to keep it closer. That fancy catering menu you were talking about? Sure, upgrade the food for the festival. It could use it, honestly. But stick to getting Rockridge Grill and Marie's to make the food. Trust that they can handle it. I promise you some of the guys who hunt would love to provide game to turn into some kind of fancy appetizers."

She smiled, the expression looking a little odd on her mouth. Nora couldn't remember the last time she'd seen it.

"Those decorations?" she continued. "Trying to do something new, all those themes? That's great too. You just need to employ people in the town to help. Aiden would have made those signs, I bet. And you know Mom loves to paint."

"Aiden is busy!" Nora let out a frustrated sigh. "Everyone is busy. They have jobs and lives and businesses to run and kids and houses to keep, and—"

"And they love this town," Caroline said gently. "They'd be *excited* to help make those things, rather than have them brought in from some out-of-town place with no special touch. I've seen some of your plans," she added. "I think they're great, honestly. You don't have to scrap everything. Just tweak it a little so the people here have a hand in it other than just setting up stuff someone else has put together."

"You've seen it?" Nora asked weakly, still stuck on how many words she just heard her sister say—

more than she usually strung together—and the fact that Caroline thought her work was good.

Caroline nodded. "You're a great event planner. Honestly, I'm proud of you. You just need to adjust your touch a little for a small town like this. Not take your hands off the wheel altogether."

For a moment, Nora couldn't speak. She was too shocked to hear her sister say that.

Caroline must have read it on her face, because she reached out, touching Nora's knee with a slight look of remorse on her face.

"I can admit that I've been in the wrong a bit," she said quietly. "I've let the stress of the inn get to me over the years, and I've been taking it out on you. No one should have made you stay here if you really didn't want to. It's not as if that would have helped anything, or made any of it better. Not because you *couldn't* have helped," she clarified. "But you would have resented it."

Caroline let out a sigh, looking across the room as if she couldn't quite meet Nora's eyes. "I've felt rather alone in running it," she admitted quietly. "I just don't like to talk about it."

"I'm sorry." Nora's words came out suddenly, but they were entirely genuine. "I really am. I don't think

I was wrong to go to Boston, necessarily, but I didn't think enough about how it would affect everything. I really want to help now that I'm back."

"Your promotional idea sounds like a great start." Caroline glanced back at her. "Mom ran some of the numbers. I think it really might work. She's considering it."

For the first time since the conversation with Sabrina, Nora felt a smile tug at the edges of her lips. "What do I do about the festival?" she asked quietly, and Caroline considered for a moment.

"Scale it back a little," she suggested finally. "Outsource the things you still need to local vendors. Showcase those businesses, instead of ones outside of Evergreen Hollow. It will mean more to everyone involved, and tourists who show up will see the best that we have to offer. Everyone will be more invested in the success of the festival, and you can still improve on past years, just on a little bit of a smaller scale."

"You're right," Nora admitted, after a moment's consideration. "All of this just got out of hand, I think. I've been so used to pulling off big events in one certain way that I didn't think about doing it differently. But... you're right."

She felt better after saying it. Her mind was already running off in three different directions, imagining how she could take the plans she'd already made and alter them to work on a smaller, more local scale.

And it wasn't just the festival that she felt better about either.

For the first time in years, she felt better about things with Caroline too.

* * *

It was going on three days since he and Nora had gotten into that argument on their walk, and Aiden still hadn't spoken to her. He'd wanted to call or text her, but he'd figured she needed some cooling-off time, and after two days had passed, he thought maybe she just didn't want to talk to him. Truthfully, he was starting to believe that Leon had been wrong.

He and Nora were probably far too different for a relationship to ever work. He'd thought maybe the years that had passed had changed things, but Nora was still a big-city girl, and he was always going to be the guy who had been happy to come back to Evergreen Hollow. It had seemed pretty clear, during that argument, that she either couldn't or wouldn't understand why that was. And while he understood why she'd wanted to go to Boston, he couldn't see the appeal of it any more than she seemed to understand what it was about Evergreen Hollow that made the residents so fiercely devoted to it.

It'll be all right, he told himself as he pulled into the parking lot of Rockridge Grill for a late lunch, jumping down out of his truck. He'd always known this was how it was going to go—he'd just let himself wonder a little too much after he and Nora had hit it off so well on their first couple of dates. But it didn't change anything, that it wasn't going to work out. He'd go back to life as it had always been, and she'd leave after the festival. Things would go back to normal, and those dates would be a nice memory in time.

He'd just about convinced himself of that when he stepped into the grill and saw her standing at the back counter, talking to Jonathan.

She turned at the sound of the bell over the door, her eyes locking with his for a moment, and his heart flipped in his chest. Never mind their argument, all it took was that for him to have to admit to himself that he still had strong feelings for her. It was going to take more than one argument to shake those loose.

They were different, there was no denying that. But in all the conversations they'd had, he'd felt a connection with her that he couldn't pretend hadn't existed.

But what he didn't know was if a connection, strong or otherwise, was enough to overcome those differences.

He sank down at a table, fiddling with the laminated menu, and it was only a minute before he heard the sound of Nora's boots clicking against the tile as she walked over to him. She stood at the end of the table, her expression soft, and he saw her fiddling with one of the buttons on her peacoat.

"Can I sit with you?" she asked quietly, and he let out a breath.

"Yes." *As if there was any other answer.*

Nora slipped her peacoat and scarf off, draping them over the chair next to her, and sank down opposite him. He saw the delicate compass necklace resting against the front of her cream-colored fisherman's wool sweater, and his heart did another of those little flips in his chest. She might have been upset—with him or because of him, he wasn't quite sure—but she hadn't taken the necklace off.

There was quiet for a moment. He wasn't angry with her, and he didn't think she seemed angry with him just then, but he could feel that she was as tentative as he was. He thought she might get up and bolt if he didn't say something.

"What are you up to?" he asked finally, the question feeling awkward. "Getting lunch?"

Nora knotted her fingers together on the table in front of her. "I was talking to Jonathan about catering for the festival," she said finally. "I'd planned to bring in outside restaurants for most of it—you know that now—but I talked with the other ladies on the planning committee again this morning. We've decided to tweak the menu a little and use local places for the food. Rockridge Grill, Marie's, and some of the other local establishments are supplying some game for the Evergreen Tasting buffet." She licked her lips a little anxiously. "We're going to shift to some local places for other aspects of the festival too."

He felt his spirits lift a bit, hearing her talk. He was glad that she'd decided to change tactics, but he kept quiet, letting her finish. He wanted to hear her out in full.

"Caroline and I ended up talking about all of this," Nora said quietly. "The festival, the inn—me going to Boston instead of coming home all those years ago. We managed to finally work some things out, I think." A small, hesitant smile curved the corners of her lips, and then fell again. "I'm sorry for getting angry with you while we were out the other day. I was sensitive from the argument with Sabrina—but it's really no excuse. You were right about all of it."

"It's all right." He meant it too. "I could understand why you were feeling that way. It's water under the bridge. Doesn't change anything." He hoped she understood his meaning. He'd never been good at being blunt when it came to romance, despite his straightforwardness in every other aspect of his life. Especially, it seemed, when it came to Nora.

"I'm glad to hear that," Nora said softly. "I wanted to know, if you weren't *too* upset with me, if you'd help me with some of the remaining preparations. I see now that this sort of festival is only successful with a *lot* of community involvement—and we're going to need help, since it's coming up very soon now."

Aiden smiled at her. "Of course I'll help," he said firmly, reaching across the table to touch her hand. "I'm more than happy to."

Nora let out a sigh of relief. "Oh, thank goodness." She pressed her lips together, her fingers curling around the side of his hand. "I'm glad I didn't ruin things by letting my emotions get the better of me."

"Nothing's ruined," he promised her.

"I feel out of my depth here, sometimes," she admitted. "I don't like to say it out loud, but it's true."

Aiden laughed at that, squeezing her hand gently. "If anything, the rest of us feel out of our depth around *you*. But we'll just have to find a way to meet in the middle."

A smile spread across Nora's lips. "I like the sound of that," she said softly.

They sat there like that for a moment, the menus in front of them forgotten, Aiden relishing the feeling of Nora's soft hand in his. Just a little while ago, he hadn't thought they'd be able to reconcile, and yet here they were. He was glad to have been wrong.

"I'll owe you for your help," Nora added, and he shook his head firmly.

"You won't owe me anything. I *want* to help you. I've got your back, and I want to help, no matter what you're doing."

Nora's eyes widened, a dozen emotions passing over her face before he had a chance to really catch any one of them. "I'm so glad I came back home," she whispered. "Or I might never have known what a wonderful man you turned out to be."

She leaned across the table, her hand on his cheek as she kissed him. He felt his heart swell in his chest, a warm glow settling there.

What a Christmas it was turning out to be.

CHAPTER TWENTY-FOUR

Evergreen Hollow was buzzing with activity the day before the festival. It was less than a week and a half before Christmas, and the festival was the week before Christmas Eve. Everyone involved was hard at work getting things ready, and Nora could feel an excited energy humming through the town that told her she'd been right to listen to Aiden and Caroline's advice. The enthusiasm among the locals was palpable.

She'd made her way over to the event center first thing, meeting with Jonathan, Marie, Leon, Aiden, and some of the others who were helping with a variety of tasks. She couldn't help but feel incredibly grateful—they'd all come together and pulled out all the stops to make sure that the festival would be amazing even at this late hour. She'd laid out all her original ideas, and they'd brainstormed to find ways to make it work on a more local scale. Everything was coming together perfectly despite all her fears, and she was glad she hadn't given up.

She should have known though. Back in Boston, she'd always told new coworkers not to judge a vendor by how expensive it was, but by how good it was. That money and cost weren't the only markers of worth. That advice had always served her well—both in saving money for clients and finding gems in the city that she wouldn't have otherwise if she'd only focused on the most expensive option.

She'd forgotten that, while she was home. But now, thanks to the collaborative efforts of Evergreen Hollow, she'd been reminded once again.

Caroline was sitting at one of the tables, discussing arranging a small petting zoo with a few other residents who owned small livestock. She'd agreed to bring a couple of their friendlier hens, along with a neighbor who had pygmy goats, and when Nora glanced over at her sister she saw an unusual smile on Caroline's face. It had been good for her to take a little time away from the inn—Rhonda had immediately encouraged Caroline to help when Nora had suggested the petting zoo, insisting that she could handle the inn for a few days on her own with Donovan's help. And it had certainly brightened her sister up a bit, getting out and about with the others.

Aiden walked in just then, dusting the snow off of his boots. "Blake and I finished getting the lights hung," he said. "We should probably test them though, just in case anything needs replacing."

One thing that no one had challenged Nora on was the elaborate light display that she'd laid out for the exterior of the event center and the festival grounds. She'd asked Leon if he could order in enough lights, and sure enough, he'd been able to. Aiden and Blake had been hard at work for two days getting all of them up, in between jobs.

"Sure thing." Nora set down her planner. "Let's go check out the generator."

She saw the grin on Aiden's face as he nodded, following her to the back room. She was pretty sure that he knew it was mostly an excuse to get him alone for a moment—she could flip a switch on a generator on her own. But with all the work that needed to be done for the festival, they hadn't really had a moment to themselves since they'd made up.

His arms slid around her waist as they stepped into the back room, pulling her close. She breathed in the scent of his shaving cream and shampoo, enjoying the moment of closeness with him. It made her feel happy, having him here with her, and she tried not to worry about what that might mean for the future. To just enjoy the moment of being there with him now, rather than worrying about what would come later.

"It's going to be so romantic being surrounded by all those pretty lights," she murmured, and felt him brush his lips against her hair.

"I'm so glad you're here for Christmas." Aiden's grip on her tightened for a moment, and Nora let out a happy sigh.

"I am too."

She reached out, flipping the switch on the generator, and—

Nothing.

Nora frowned, flipping it back off and on again. "Oh no," she said softly, disentangling herself from Aiden's embrace to peer at it more closely. "Can you take a look at this?"

It only took a moment for Aiden to tell her what she had already been fairly sure of—the generator was busted.

Nora pinched the bridge of her nose between her

fingers. "We're going to need another generator." She let out a huff of frustration.

"Didn't you say something a couple weeks ago about ordering a backup?"

Nora's lips thinned. "I was going to. But Sabrina canceled the order and said it wasn't necessary. I didn't get a chance to try to override that with the committee before."

She flapped a hand uselessly, indicating the arguments that had broken out before everything had been smoothed over.

"I'll have to go pick one up in Bronston. The hardware store there should have one." It was common to go to the next town over for emergency supplies that anyone in town couldn't wait for Leon to order in, and she felt sure they'd have what she needed.

"I'll go with you," Aiden offered immediately, but Nora shook her head.

"You and Blake still need to finish building the space for the temporary petting zoo. And we still need some more signs." She let out a sigh, giving him a faint smile. "I'll just go. It's no big deal."

"You're not used to driving a truck. Especially on country roads in the snow." Aiden looked worried, and Nora gave him a reassuring smile.

"I'll be fine," she promised.

She took off shortly after filling everyone in on what was going on, borrowing Donovan's truck to make the drive, a tarp thrown in the back to cover the new generator with. She found a station on the radio with cheery Christmas music, not finding it grating any longer, the way she had when Melanie first picked her up from the airport. She'd managed to thoroughly get into the holiday spirit over the past few weeks.

It was a bit of a drive, and traffic was worse than she would have expected. She managed to get the generator just before the hardware store closed, enlisting one of the employees to help her get it into the back of the truck. She tied down the tarp over it, hopping back into the cab, peering at the starless night sky. Snow had started to fall when she'd first gone into the store, and it was getting thicker now, enough that she put on the truck's windshield wipers and was careful as she eased her way out of the parking lot. It was picking up quickly, and she felt a quiver of uneasiness in her stomach.

The storm didn't let up. The snow started to come down harder as she drove home, the wind picking up too, blowing the snow around the truck and obscuring her vision. It was getting harder and harder to see, and she bit her lip, feeling a little silly as she flicked the overhead light on and took Aiden's compass necklace off. She knew which way she needed to get home with the map, but a part of her missed the GPS she had in her car back home. As long as she could use the compass to make sure she was going the right way.

She was *pretty* sure that she was. She took a turn, anxiety swirling in her stomach as thickly as the snow outside.

Her visibility had lowered to only a few feet in front of her, the lines on the road obscured with the settling snow, and she wasn't as familiar as she used to be with the area around Evergreen Hollow. She took another turn, biting her lip as she leaned forward to peer out of the windshield. The road looked as if it were getting narrower, but it must be an illusion from the snow.

It *was* getting narrower. She felt the truck tires slip on the ice, and she overcorrected, trying to figure out where the lane began and ended. The truck started to slide, and Nora let out a small scream as she slid off the road and into a snowdrift with a heavy *thud*.

The truck was very still. The engine was still running, but all she had to do was look at the height of the drift to know she wasn't getting out of this on her own.

Her heart was racing with adrenaline. She reached for her purse, fumbling for her phone to call Aiden. She'd call him and try to explain where she was, and then he could come and help.

But there was no reception.

Not even a single bar when she held the phone up.

Nora's heart sank as she looked out into the swirling darkness, with no idea what to do.

* * *

It was well after dark, and Aiden was starting to get worried.

Nora wasn't back yet, so far as he knew, and he couldn't get ahold of her. He hadn't wanted to text her, worried about her answering back while driving, so he'd tried to call instead. But she hadn't picked up at all.

He remembered all too well how directionally challenged she'd been on their hikes. She probably wasn't as familiar with the roads as she might have been before she'd moved away, and he wasn't certain how good she'd been at getting around with a map back then. One glance out of his living room window told him that the snow was beginning to come down at an alarming rate.

He'd wanted to go with her in the first place. Now, as the storm intensified along with his worry, he couldn't stop himself from going *after* her. He didn't know exactly where she was, but he knew the direction of the town she'd been going to, at least.

He'd head that way, and make sure she was all right, he reasoned. Once he saw her truck—probably one of the only vehicles out on the road at this point—he'd follow her back and make sure she got back to The Mistletoe Inn safely. Help her unload the generator, if she needed it.

His mind made up, Aiden headed out to his own truck and pulled out onto the main road. The storm was picking up even more, and he drove slowly, taking his time as he made his way in the direction Nora had gone. Visibility was low, and he almost missed the tire tracks that he saw about an hour out of Evergreen Hollow, veering off onto a side road.

That might have been Nora.

He couldn't take a chance that it wasn't. He turned, following them, and sure enough, about a half mile down he saw her truck wedged deeply into a snowdrift.

He slowed to a stop, putting on his hazards, and slid out of the driver's side. A moment later, Nora leapt out of the truck, making a beeline toward him.

She threw her arms around him, pressing her head against his chest. "I'm so glad to see you," she breathed, and he put his arms around her too, squeezing her tightly.

"I was so scared. The truck just started sliding, and I think I took a wrong turn, and then there was no cell phone service and I felt so isolated out here, all alone. I had no idea how I was going to get out, and I worried I'd run out of fuel and not have heat, and I—how did you know to come out here? I can't believe you're here." Nora's words tumbled over each other, coming out in a torrent before finally sliding to a stop as she looked up at him. "How did you know?"

Aiden rubbed a gloved hand over his face. "Well, you weren't answering any of my calls, so I figured you weren't getting service. Using a map to get back, then. Saw the storm was picking up and thought you probably couldn't see well, and considering how easily turned around you got on our hike..." He shrugged. "It didn't seem like too big of a leap to think that you might have gotten lost out here on the back roads getting home."

He could see her face flush even in the dim light from the headlights.

"That was a very educated guess," she said with a small, embarrassed laugh. "Thank you for coming after me."

He hugged her again. "I'm glad you're safe is all."

Nora let out another small, chagrined laugh.

"I've always been the type of woman who has everything under control, you know?" she said softly. "But if there's one thing I've learned since I've been back here, it's that depending on others for assistance isn't always a bad thing. And I think I've learned that lesson again tonight. I shouldn't have tried to make that generator run myself. But I guess I just wanted to prove myself to the town. That I'm as tough and capable as anyone who lives here full-time."

Aiden's chest tightened. He reached down, brushing a piece of hair away from her face. "You don't need to prove yourself to the town," he told her gently. "Everyone here knows how amazing you are, Nora Stoker. I certainly do."

Her eyes were wide as she looked up at him, a soft vulnerability in her face that tugged at his heart in a way that was becoming familiar. "Do you really mean that?"

"I do." A small smile twitched at the corners of

his mouth. "I had a terrible crush on you in high school, by the way. If we're admitting things. Just in case you didn't know."

Her blush deepened. "I wish we'd found our way to each other sooner." Her mittened hands closed around the front of his coat, tugging him closer. "But better late than never, right?"

Aiden grinned. "I couldn't agree more."

He leaned down, kissing her softly in the middle of the swirling snow. When he felt her shiver, he pulled back, giving her truck a measured look.

"I can hook my car up to yours," he said. "And get it out of the drift. Then you can follow me back, if you like."

"I think that sounds like a good idea." Nora laughed. "Thank you."

Aiden smiled at her. "Anytime," he promised.

And he meant it.

CHAPTER TWENTY-FIVE

Nora woke up early the morning of the festival, just after the sun came up. She'd barely been able to sleep all night, caught between excitement and nerves.

After Aiden had pulled the truck out of the snowdrift the night before, she'd followed him back to town, and they'd dropped the generator off at the event center. Despite how late it was, he'd helped her hook it up and made sure it worked—and it had, perfectly. He'd come back to The Mistletoe Inn with her then, sitting up late with her and helping her go over last-minute things. It had been nice. Just the two of them with cocoa and cookies, going over all of her lists and checking them twice.

She had to admit that he and Sabrina were right.

The festival was going to be amazing, and more so because of how it had ended up coming about. Doing it the way that had been suggested to her—involving the town and all of the locals—meant it had been as much about the journey to get there as the destination. Everyone had gotten to pitch in and help, and instead of it being a burden, it had only made everyone that much more excited to enjoy the final product.

Nora got up, putting on jeans and a Christmas-y red sweater, along with her trusty peacoat, scarf, and Aiden's necklace. She put on her Hunter boots instead of her ankle boots this morning, figuring she'd be doing a decent amount of walking around in the snow. She could already smell breakfast from downstairs, telling her that her mother had been just as much of an early riser today.

She grabbed an apple-cinnamon muffin and a coffee-to-go downstairs, giving her mother a quick hug and her father a smile. "I'll see you at the festival!" she said excitedly, catching Caroline's eye as her sister came in from the backyard. Caroline was always up early to take care of the animals, and today was no exception.

Rhonda and Donovan waved at her, Donovan smiling at his daughter over his morning paper. "See you soon," they both said, and Nora went into the living room, grabbing the reindeer costume that she had ordered a few days ago. Bethany had finally talked Aiden into wearing his, and she'd thought it would be fun to get one to match.

"I never thought I'd see the day," Caroline teased, walking in just as Nora was zipping it up. "My fashion-forward sister dressed as a reindeer. Love really gets in your head, doesn't it?"

Nora rolled her eyes at the good-natured teasing, choosing to ignore the last part. It made her think of what might happen between her and Aiden after the holidays were over—or rather, what might *not* happen, and what she actually wanted. All things she wasn't prepared to face today, of all days.

"I'll see you there," she said instead. "Don't forget the chickens!" she added, flashing Caroline a grin, and her sister shook her head, still laughing as she retreated into the kitchen.

All ready to go, Nora headed to the event center. The early morning went by in a flash, as she and Bethany and the other ladies finished all of the last-minute things needed to set up. The festival started at ten, and they had the lights on and the morning booths set up just as people started to arrive.

The excitement buzzing through the festival was

palpable. Nora could feel it everywhere she went—in the townspeople manning the booths and events and the ones participating, in the tourists and visitors from the surrounding towns, all eager to see the Evergreen Snowman Festival. The space was packed, inside and out, and everyone was enthusiastic, laughing and having a good time. Nora felt the warm glow of it as she went from place to place, helping with small fixes and replenishing food platters and giving vendors a small break if they needed to run to get a snack or visit the bathroom. She couldn't remember ever having had so much *fun* at an event, and it made her happy to hear the talk of how much bigger the event was this year than any year before. All the talk and buzz surrounding it that they'd managed to generate had paid off.

Aiden stayed with her for most of the day, helping alongside her, and everyone who saw them loved their matching reindeer costumes. On any other day, Nora would have felt silly, but she didn't. It felt normal and fun, the kind of thing she never could have done with anyone else.

"Our past selves could never have imagined this," Aiden joked in the late afternoon, as he passed her a foam cup of hot cocoa with marshmallows. "Before you came back? Never. I would have thought you were way too cool to wear a reindeer outfit."

Nora took a grateful sip of the hot drink. Her lips were starting to feel a little numb from being outside for so long, despite how busy she'd been. "You have no idea how nerdy I can be," she teased.

"I'm looking forward to finding out." Aiden smiled at her, and her stomach fluttered. She liked the idea of that, she realized, as she looked up at him. She liked the idea of learning all of his little idiosyncrasies, and him learning hers. Of getting to know what their day to day would look like, if they were *really* together.

But that would only happen if they had more time together.

The thought stuck with her, as it had after Caroline's offhand comment that morning. But the day was going by in a blur, and she couldn't dwell on it too much in the midst of all of the fun and activity of the event.

"Nora!" Her mother came up to her, breathless, her cheeks pink above her scarf. She was glowing, and Nora looked at her, wondering what had gotten her so excited—beyond just the festival itself.

"What is it?"

"Your advertising campaign for the inn has

worked wonders!" Rhonda smiled broadly at her daughter. "We're all booked out. The idea of centering it around the festival was perfect!"

Nora felt a warm glow, a matching smile spreading over her face. "I'm so glad." She gave her mother a quick hug, feeling happier than she would have thought possible a week ago. Everything was turning out better than she could possibly have hoped.

"We're almost out of fliers advertising it. We might be able to do some later bookings if there's still interest. Can you go over to the *Gazette* and print more?"

"Sure." Nora finished her cocoa, tossing the cup in the trash. "I'll be right back."

The music and festive sounds faded into the background as Nora headed over to the *Gazette*. She pushed the door open, heading down the hall to see about reprinting the file for the fliers. She doubted anyone was in today, but she could figure it out on her own.

She heard what sounded like soft sobs from Sabrina's office and stopped dead in her tracks.

The door was cracked open, so she couldn't help but see. To her surprise, Sabrina was sitting at her desk, tears streaming down her face. She looked miserable.

Nora didn't particularly like the woman, but she couldn't help feeling bad for her. Everyone was out having an amazing time, and for some reason, Sabrina was tucked away here, sobbing.

"What's wrong?" Nora nudged the door open, and Sabrina looked up, startled.

"I..." Her face flushed, and she looked away for a moment. "I feel so guilty."

Nora frowned, confused. "For what?"

"For endangering your life last night." The words came out quick, rushed, as if Sabrina could hardly bear to say it. But it didn't make Nora any less confused.

"What are you talking about?"

"I canceled the backup generator." Sabrina dabbed at her cheeks with a tissue. "I meddled with your plans for the festival. If I'd stayed out of it, you wouldn't have had to venture out in a snowstorm to keep the festival from falling apart. It's my fault, and—"

"It's not your fault," Nora said gently, walking a little further into the office and stopping at the edge of the desk. "Look, I understand now that I was going overboard with the event. You were right, I was losing sight of the point of it. I understand now why you did what you did, a little better than I did before, at least. But..."

Nora hesitated. *Might as well get it all out now.*

"I don't understand why you seemed to have such an issue with *me* though," she continued. "It felt personal, not just about the festival. Even things that shouldn't have been a problem, like the generator, were still an issue. Do you just not like me?"

It was a blunt question, but it seemed to calm Sabrina down a little. She let out a long breath, wiping at her eyes, before refocusing on Nora.

"I was jealous," she admitted. "Truthfully? I always wanted to move somewhere like Boston—a big city—and level up my career the way you did. I wanted to work at a big newspaper, have all of those big career goals and meet them. But I didn't. Some of it had to do with my family, feeling like I needed to be here for them, and some of it was that I guess I just didn't have it in me. I didn't have the chance—some of it because of me, and some of it not. But I was jealous of you because you just took the leap and did it. Regardless of what anyone else thought or wanted."

Nora blinked, surprised. "I had no idea." She

glanced around the office and back at Sabrina. "You do an incredible job, running this newspaper. You could do amazing things if you wanted to try and do exactly that. But—"

She let out a breath, almost surprised at what she said next. "I wanted nothing more than to get out of here. To break free of Evergreen Hollow. Everyone knows that. But now that I'm back, I'm seeing how beautiful it all really is. And I've learned that sometimes chasing after what you think you want doesn't always lead to the fulfillment that you think it will."

Nora leaned against the desk, meeting Sabrina's eyes. "I got really caught up in that chase for something bigger and better, all the time. And I forgot to just look around and appreciate what I already had. It never felt like enough. But since I've been here, I've recognized the need to share in a victory and work together toward it. You're a big part of the community here. And you were a big part of the festival's success, whether you feel like it or not. I might not have seen all of that if you hadn't forced me to," she admitted.

Sabrina brightened a little, wiping away the last of her smudged mascara. "I'm sorry for being difficult."

"This entire Christmas season has been about resetting for me." Nora smiled encouragingly at her. "So why don't we reset and start over? I need to print some more fliers, and then let's go back to the festival and enjoy it."

Sabrina smiled. "Okay," she said, standing up and putting a hand out. "I like the sound of that."

Nora shook her hand, laughing a little. And then the two of them went to get the fliers and head back to the festival that they'd both put so much work into planning, reconciled at last.

A Christmas miracle, Nora thought wryly as they headed outside. But one that she was happy for.

It was shaping up to be the best Christmas she'd ever had.

CHAPTER TWENTY-SIX

It was Christmas Eve, and Nora was sitting by the window in the front room of the inn, looking out at the thickly snow-covered landscape. There was a fire burning cheerily in the fireplace, a plate of snickerdoodle cookies next to her on the small table, and a pile of gifts under the brightly lit tree waiting to be opened the next morning. She felt happier than she had in a long time.

She glanced back at her laptop, re-reading the email that she'd typed up to send to her boss. One more look, and it was ready to send.

She wondered if she was being too hasty, putting in her notice. But the truth was, she didn't want to go back to Boston. Now that she had come back home, found a burgeoning love and a renewed sense of what was really important to her, she didn't have any desire to return.

Nora heard footsteps and looked up to see Caroline walking into the living room. Her sister looked less tense. Ever since their conversation, Nora had noticed her actively trying to be less constantly busy, and slowing down to enjoy the holiday a bit more.

They'd both helped each other in different ways. Nora had been trying to pitch in more around the inn too, once the festival was finished, helping with rooms and trying to learn how to cook. The outdoorsy work and maintenance of the inn was still beyond her, but she was sure she could learn. It was a group effort to keep the inn running, she'd found, and she wanted her sister to feel able to relax.

Caroline came to sit down next to her, setting down two large mugs of white hot chocolate with marshmallows. "What are you working on?" she asked curiously, as Nora picked up her mug and took a drink. "Now that the festival is over."

"An email to put in my notice at work." Nora felt a wry smile on her face at her sister's surprised expression. "I know it feels a little soon. But I've learned so much about myself since I've been back here. And I feel like I've found a new path. One that will make me happier in the long run."

Caroline sat back, looking at her sister. "Well, I'll support you whatever you decide. But I really have enjoyed having you here, back home with us. I'd love if that continued." She hesitated. Talking about her feelings still didn't come easily. "I missed you. I'm glad that you coming back mended things between us. Improved them, even."

Nora reached over, squeezing her sister's hand. "I am too."

That moment felt like the final push that she needed. Going back to Boston would put distance between her and all of this again, and even though she could come back and visit more than she had before, it didn't feel like enough. She wanted to stay close, to grow closer to her family and make up for lost years, to pursue everything that being back in Evergreen Hollow would allow her.

It didn't feel like a trap any longer. It felt like a new opportunity. And she had always loved those.

She took a deep breath and hit *send* on the resignation email.

Caroline nudged her, an oddly mischievous grin on her face. "Isn't there someone else that you should tell that you're staying?"

Nora's stomach fluttered. "You're right," she said weakly, feeling nervous as she reached for her phone. Her sister drifted off, giving her privacy as she called Aiden.

He answered on the second ring. "I have some news for you," Nora said, sure that he could hear how nervous she was. "But I want to tell you in person. What do you think about a Christmas Eve hike?"

"Sounds like a perfect idea to me. I took the day off, so you just tell me when."

"How about as soon as you can get here?" She wasn't sure how long she could keep the news in—she wanted to tell him as soon as possible, and know what his reaction would be, one way or another.

"I'm on my way."

Twenty minutes later, Aiden was at her door. Her heart had felt like it was racing in her chest the entire time she'd waited for him, and she hurried outside as soon as she heard his tires crunching into the snow, hopping into the truck so that they could head to their hiking spot.

It was the most gorgeous evening she could have hoped for. The maples were a bright burning red against the evening sun, the snow packed hard and glittering. It took her breath away, the perfect white

Christmas, and it only reinforced how right Nora felt her decision had been. Out here in the nature surrounding her hometown, with Aiden—the man she never would have thought would be hers, and yet somehow always had been—she knew she had made the right choice. She had just needed the right timing to know it was where she should be, and it had finally come.

She smiled as they walked up the hill, thinking of the unexpected route that had brought her here. A breakup that had turned out to be the best possible thing for her, a phone call to a friend that had urged her to come home. A sequence of events that had led her here, to a moment happier than any she had imagined.

They made their way up to the top of the overlook, just in time for the sunset, and Aiden turned to look at her. "I've been trying to be patient this whole time," he said with a laugh. "But I'm dying to hear your news."

Nora felt a sudden rush of nerves. *What if this was all based on him knowing I'd leave eventually?* Maybe it had been easier for him to open up to her a little, knowing it wouldn't last. But she had to hope that wasn't true.

She hesitated for a moment, then blurted it out.

"I've decided to stay here. I sent in my resignation today."

The nerves she had felt were gone in an instant when Aiden swept her into his arms, holding her close in a tight hug. He bent down, kissing her swiftly, his face radiant with happiness when he pulled away. "That's what I hoped you were going to say."

Nora grinned, a different kind of butterflies swirling in her stomach. She felt as if she were glowing with happiness, the last thing that she had wanted falling into place.

Aiden reached down, brushing a little of her hair out of her face in a sweet, familiar gesture. "If you're staying," he said with a smile, "I'd like to take you out on many, many more dates. How do you feel about that?"

Nora's smile spread across her face. "That sounds amazing."

He put his arm around her, pulling her close as they looked out over the landscape, the colorful sunset blazing over the snow. The chill of the evening was creeping in, but Nora couldn't feel it. She was happy and content and full of warmth, more so than she had ever been, and she felt as if she could have stood there forever with him.

"Caroline must be happy you're staying," Aiden said, and Nora nodded, leaning her head against his shoulder.

"She was really glad to hear it." She smirked, pulling back a little to look up at him. "And now that I'm staying, my new goal is going to be finding Caroline a man. I can tell she's a little lonely, even if she'd never admit it."

Aiden laughed at that, the sound echoing in the forest around them. "Good luck. I'll help if I can."

Nora grinned, sliding her arms around him. She had found so much happiness, she thought to herself, by opening up her heart again. It had been risky, and scary, but so, so worth it. She was home now, with everything she could have ever dreamed of, and a future ahead of her that she was sure contained so much love.

She hoped her sister would find the same someday.

* * *

The series continues in *Snowflakes and Surprises*!

ALSO BY FIONA BAKER

The Marigold Island Series

The Beachside Inn

Beachside Beginnings

Beachside Promises

Beachside Secrets

Beachside Memories

Beachside Weddings

Beachside Holidays

Beachside Treasures

The Sea Breeze Cove Series

The House by the Shore

A Season of Second Chances

A Secret in the Tides

The Promise of Forever

A Haven in the Cove

The Blessing of Tomorrow

A Memory of Moonlight

The Saltwater Sunsets Series

Whale Harbor Dreams

Whale Harbor Sisters

Whale Harbor Reunions

Whale Harbor Horizons

Whale Harbor Vows

Whale Harbor Blooms

Whale Harbor Adventures

Whale Harbor Blessings

Evergreen Hollow Christmas

The Inn at Evergreen Hollow

Snowflakes and Surprises

A Christmas to Remember

Mistletoe and Memories

A Season of Magic

The Snowy Pine Ridge Series

The Christmas Lodge

Sweet Christmas Wish

Second Chance Christmas

Christmas at the Guest House

A Cozy Christmas Escape

The Christmas Reunion

For a full list of my books and series, visit my website at www.fionabakerauthor.com!

ABOUT THE AUTHOR

Fiona writes sweet, feel-good contemporary women's fiction and family sagas with a bit of romance.

She hopes her characters will start to feel like old friends as you follow them on their journeys of love, family, friendship, and new beginnings. Her heartwarming storylines and charming small-town beach settings are a particular favorite of readers.

When she's not writing, she loves eating good meals with friends, trying out new recipes, and finding the perfect glass of wine to pair them with. She lives on the East Coast with her husband and their two trouble-making dogs.

Follow her on her website, Facebook, or Bookbub.

Sign up to receive her newsletter, where you'll get free books, exclusive bonus content, and info on her new releases and sales!

S0-FPI-266

No part of this publication may be reproduced, stored in a retrieval system, or transmitted in any form or by any means, electronic, mechanical, photocopying, recording, scanning, or otherwise, without the prior written permission of the publisher, except in the case of brief quotations within critical reviews and otherwise as permitted by copyright law.

NOTE: This is a work of fiction. Names, characters, places, and incidents are a product of the author's imagination. Any resemblance to real life is purely coincidental. All characters in this story are 18 or older.

Copyright © 2019, Willow Winters Publishing. All rights reserved.

Kisses and Wishes

Willow Winters
Wall street journal & usa today bestselling author

From USA Today bestselling author, Willow Winters, comes an exclusive collection of novellas!

Romantic. Addictive.
Second chance wishes and first time kisses. Everything you need for a cozy read.
You'll devour each of these winter reads down to the last page.

The previously released stories available in this collection are:

One Holiday Wish

Collared for Christmas

Stolen Mistletoe Kisses

One Holiday Wish

Chapter 1

Carla

The light dusting of snow steals my attention as it blows in the bright lights of my headlights and across the sidewalk. It's dark already, even though it's only six, but I'm wide awake with the nervous butterflies in the pit of my stomach.

The sound of the keys jingling is all I'm left with as I turn off my car and sit in the driver seat. Rustling in my bag, I find the stick of sheer berry lip gloss. It matches my nails that I just had done yesterday too. I spent way too long thinking about what I was going to wear. It's just a holiday party, and hosted by my best friend, Lauren. So it shouldn't matter.

Every other Saturday I park my car right where it is now, and head straight into her house without an ounce of makeup on and only in my PJs. I have no shame when it comes to girl's nights. And a holiday party of just close friends normally means making sure I'm wearing real clothes, complete with a bra – even though I hate bras. Not the designer skinny jeans and flowy white silk blouse I picked out just for this night.

My phone pings with a text from Lauren just as I'm smacking my lips together: *You here yet?*

Just pulled up.

My phone buzzes again with: *Shit, I have no red wine!*

My lips quirk up into a grin as I snap a picture of the two bottles in my passenger seat and send them to her with the line: *Got you covered*.

You are the fucking best. My smile widens but with her next message, it falls.

Now get your ass in here!

Deep breaths. Dropping my phone into my bag, I open my car door and grab a bottle of wine in each hand which means I have to bump my car door shut with my ass.

It thuds as it closes and so do my heels in the bit of snow.

My coat's not shut tight enough with the loose tie, but even with the chill, I'm burning up with nerves.

He's going to be there. I swallow down my anxiousness as my heels crunch down the snow and I get closer to the front door. I can hear the laughter, the chatter, the faint sounds of Christmas music.

I should be excited, - *merry*, so to speak – but I can't shake the apprehension, knowing Michael Davis, my high school boyfriend, my college on-again-off-again-can't-keep-my-hands-off-of-him-when-we-run-into-each-other-occasional-fling is going to be there.

All of these nerves because of one very important detail.

He's coming back home; he's moving in down the street from me, back into his old house. It was one thing when I could travel a thousand miles and put distance between us after we had a rendezvous. It's completely different when he's a block away and we'll run into each other constantly.

I don't know how I'm going to keep my hands to myself. I don't know if I want to try to pretend like I don't still want him.

Ringing the doorbell, I tell myself the scary truth that has me shaking in my cherry red heels, I don't know if he wants me at all now that he's back. That's the part that makes the butterflies in my stomach beat their wings a little too hard.

Chapter 2

Carla

"It's irrationally hot in here," I tell the back of Lauren's head as I plop both bottles down on her kitchen table, knocking the bowl of Tostitos ever so slightly.

"Wine! My hero," Lauren drags the "o" way too long as she gives me a hug without wrapping her arms around me because she's got a Solo cup in each of her hands.

"You started without me," I jokingly scold her and slip off my jacket as someone comes into the kitchen from behind me.

"Pre-gaming was like hours ago girl. You and that bakery," she's back to filling the cups as soon as I let her go.

"I'll be in that bakery every day until I die," I respond

and my words are full of pride. It's my family's bakery and I'm the one who inherited it from my grandmother. My mother's a nurse and my father married into the family with a career in law. So the bakery – and all the memories that come with it – are all mine. "I wouldn't have it any other way."

Lauren rolls her eyes at me but then winks and gives me a nudge to look behind.

Shit. I almost say the word out loud; I wasn't ready for this. I should be or maybe I should know I never would be. But dammit, I thought I'd at least have one minute… to down whatever is in that Solo cup in Lauren's left hand.

Michael is standing right there behind me, telling something to James that makes him laugh as the two of them open the caps of their beer and toss them in the trash can next to the counter. As Michael lifts his beer to take a swig, his eyes catch mine.

My heart pounds in my chest.

The second he lowers his beer; he smiles at me. Charming, sweet but he fails to hear whatever James said. My floosy of a heart picks up her pace.

"Are you listening?" James questions Michael, clinking the bottom of his beer against Michael's.

"What?" Michael's attention is stolen by James and it's only then that I let my own smile show. Even though

I know the blush will stay right where it is and I won't be able to hide that.

"Dude," James shakes his head in disapproval until Michael nods slightly my way. I see him do it and stupidly, I stay put, a hand on each bottle of wine as if they'll save me from this awkward moment.

The movement doesn't go unnoticed and Michael lets out a soft chuckle before pulling his bottom lip into his mouth and biting down on it slightly, shaking his head at me.

Instantly, those butterflies move lower, so does every bit of heat in me. It's his broad shoulders, I think, that does it. Lauren and I narrowed it down based on my celebrity crushes. The way he hovers over me, dominating my space and closing me in. I am a helpless victim to it.

And that lip that's trapped in between his teeth right now, I'd like to bite it too. In fact, I have. On multiple occasions.

"Carla!" James is the first to speak. He and Michael roomed together at college. He knows every sordid detail of what Michael and I have done, and unbeknownst to Michael, he also kept me up to date when I wasn't there, filling me in on any and every detail of any girl Michael could have gone after. He never did date anyone else though, even when I broke it off, admitting that the distance was too much. He had school. I had the bakery. It wasn't going to work.

But James and his wealth of information are the reason I always fell into Michael's bed whenever Lauren went to see James, her brother, and she needed a travel companion, or whenever Michael came back here, to this small town. James is the one who told me I was all Michael ever talked about and said he didn't want anyone else.

I didn't want anyone else either. But when we hooked up that first time after the break up, I didn't want to put a name on what we were. So it was on-gain, off-again, whenever we were around each other, or miles away. Just hooking up, but I didn't want to hook up with anyone else.

"Hey, I heard you were coming back," I say off handily, peeking up at Lauren to save me, but she's busy gathering a bag of chips from the cabinet.

"So that's how you're going to play it?" Michael's question catches me off guard.

"What do you mean," I play innocent and peek at James just as Lauren bails on me, practically running out of the kitchen with a twinkle of mischief in her eyes and the widest smile I've ever seen. Michael asks James to leave us for a minute and before I can even turn around, we're alone.

"So you don't want them to know?" Michael asks and I stumble on my answer.

"Know what?" Adrenaline races through me. We've never talked about what we do and I sure as hell don't spread the gospels about how I still spread my legs for Michael.

It only takes three foreboding steps from Michael. One. Two. Three. Until he's standing over me, invading my space and making me crane my neck to look up at him. I can smell him, feel the heat radiating from him. I could taste him and that lip of his if I wanted to right now.

"That I fucked you last week on my sofa... and then my desk. And that you already know I'm coming home because I mentioned it before you left."

"They don't know." I answer him with a shake of my head. Michael's facial expression gives no hint of what he thinks about the fact that I kept it a secret. Whether he likes that I've kept it a secret or otherwise. His statement is simply matter of fact ... and dripping in sex appeal. Until he clarifies with another question.

"So you haven't told anyone?" His eyes flash with something. It's gone as quickly as it came, and too soon for me to place it. Maybe guilt? I feel it too. Everyone in here knows what we used to be and I don't want them coming between what we have now simply because I'm happy with the way it's been. Even if we don't have a title.

Or I was... until he decided to come home. Still, we don't need the opinions of the peanut gallery.

If my nerves would calm the hell down, if I could breathe whenever Michael gets close to me, I'd be a better fighter in this battle of flirtation. But as it is, Michael dominates every piece of me the second I smell his woodsy scent, or see that dark stubble that lines his sharp jaw all the way down his neck.

"You're staring at my lips, Carla," Michael's voice is deep and husky, and the way he speaks sends a heat straight to my core. "You want something?"

I only nod, and let my fingers reach up to the last button on his long sleeved Henley. The deep groan that slips from him is accompanied by a roar of laughter from just on the other side of the wall in the living room. Lauren's house is small, it's all her own, but this is a tight space to hide something like what I want to do with him.

"You want to go upstairs?" Michael asks me, glancing behind him and I follow his gaze. No one's there but the shadows of people are coming.

The second I nod, his hand is on mine and I creep up the stairs of Lauren's two-bedroom townhouse as quietly as I can. "We won't have long," I whisper and wish I'd had at least one glass of wine so I can blame this on that, but the way Michael looks when he pulls me in closer to him at the top of the stairs has me drunk on lust already.

"We can be quick here," he leans down to nip my bottom lip before adding, "And then we have all night."

Chapter 3

Michael

I missed the slower pace of this town and how everyone knows everyone.

I missed being able to walk everywhere and know that every single building has a story to tell.

I missed all of this when I left for college.

But most of all, I missed her. My Carla.

Pushing my hip against her belly, I back her up until her back hits the wall. Grabbing her wrists in my hand, I pin them above her head. No one can see us here, but if anyone came up the stairs, they'd have a view of everything.

Carla moans into my mouth and my cock is instantly

hard. I rock it against her, making sure she can feel what she does to me.

She breaks the kiss before I'm ready, leaving my heart racing. As I trail my finger down her arm, still keeping her wrists pinned, I watch the goosebumps spread across her body and her nipples pebble through that thin bra and loose blouse she's wearing.

"Did you wear that for me?" I ask her and my voice comes out huskier than I meant. I have no control when it comes to Carla.

She nods and pushes herself against my leg, grinding into me. "All for you," she nearly whimpers as her back bows and she rocks herself harder against me.

Releasing her wrists, I cup her pussy through her jeans and my other hand goes to her hip. My lips trail down her neck until I can nip the lobe of her ear and whisper, "I need to be inside you in the next two minutes or I'm going to lose my shit."

Carla's eyes widen, as if registering what we're doing for the first time. Her lips purse as she glances behind us, to Lauren's bedroom. "We can't. Not in Lauren's room and the other is where her sister is staying."

I back up slightly, wishing a third room would appear when I see the wide hall closet. So wide it's two-doored. Not hesitating, I swing the closest door open and pull a string to turn on the old light. There are only a handful of coats on left side and plenty of room on the right to take care of Carla and the hard on that never goes down when she's near.

"I need you to be quiet," I warn her and open the door wider. it's not until she takes one last peek down the stairs before she grins at me. A mischievous and sexy grin that has my cock aching to be inside of her.

"I can be quiet," she whispers and lets out a giddy feminine laugh as I come in behind her. "Liar," I tease her and close the door behind me.

Before her back even hits the wall, her lips are on mine, sucking and nibbling. I don't waste any time either, pushing my hand up her blouse and rolling her hardened nipple between my forefinger and thumb.

She moans, loud, breaking our kiss and I pull back on her nipple in punishment since I know that mix of pain and pleasure is delivered straight to her core.

"I bet you're wet for me," I taunt her in a low breath.

"There's only one way to find out," she teases me back and as my hands find the button of her blue jeans, she does the same to mine.

The button, the zipper, the jeans in a mess around our ankles.

I groan in the crook of her neck as I tear off the thin lace that separates her hot cunt from my fingers and learn that I guessed right. "You're so fucking ready." I leave an open-mouthed kiss on her throat and then on the back of her neck as she turns around for me, slowly and with intent. It's more difficult with the jeans still around her ankles, but she does it well like the little minx she is.

"We've got to be quick," she whispers as I wrap my hand around my cock and stroke it.

"I should have stopped by the bakery before coming here." I'm only joking, but the serious side of Carla comes out when she answers me, "Not going to happen in the bakery."

The smirk on my face is uncontrollable. "That's what cars are for, baby." I playfully answer and smack her ass before telling her, "stay quiet," and shove my cock inside of her in one swift stroke.

Fuck, my eyes nearly roll back into my head. Not just because she feels like heaven, but because of the look on her face right now. Eyes closed and her mouth open with a silent scream of ecstasy.

With every buck of my hips, I brace her against me so her body doesn't hit the wall.

I could give two shits if they know we're fucking up here, but I know Carla doesn't want anyone to know.

I'm sure they're thinking we're doing something else right now. That I couldn't wait to ask her. And that's fine by me if that's what they think. They should know better at this point.

"The two of us can't be in the same room together without getting inside each other's pants," I whispers to Carla and as she smiles, I slam inside of her. Again and again.

She's trying to grab on to anything at all, but there's nothing but bare wall in front of her.

It's hard to control myself as I slam inside of her, still bracing her against the wall. Feeling her cum around me, the heat, her arousal, the way her cunt grabs my cock. Fuck. I'm going to cum and I'm not ready. I want to fuck her how she likes, rough and hard. For hours.

"Tell me I can have you again tonight," I barely groan the words out at the shell of her ears and she shivers, shivers from her shoulders and down, all the way down, in a way that leads straight to my cock.

"You can have me," she gives me just what I need and lets her head fall back against my chest. Her cheeks are full of color, her lips still parted and her eyes half lidded.

"One more," I whisper against her heated skin and reach down to rub the rough pad of my thumb against her clit.

Her hands come up to her mouth; she bites on her thumb to keep from screaming as I fuck her recklessly, harder, faster, waiting to feel her cum one more time.

The second she does, all the tension in her body

leaves her and I feel my own release with her. Gripping onto her with a bruising force, I let go of everything and cum with her, feeling my balls draw up and the tingling in my spine. My toes curl as the pleasure rocks through me in waves.

I can barely breathe I cum so hard.

I pull out of her, wishing we had more time and use her underwear to clean her up and then shove them quickly in my pocket. She's still panting against the wall and I have to help her pull her jeans up. I have every curve of hers memorized. The way she leans her head against the wall is exactly how she does it on my pillow. And her fingers come up to rest in the little space below her collar bone, that little divot she loves for me to kiss. She does that every time too.

Time ticks too fast. I want to stay in this moment forever. But that's a holiday wish that won't be gifted.

"Is this going to be something we do one last time? I don't know that I can handle..." Carla asks me quietly, one hand on the doorknob and the other on my hip. Her eyes reach mine, and I hate that she has any insecurity. It's always been her. I knew if I didn't push, I'd hold on to her until I could come back and be here for her how she wanted all these years.

"Carla, I have one question to ask first."

My heart hammers in my chest. It's now or never. As

my bottom lip drops to ask her the one question I need answered, the door to the coat closet flies open, bringing with it the bright light of the hall way and a not-so-shocked Lauren who somehow manages to bother grin and scream out, "I knew it!" at the same time.

Fuck.

Chapter 4

Carla

"Everyone!" Lauren's screaming through her house with a shit-eating grin that won't budge. The thud, thud, thud of her pattering down the steps as quickly as she can is far faster than mine because of these heels.

"Lauren!" I scream her name and add, "Don't you dare!" as I bend down on the third step to grab my heels so I can catch her barefoot before she can go shouting to everyone what she just saw. I have half a mind to throw them at her as she lands on the bottom step.

"Guys!" Lauren squeals as she rounds the corner, leaving me in a view of only her hand. My chest is heaving in air by the time I catch up to her in the small living room crowded with James and four more friends for years and years. Friends who have been my family and know every detail of my life. Including the bits about Michael. The very large bits that have made up most of my life since the tenth grade.

All of their eyes are on me, I can feel them burning into me as I hold up a heel at Lauren, ready to tell her to shut it just as she announces, "He totally gave it to her already!"

Gave it to her. My mouth drops just like the shoe in my hand. How could she? Betrayal rips through me like I've never experienced in my life and instantly tears prick my eyes. Were they betting on how long it would take before I fell back into bed with him? Fuck. That hurts more than anything ever has. Embarrassment doesn't even register. It just hurts.

"Lauren, I didn't ask yet!" Michael's voice booms down the stair case. I barely notice the thumps pounding down the steps and coming up behind me.

"Fuck," Lauren covers her mouth before closing the distance between us and grabbing my shoulders. "That sounded so wrong. I thought you two were up there because he asked you. I'm so sorry. Don't take those words like the way they sounded.

"You really put your foot in your mouth," James laughs at Lauren, no sense at all

"I thought he asked her!" Lauren raises her voice and directs her guilt on James who shakes his head comically. "You're a mess," he jokes and my friends in the room chuckle. Everyone still jovial as if nothing's wrong in the least.

"Ask me what?" I breathe the words and turn around to face Michael, his soft blue eyes piercing me like they always do.

"Oh my God he's going to do it now," I hear Lauren's words rush out of her mouth as she steps away, giving us room and letting everyone else see the two of us.

My heart beats fast, my body heats and my lungs stay perfectly still, refusing to let me breathe as Michael takes my hand with one of his, running the rough pad of his thumb over my wrist and reaches into his pocket to pull out a small black velvet box.

Oh, my fucking God.

My bottom lip wobbles slightly as my eyes glance at the box, then back to his eyes.

Michael lets out an uneasy breath, "I wanted to ask you in private." He clears the nervousness from her voice with a small cough before continuing. "I wasn't sure what you'd say, but I guess in front of all of our friends is a perfectly fine way to do it."

"You remember how you asked me what my holiday wish was?" he asks me but my mind still isn't functioning quite right and I can only stare back at him, feeling so much excitement, nervousness, so much hope that this means he wants the same as me. Michael glances at everyone behind me before leaning forward and reminding me, "Last week when I saw you, do you remember when I asked you and then you asked me back?"

Blinking away the buzz of this frenzy I nod vigorously and Michael smiles at me, it's a lop sided grin that makes him that much more charming. "You've got to help me here," he whispers just for me, "I'm nervous."

Rocking onto my tip toes I steal a quick kiss from him, feeling the blush rise into my cheeks, "Sorry, I swear I'm paying attention." He laughs as I rock back down onto my heels and look up at him with a warmth flooding every bit of me.

"You're my holiday wish." He stares into my eyes. "I just want you and this can be whatever you want it to be, if you want me too." His words come out faster as he goes on until he takes a moment to breathe, opening up the small velvet box for me to see. "A promise ring or more, I'm not sure," he lets out a long breath as I peek at the sparkling ring.

Tears cloud my vision of the rose gold diamond ring with floral details surrounding it. *Or more?* I never expected this.

"I'm not sure what you want, proposal or a promise, or to get married tonight. I just want you and this is for you."

"Tonight!" the word shrieks with glee from behind me and I look over my shoulder to see Lauren barely being held back by James. She covers her mouth with both hands and I have to laugh at her antics. She's always said we were meant to be together, that even a thousand miles wouldn't keep us apart.

"Not tonight," I say mostly to get that thought out of Lauren's head before looking back at Michael. "Not tonight," I repeat and hold his hand tighter. "And if it means I get another, this is just a promise ring," I bite down on my lower lip to keep my grin at bay, but it doesn't work.

Michael's shoulders shake as the tension around us eases and our friends laugh from my answer.

"Told you!" this time it's James who pipes up.

"I'll get you another then." Michael's voice is soothing, and the look in his eyes is everything right now. Devotion, love, the way he looked at me when we shared our first kiss, our first time, all of our firsts. And the way he looked at me when I left him, thinking I couldn't be the only one who felt this between us, but too scared to ask. "When you're ready."

"Let's just be us, for now."

"That's all I want." He lowers his nose to mine, and gives me another kiss as the chatter and cheers pick up behind us. It turns to white noise when he whispers though, "I love you Carla. I always have and I always will."

My lips press against his for a short kiss and then I whisper in the warm air between us, "I love you too."

Collared For Christmas

Chapter 1

Joshua

I sigh heavily at my desk knowing I shouldn't be doing this. But I fucking want to. I lean back in the leather chair, staring across the room with the tips of my fingers tapping on the Mahogany desk.

It's been years since I've seen her and now that I've had a glimpse of my sweet cherry, I can't get her out of my head.

What's worse is she didn't even see me. Or maybe it's better that way. I'm not sure.

It was her voice that made me turn. The soft cadence that spilled from those beautiful lips. Had I never heard her, I wouldn't have seen her. It's incredible how sometimes fate gives you just enough of a glimpse to change everything.

I close my eyes remembering the sweet sound of her voice. She ordered a salted caramel coffee and a blueberry muffin to go. I huff a small laugh at the memory. She always had a sweet tooth. Her pale pink, A-line dress flowed below her hips as she moved across the glass display case, smiling sweetly as the young man handed her the muffin.

She nibbled on the muffin as she waited for her coffee. Those plump lips parting ever so slightly as she pushed a stray crumb into her mouth and sucked gently on her finger. She'll never know just how tempting and sexy she is without even trying. The sight made my dick twitch. I remember how she wrapped those lips around my cock and owned me as she sucked me off. I groan in my chair trying to push the past out of my mind.

I was stuck there, in my seat at the far corner of the coffee shop, frozen in time, watching her as though I weren't really there. The paper in my lap and an espresso on the small, white table in front of me, I stared at her with desire.

I couldn't believe she was there right in front of me. As if the time hadn't passed and we hadn't parted all those years ago. I sat there in awe until she accepted her coffee with a smile, taking a sip as she strode to the front, shifting the purse on her shoulder as she pushed the door open and left, blending into the hustle and bustle of the city.

I smile at the memory, back when we were together, she never drank coffee. It doesn't surprise me that she ordered it flavored and added so much damn sugar to it.

I had no idea she'd moved to the city. I had no clue she was anywhere near me. *My Cherry.*

I'm ashamed to remember how I followed her to her office building. The winter air blowing in my face and the Christmas carolers already out in the morning on the corners of the busy streets. I walked into the sleek skyrise with shiny steel and tall glass windows. I've driven past this building a thousand times. I remember thinking there's no way she's been this close to me all this time.

I walked in behind her and watched as she walked through the marble floored lobby of Parker-Moore and confidently strode towards the elevator. I walked to the fountain in the center of the lobby and watched as she took small bites of what was left of the muffin, waiting for the elevator to ding and take her away from me.

I look back to the screen on my computer. All of her information is there. Alena Morgan. She's a chief advisor for a prominent sales company now. After years of schooling and a prestigious internship. Now she's back. Back in my life with her dreams accomplished.

And according to her background check, her name is the only one on the lease.

Which means she's single. As far as I can tell she is.

I fucking hope she is. I want her now even more than I wanted her then. I knew I'd hold her back, I knew she needed more from life than what I had to offer back then. Fuck, we were only just experiencing life and I wanted to keep her all to myself. I felt selfish and like an asshole for making her feel like she needed to run. And when she walked away, I let her go without fighting.

The day she left me tore a hole in my heart, filled only by my work. I worked in private security with a good friend of mine, Isaac. Every fucking day, I was working. Trying to ignore the fact that I'd let her slip away.

She was mine. Had I told her no, she wasn't leaving, I think she would have rebelled, but I could have disciplined her and she would have fucking loved it. She would have seen how good it felt. How much she wanted it as much as I did. We could have made it work. But back then, I wasn't the man I am now and I sure as fuck wasn't the Dom I am now.

She wouldn't have understood her feelings and I would have failed at explaining them to her. She was degrading what we had by thinking her submission made her weak. It doesn't make her any less of an equal to submit. If anything she has the upper hand. I'm the one who needs to know the limits, her limits. The limits that *she* sets.

But she didn't accept that. She wouldn't. She left me and I let her go, burying myself in work as a punishment more than anything else.

Until I met Lynn and created this place. *Club X.*

A smile curls my lips up.

I never dreamed it would grow to be something so ... powerful. This lifestyle has always been a passion of mine. The darkness may have been hidden and subdued, but it's always been there. I didn't know how lucrative my expertise would turn out to be.

This rebuilt mansion is an escape to debauchery and sin for the rich and powerful. Our security and use of non disclosure agreements as well as the clientele make Club X unique and desirable. We're exclusive and that makes the members even more eager to join. Most only know of Club X through word of mouth. We don't have a website and we aren't interested in advertising. With a ten thousand per month membership fee, we don't need more business.

This club may be my profession, but it's so much more than that.

It's something I want to show my cherry. I know she'd love it. She's the most submissive woman I've ever met. She's confident and professional, but she craves an escape from responsibility. She loves handing over power to those she can trust. She may not be aware of it, but it's liberating for her.

I need that exchange of power. I need her back in my life.

I haven't had a steady relationship for years. I haven't even had a submissive or played downstairs for months. I haven't *wanted* like this in so damn long.

Not since she left me.

I click to my email and hover the mouse over send. But I can't do it. I can't let her know that I'm here just yet. I'm afraid she'll run.

I stare at the screen, feeling pissed off to even be in this predicament. I know one thing for sure, as soon as I get her in here, I'm not letting her go.

At that thought, an idea strikes me.

"Lynn?" I call out of my office and my business partner, the face of the business really, peers into my doorway.

We met years ago and hit it off right away as friends, good friends too. We aren't anything more than that, and we both like it that way. In this line of business, that makes what we do much easier.

"What can I do for you Joshua?" she asks, walking in but only taking a few steps into my office.

I don't want my sweet Alena, my Cherry, knowing I want her here. I want her to come here on her own.

I tell her, "I need you to send an email for me."

She tilts her head with her forehead pinched, "am I your secretary now?" There's a touch of humor, but also slight disbelief.

"It's an invitation and it can't come from me." I tap my knuckles on the desk, debating on whether or not I should tell her.

Judging by the smile on her face, she doesn't need to know more. Lynn is an expert at judging facial expressions and apparently I've given more than enough away.

"I'm happy to help," she says with a twinkle of mischief in her eyes.

Chapter 2

Alena

I swallow thickly looking up at the large wooden doors. This is for me. A Christmas present of sorts for myself. I'm finally going to go through with it. My heartbeat races and my palms are sweaty. I've never done anything like this. I haven't even been with a man in years.

As pathetic as that sounds, work has taken priority. I'm more than ready for this.

I had a boyfriend, Joshua, years ago, who made me want this. He was my first in every way. He teased me with the idea of being a submissive. Really, I teased myself. He wanted me to kneel, to crawl to him, to obey his commands and let him tie me up. I'm wet just thinking about him and his dirty words.

I was convinced that lowering yourself to be submissive was wrong and dirty. That it was degrading.

But I'm obsessed.

Even more, I'm turned on by the idea.

"Come here Cherry, be a good girl for me," his seductive words echo in my memory and I have to close my eyes and sink my teeth into my bottom lip. My heart clenches at the memory, so does my pussy. Joshua was good to me.

But he didn't last. Your firsts never do. We each wanted different things and moved on, going our separate ways. It was hard at first, even if it was my decision.

After all, I was falling for him, I was weak when I was with him. I craved to submit to him and I know how badly he wanted it. But I wasn't ready back then. I didn't know that I ever would be. Almost ten years later, ten years wiser and more established, now I know what I want.

And now I'm standing out in front of Club X. It's not well known. It's full of powerful men and rumored to be the hottest BDSM club there is. But it's secretive for a reason. From outside it almost looks like a mansion. It's large and intimidating, but aged with beauty. There are details in every aspect of the architecture and landscaping.

It's a gorgeous building, but I have no idea what it looks like inside. Pictures are forbidden. The only ones I've seen are from the emailed invitation I was sent.

And I certainly didn't focus on the architecture in those pictures.

I almost didn't open the email. I had no idea who Madam Lynn was and it's only out of curiosity that I clicked. It was a personal invitation. Somehow she knew what my dark desires were.

My blood heats at the memory. It's been two weeks since I got the email. Two weeks of warring with myself. But I'm a grown woman. I'm successful and I have everything I've wanted out of my professional life. But my love life is non existent and I don't even know how I'd find a boyfriend.

Nor if I'm interested in one. But I can't deny my curiosity.

It's only two on Tuesday, so I'm sure it won't be packed. I'm surprised they're even open.

I wanted to see what it was like on my own. I just want a small peek to see if I'm really tempted. I want to know if I can actually do this. The thought of being a submissive is intoxicating; it's a fantasy. I don't know if I can go through with it. But I have to try in order to find out.

I ball my hand into a fist and knock against the door. The cold air makes my knuckles hurt at the hard contact. It's only when I'm pulling my hand away that I see the black cast iron knocker.

I roll my eyes at my stupidity. But before I can dwell on it, the doors open and I sucked in a breath.

A large man, opens the door. I have to crane my neck to look him in the eyes. I am a step lower than him, but still, his broad shoulders and towering height are intimidating. He's handsome enough, but not really my type. He looks down at me and cocks a brow, "Are you a member?" he asks. "I don't recognize you," his eyes travel down my body, "and I'm sure I would had I seen you before."

"I-" I almost stutter from the nerves, my cheeks heating with a violent blush, but I clear my throat and grab a hold of myself. I shake my head, "not yet." I'm proud of how firm my voice is, but my heart is trying to climb up my throat and my body is humming with anxiety.

This is my choice. I can always leave if it's not what I expect.

"Welcome," he says with a smirk on his face, opening the door wider and allowing a warmth to flow through the door, urging me to enter.

Seductive music lures me inside. I give him a small smile and blush again when I catch him blatantly staring at my ass. My heels click on the stone floored foyer. The ceiling is domed and there's a large desk to my right, a coat check on my left. Beyond the foyer, the deep red carpet mutes the sound of my heels as I step forward, drawing me to the large open ballroom beyond the lobby. Or is it a dining room? There are tables and what looks like a stage behind a thick velvet curtain. I unconsciously step forward drawn in by the elegance and mystery and, to be frank, disbelief.

It literally takes my breath away.

"Miss?" A woman calls out after me. Her voice breaks me out of my reverie and I turn to face whoever's calling me.

A gorgeous woman walks towards me with a confidence I can only wish I possess in the boardroom. Her blonde hair is pulled back into a bun and her makeup is flawless and natural with the exception of a slight cat eye and thick long lashes that must be fake. There's no way those are real.

Although she's not young, she has a better figure that most and she strides towards me in her Louboutin heels as though she's owning a runway, the scarlet colored dress clinging to her curves the entire way.

Madam Lynn. She must be the Madam of the club.

I take a step forward and hold my hand out, moving my coat to the crook of my arm. "Madam Lynn?" I say, although it's a question.

The woman pauses, accepting my hand and smiling with a twinkle in her pale blue eyes.

"You've finally come." She says accepting my hand shake and taking me in. "Alena, correct?"

I nod my head and return her smile although my heart's still pounding in my chest. "Yes, I'm here."

"I'm glad you've accepted the invitation." She looks at my coat and then back to my eyes. "May I?" She asks while reaching out for it.

"Oh sure, of course." I hand her the coat and she immediately takes my hand and leads me back out into the lobby.

"I know you're going to want to look around and," she looks over her shoulder at me with a mischievous grin, "have some fun." She stops at the desk and waves over a young woman in a silk black jumpsuit, "but let's get you checked in first." My cheeks color with slight embarrassment.

"Yes, Madam Lynn," I say just beneath my breath.

She looks back at me with slight surprise and tilts her head. "Oh he was right about you."

I take in her words, letting them resonate in me slowly, as she walks behind the desk with the other woman tapping on keys at a computer.

Who is 'he' and what the fuck was he right about?

Chapter 3

Joshua

I watch on the screen in the security room as Dominic let's Alena in from the cold and takes a deliberate look at her ass. It would piss me off if I wasn't feeling so fucking confident.

She's here because she wants this. She wouldn't have come otherwise. She had one day off this week and she chose to use it to come here.

I should be ashamed that I hacked into her emails, but I'm not. It's something that's almost natural at this point. With every application we do a background check. And that includes some digging that's on the other side of the law. But we have to be careful.

And with Alena, I had to make sure she was single and that she was still the same woman I once loved. The thought strikes me like a hit to the chest. *Love.* It's been a long time since I've said that word. With no family and no relationship, I haven't had a reason to. I huff a small laugh as I realize the last woman I ever told those three little words just walked into my club.

I remember her whispering it with such sincerity after I took her for the first time. It was slow and sweet and I hadn't revealed how much more I needed from her. I was desperate to have her and I wish I'd told her sooner. Regret starts to creep up on me, but I shake it off.

She's here now and that's what matters.

I watch the screens in the control room as she walks into the dining hall. She's beautiful in her cream chiffon pleated dress. She looks innocent and naive wearing that in here. If it were any other time, she'd be struck with surprise at how out of place she is. We usually don't let anyone into the building this early. Some Doms have keys to the private rooms that work from the entrances outside, but not in here.

When she emailed back asking to come, I allowed it. I'm already breaking rules for her. I'll break them all to get her to submit to me.

Madam Lynn is getting her set up. Watching the two of them interact makes me uneasy. Lynn knows how much this means to me. I turn on the volume for the mics and listen in as they walk through the hall and into the play rooms. There are several on the first floor, and even more in the dungeon.

Alena never struck me as a woman who'd care for the dungeon. She doesn't want pain. She just wants to give up control. Even if she doesn't realize it.

My thumb rests on my bottom lip as I watch the screen.

They're quiet as they walk into the first play room and she eyes the Andrew's cross in the back of the room.

There are two crosses as well as some other furniture meant for BDSM interaction.

I can see her tied to one. Bound and helpless. Her eyes widen slightly and I can see her breath hitch as she realizes that's what it's for. She pauses mid step and looks at the dark raw wood beams as though they may bite her.

I lean forward watching her every move and willing her to explore.

I don't want her to be scared off just yet. She would enjoy it.

As if hearing my thoughts, she takes a few steps forward and gently touches the wood. Running her fingers down the side of it and eyeing the leather cuffs attached to it.

I can see the wheels turning in her head and finally, those plump lips part with lust clouding her eyes. *Yes!*

She turns abruptly and clears her throat.

"How are the..." she looks away and then back at Madam Lynn. "How do the Dom's choose their subs?" she asks. My skin prickles with excitement.

"Well," Lynn takes a seat on the dark brown leather chaise and crosses her legs as she leans against the back of it. "Submissives and dominants are free to roam so long as they're wearing the bracelets that signify their interests.

"So as long as I have no collar and wear this," she raises her arm, showing off the three layered bracelet, silver, black, silver, bands. "Then the dominants will know?"

Black for carte blanche. A smile slips into place. I have so much to explore with her. So much to teach her.

Lynn nods her head. "That's correct." She gestures to the cross. "If you'd like to go up there, you can simply kneel by it and wait for a partner.

Alena's head whips to the side. "Just wait?" she asks with a higher pitched voice. Her face is etched with insecurity. "What if no one wants to."

Lynn laughs at the absurdity. It pisses me off that she thinks no one would want to accept the offer. She'd have men lining up for her.

My hands ball into fists. That's not going to happen though. I'll kick all those fuckers out before I allow that.

She's mine.

My anger dissipates entirely as Alena asks, her voice laced with fear, "what happens if they just leave me there or-"

Lynn's quick to cut that off, and I'm relieved she's there to put cherry at ease. This was good. I was right to handle it this way. Lynn isn't intimidating in the least. This is the perfect introduction for Alena.

"We have security in each of the rooms at all times. All you'd have to do is safe word. If you're gagged, then you can use a hand signal."

I can see Alena taking in the information and letting it calm her down. She nods slightly and looks at the other trinkets and toys around the room. Most items are in packages because of the nature of their use. Vibrators, plugs, nipple clamps. Some paddles and whips aren't packaged. They can be wiped down and sterilized.

"You can always go up for auction," Lynn offers out of nowhere. Every hair on my body stands upright, the breath stolen from my lungs. Once a month we hold an auction. It's a one month long contract. Lynn's eyes meet the camera in the room and I know that comment was meant for me.

I grunt and sit back in my seat. Fuck that, cherry's not going up for auction .. although. If I bought her she couldn't say no. I'd have her to myself for an entire month.

She'd have to sign the paperwork afterwards though. And the next auction isn't for two weeks. I'm not waiting that long or risking her running when she finds out that I'm the one who bought her. Waiting this last week was too much as it is.

I've waited long enough.

She wants a Dom and I want her. That's all that matters.

I watch as Alena shakes her head, although her eyes are hazed with curiosity. "I don't think an auction is what I'm looking for." *Good girl.*

I rise from my seat. Muting the microphones and buttoning my suit jacket. It's time for me to take over the tour and show Alena what she really needs.

CHAPTER 4

ALENA

The second play room is even more interesting than the first. It seems more private since it's smaller and there's only one of everything ... but there are so many items I'm not sure if multiple couples play together or not.

"How many people are usually in here?" I turn to Madam Lynn and ask. I love the idea of being at a Dom's mercy. But I'm not sure how I feel about other people watching. Especially at first, when I'm just learning. All of this is overwhelming to see in person.

I just don't think I could do it if strangers were watching. And the insecurity of it all is making me wonder if I can do this at all. I swallow thickly and wait for her to answer.

She's been patient and I really appreciate the tour. I didn't expect it. I also didn't expect it to be so empty.

"The play rooms are usually packed." My lips purse and my brow raises. Shit. I don't think I can handle that. I look around the room at the benches and sex swing and try to imagine being fucked mercilessly while tied down and having people watch. The first part heats my blood and makes desire stir low in my belly, but the second ... it kills the fantasy for me.

I can't lie. I've been mused about this for a long time. More so recently since getting the email. I've touched myself to the thought of what it would've been like had I let Joshua dominate me like he wanted.

It caught me off guard back then. I kept thinking it was wrong and that he must've thought less of me. But now that I look back on it, he never treated me differently. He was just more aware of what he wanted. He shared his desires with me and fear kept me from submitting.

I wonder what it would have been like if I'd let him cuff me to the bed like he wanted to. What he would have done to me. I stifle my moan at the thought of him strapping me down and spreading my legs while I'm bound and helpless.

Madam Lynn's cough makes a blush stain my cheeks.

I turn and ignore the fact that my thoughts must've been obvious.

A frown pulls at my lips as I take in the room, remembering what we were just talking about. Coming here would be nothing like what I fantasize about. I'm not interested in an orgy or voyeurism. Whatever it is that they call it.

I was hopeful that this was going to fulfill my needs, but all this tour has done is fill me with regret. I wish I'd never ended things with Joshua. I let my fear push him away.

I bite the inside of my cheek.

"I wouldn't worry too much if I were you," Madam Lynn says, her seductive voice grabbing my attention and bringing me back to the present.

"Why's that?" I dare to ask.

She may be elegant and graceful, but Madam Lynn seems to be a woman of secrets. She has a look in her eyes and a manner of speaking that makes it obvious that she knows more than she's telling you. I'm not sure I like that, but considering her profession, it's admirable.

"I have a feeling you'll be spending most of your time in a private room." My shoulders relax slightly at the thought. Yes, I think I'd much prefer privacy.

I open my lips to ask to see the rooms, but my body freezes as my eyes catch sight of *him*. My heart, my blood, everything slows and heats to a nearly unbearable degree.

I blink a few times. Not believing he's here.

"Alena," Joshua steps into the room, proving that he's not a figment of my imagination. My entire body feels as though it's on fire.

Holy fuck!

Ten years ago he was a hot-as-fuck twenty year old. The years have aged him beautifully. His strong jawline and broad shoulders heighten the severity of his suit. Joshua has always radiated power, sex appeal and authority to me. But in this moment he is the epitome of dominance.

I almost take a step back as he walks closer to me, out of sheer instinct. But my lust for him has me frozen in place. I can hardly breathe as the images I was just conjuring flash before my eyes.

Prickles of want travel down my body, hardening my nipples.

Desire stirs in my core.

"I have more work to attend to," Madam Lynn says to no one in particular and not waiting for a response. she gracefully, yet quickly leaves me alone with Joshua.

This is not good.

As she closes the door behind her, the only thing I can think is that I am so fucked.

Chapter 5

Joshua

I excel at reading body language. And right now my Cherry is looking to bolt, but more than that, she's turned on. I have to resist the urge to smile. I want her. I want her badly. And it's obvious that she wants me too.

"Do you want to try it out?" I ask her as she tries to right herself. She still hasn't spoken and I can practically hear the questions on the tip of her tongue.

There's a spark between us, a recognition of desire and want. But our past is in the way and all I want is for it to move aside so I can take her like I'm meant to.

"Joshua," she finally says my name as I walk closer to her, standing at a safe distance, but close enough to talk easily.

"How are you Alena?"

She nods her head as her fingertips roll the hem of her dress nervously and she glances behind me at the door. Her cheeks are colored with a violent blush that looks beautiful on her.

"How did you-" she starts to ask, but she doesn't complete the thought.

It could be one of many questions.

How did I get here?

How did I know she was here?

I decide to lay it all out for her and let her choose what to do with it.

"I knew you were coming." I answer her. My heart races as her eyes widen. "In fact, I asked Madam Lynn to send you the invitation." I spot the large wing back chair and decide to take a seat. It will be less intimidating for her if I'm sitting.

Her lips part with a question and then slam shut. She blinks several times.

"I saw you a few weeks ago in the city and I couldn't believe you were here." I sit back in my chair, "I thought this may be better." I look her in the eyes and wait for a response. It may have been easier to stop her from leaving the coffee shop, to walk up to her at the elevator before she went to work. But that would have set the wrong precedent.

This is the relationship I want. And the one she needs.

Our needs have to be established. Without it, without her willing to give both of us what we need, this relationship will fail like it did before. This time I'm going to fight for it. I want her badly enough to convince her to give this a chance.

"I wanted to see you here. I wanted to offer you this." I gesture around the room.

She blinks several times and then a small breath leaves her and her eyes gaze with lust.

"You want this?" she asks me as though she's shocked by the truth. Her hands reach up to her collarbone and she looks at me with a raw vulnerability I've only seen in her eyes once. The night I first made her mine. All those years ago.

I nod my head once. "I want this with you."

She seems to come out of the lust filled haze and realize she's in a room with me, a man who she's hardly spoken to in years. But I'm still a man she once loved. A man who knew her better than anyone.

"You don't know me, Joshua," she starts to say although she's obviously bothered.

"I knew you well enough to know you'd want this." I know she's going to fight at first. She's not used to submitting, but I'll earn her trust, I'll show her it's worth it.

It's quiet for a moment as she takes in my confession. "Do you come here a lot?" she asks, changing the subject.

"I'm a partner in the business." Her mouth drops some and she looks around the room with more unease than before. Insecurity obvious on her face.

This is a turn for the worse and I don't understand why. I wasn't expecting it.

"What's wrong?" I ask.

She shakes her head and almost refuses to answer.

"What did I say?" although it's a question, there's a command in my tone.

She recognizes it and considers me for a moment. She may not know it, but this is just like any other submission. She can choose to trust that she can trust me and answer the question honestly, or she can blow it off or hide from it and run without giving me a chance. I wait with baited breath for her choice.

And finally she answers, "I just didn't realize you did this a lot."

It doesn't take me long to read between the lines. I stand and make my way over to her, holding her gaze. "Do you think I fuck a lot, Alena?" I walk close enough to touch her, but I don't yet. "You think this is a game for me and you don't want to be used and tossed aside?"

I know that's exactly what she's thinking. And why

wouldn't she? I work in the business of selling sex and she's going to want a commitment. She needs one.

"I don't." I tell her the truth. "This isn't about a quick fuck for me. I'm not a playboy. I didn't bring you here to toy with you. I want to see if this can work between us." I'm not ready to fall back into the deep relationship we had before. Not just yet. But I won't lie and say it's not something that's on the forefront of my mind. I want her as a submissive, but I can give her more than that.

I can give her everything, if only she'll let me.

"What do you want from me then?" she asks.

"I just want a chance. One I never got before." I take a step closer and gently brush my hand along her jaw, leaning in so I can whisper against her lips. "I want to show you how much you'd love it."

Her eyes close and I know she wants the same.

As she leans in, I pull away slightly. I need her to submit before I can give her anything else. She opens her eyes instantly at the loss of my touch. Her breathing is heavy and I know she's feeling insecure. I don't want that. But I need this first. It's too big a part of my life and my desires.

"Do you want to try it?" I ask and gesture to the bench behind her. It's a spanking bench made of plush leather and steel.

She turns to look behind her, pushing her soft

brunette hair out of her face.

"Right now?" she asks.

I nod my head once, "right now."

She may not be ready just yet. And I can wait, I can take it slow. But she's in need and I'm desperate to fulfill those needs.

"I don't know," she answers honestly.

"What don't you know about?"

"I don't think I trust myself right now," she smiles slightly letting out a small nervous laugh.

"You don't need to, just trust me." I look into her eyes and plead with her to give me this. To give *us* this. "I still want you Alena. I've never stopped wanting you."

She takes in a sharp breath, her hazel eyes heating with a lust that makes my dick harden.

"I want to," she whispers.

"What do you want?" I ask her.

"I want to… try it out." She barely gets the words out, but I heard them and it's all I need.

Chapter 6

Alena

My heart is racing out of my chest.

What am I even doing?

I feel drunk from the pure seductive nature of this atmosphere. And from *him*. He always made me weak and he's doing it again right now.

Seeing him in this very room is a dream come true. But it's terrifying at same time. I feel like a naive girl all over again. I close my eyes and walk over to the bench. I want to do this. This is why I came here in the first place

This is for me. I need this.

I open my eyes at the thought and the look in Joshua's eyes pins me in place. It's predatory and full of lust. The desire evident on his face, but also… lower. His massive cock is hard and the outline of it is pressing against his suit pants.

I close my eyes again as he walks forward.

"Look at me, cherry." The command in his voice is hard and on edge. It's a tone he's only used with me once. I refused it then, but I won't now.

My eyes meet his piercing gaze.

"Yes?" I almost say sir. Simply because I know the language. I've done some research over the years. I'm familiar with this scenario and I want it. I want it desperately. Even if it's just for now.

Just this one time.

"I want you to lay down on your back on the bench." My body stiffens at his command. I'm not used to it. It's not what I anticipated either. I turn to look at the leather seat as my hands drift to the buttons on the top of my dress.

"I didn't tell you to undress," my eyes snap to Joshua's at his words.

"Yes, sir." The title slips out without my consent and the look on Joshua's face makes me want to say it again. And again and again. He's obviously pleased and that makes pride and motivation flow through my body. I hold onto them as I gently lay down on the bench. It's angled slightly, so my head is lower than my ass and it feels a bit awkward.

"That's my sweet cherry." Hearing the praise in Joshua's voice and the nickname he gave me so long ago fills me with warmth. *Cherry.* I loved it when he called me that. My thighs clench and my eyes close at the sweet memories of what we once had and what I walked away from all those years ago. But now I have a chance to have it back. I can give him what he's always needed. I know I can.

As I think the words, he brushes his hands up my thighs and loops his thumbs around my panties. I lift my hips as the thin fabric slides over my ass and he slowly pulls them down my legs. Goosebumps follow his path and my body ignites with an intense need for more.

"If you want me to stop, you'll say red. Do you understand?"

"Yes," I breathe the word.

I can't breathe as he takes them off me and tosses them onto the chair behind him. Oh fuck.

I swallow thickly and wait for his next command. My clit is throbbing with need and my nipples are hardened into peaks. I want him so much, it takes everything in me to just lay here and wait patiently for him.

His large hands grip the inside of my knees and spreads my legs wider. I grip the edge of the bench harder as he lowers himself closer to my bared pussy.

I'm fully exposed and feeling a mixture of desire and insecurity. It takes me back to our first time. It's just like that. All over again.

He pulls my dress up slightly over my hips and stares at my pussy with a hunger I've never seen on another man. My lips part with lust. I love the look in his eyes. I've missed it. I've missed *him*.

He kneels on the floor and grips my hips, moving my ass and tilting me so I'm where he wants me.

Oh, fuck. My neck arches and I want to watch and I want to run and hide all at the same time.

"Fuck, cherry," Joshua says as he trails a finger down my clit to the opening of my pussy. "You're soaking wet for me."

My clit throbs as he leans down and takes a languid lick. My neck arches and my mouth opens with the unexpected pleasure.

"Hold onto the bench," he says firmly and I look up at him and realize my hands are on his shoulders. I nod and quickly follow his command.

As soon as I do, he thrusts two thick fingers deep inside of me, making my back bow and sending spikes of pleasure shooting through my body. *Fuck, yes!*

My nipples harden and I instantly remember how he used to control my body. I know now why sex has never been the same. My body is a slave to his touch. *Only his.*

I writhe on the bench, but his firm grip on my hip keeps me pinned in place.

I can't help the moans spilling from my lips as he strokes my g-spot over and over again, making me climb higher and higher. Soft cries fill the room as my head thrashes.

So close. I'm so close.

As he sucks my clit into his mouth, massaging it with his tongue, my body ignites, coming alive with a pleasure that's unmatched. White spots flash before my eyes as I cry out my release.

My back arches and my hands reach up to grab his hair and push him closer to my pussy, but I'm quick to go back to the bench and obey him.

I grip onto the bench as hard as I can while he continues to suck my clit and fingerfuck every last bit of my orgasm out of me.

I gasp for air as my head falls to the side. Every inch of my body tingling with desire. I struggle to breathe and finally calm down as I hear a zipper. I look down my body and see Joshua's thick cock and my heart stops.

"Turn over cherry," his voice drips with desire as he gives me the command. He holds my hips, steadying me as I quickly do what he says and get into position even with the intensity of my orgasm still racing through my body in dim waves.

His deft fingers quickly strap the cuffs to my wrists and ankles and my heart races. I trust him. I do. I'd be lying if I said I wasn't partially scared, but I want this. I want to get over my fear. I want to *enjoy* this.

His hot breath on my ass makes me want more. He leaves a kiss on my right cheek as the trembling in my legs settles.

I can hardly breathe as he kisses up my body, pushing the dress above my waist, his fingers trailing softly up my body. A shiver runs down my body and I just want him right now. I don't want to wait.

His soft touches are torturous.

"I want you Cherry. Let me have you just like this, with nothing in-between us." His voice drips with lust and desperation as he gently sets his hands down on my hips. It makes me feel powerful. Even though I'm bound, it's my limits that he has to abide by and the knowledge makes me yearn for more. "It's what I've always wanted." He barely speaks the words.

I've been dreaming of this for so long.

"I know you want it to," he whispers into my ear. His hot breath sending shivers down my entire body.

I pull against the straps and moan, arching my neck to let his teeth graze down my neck. I give in to him like I want to. I trust him and I want him. It's now or never.

"Yes, Joshua. Please. Take me."

Chapter 7

Joshua

I've wanted this for too fucking long.

I line my dick up at her entrance and slam all the way in without hesitation. The bench tilts forward slightly, but it's bolted to the floor. I can fuck her as hard and fast as I want. And there's nothing to stop me from giving her just that.

She screams out a ragged cry of pleasure as I hammer into her tight pussy over and over again. I'm rough with her and ruthless, it's a hard fuck, but it's how I want her and I know she'll love it. The sounds of her pleasured moans and my hips slamming against her ass, fill my ears. I fucking love it.

I'm going to give her everything. I want her so consumed with pleasure that she can't think straight. I want her so sore tomorrow that she can't sit without remembering this.

She's mine.

I want her to know it with everything in her. I want to own this tight pussy. The thought makes me groan as she writhes under me as best she can although she's bound. It's a useless effort, but instinctual.

Fuck, she feels so good. Too good. I groan as I lean forward and nip along her shoulder, keeping up a relentless pace.

Her strangled cries of pleasure fuel me to push harder and deeper.

"Joshua!" she screams out my name as I push her limits. Yes! My name.

Her breathing is ragged and I love it. The sound fuels me onward.

She pulls at the leather cuffs on her wrists and I nip her earlobe, "stay still while I fuck you just how I want." If she pulls any more, the leather could rub against her wrists. I don't want that. Even more so, I want her to obey me. I want to give her a command that she can obey, even if it is against her instincts.

She bites down on her lip as I pound into her over and over. Fuck yes! She's perfect. She's trying so hard to stay still. Her head thrashes from side to side and she's holding her breath as her mouth opens into a perfect "O". She's so close.

"Scream for me as you cum on my dick, cherry." At my words, she cries out my name, her pussy spasming on my dick. Yes! My name! Because she's *mine*. I ride through her orgasm, hammering harder into her as I grip her hips. My blunt fingernails dig into the soft flesh and I piston my hips.

"Joshua!" she screams again and sucks in a sharp breath and it only fuels me to go faster, to take her over the edge again. I want to give her everything.

I need to. This is my one chance to have her and show her how good this is going to be. How easy it is and how much she'll enjoy it.

I keep fucking her, over and over with hard, fast strokes, taking her to the edge.

My balls draw up and a cool tingling sensation grows at the base of my spine. Fuck, I'm going to cum. She's so tight and so good, I can't fucking hold it any longer.

"Cum for me again," I tell her with my eyes firmly on her gorgeous face as my hand reaches between the bench and I gently pinch her clit.

Her face scrunches and her body tenses as her orgasm rips through her body. She pulls instinctually at the binds, but she's quick to correct the behavior. Fuck, she's so good. Knowing that even as she's overwhelmed with pleasure, she's still trying to obey me, makes me lose it.

I bury myself to the hilt and pump short, shallow thrusts until we're both spent and left panting with our combined cum leaking onto her thighs.

My body is still humming with the afterglow of my release as I grab a few tissues from beneath the bench and catch my breath. I tuck myself in, watching as her legs stop trembling and the effects of her orgasm dims.

She was perfect. Everything I've dreamed of having in a submissive. From the moment she decided to walk to the bench and give this a real try, she gave herself completely.

I kiss the small of her back as I wipe the cum from between her thighs and then unbuckle the straps on her ankles. Her wrists are next and she immediately sits.

I pick her up in my arms and she leans into me, her body still trembling. I lean back and sooth her, running my hand down her back and kissing her hair. She's so beautiful. The years have only made her more of a woman. After a moment she moves from my lap, not looking me in the eyes. I don't like it. Aftercare is important, but I let her get up and move to the chair where her panties are.

I regret letting her get up when I see the look in her

eyes. She's on edge and nervous. She's thinking too much. Worrying about what's going to happen.

If she was my sub she wouldn't have a worry in the world. And I want her to be just that.

She leans down and pulls her panties on and up her lush thighs without looking at me.

I bet she's wondering what this meant to me and if it's over.

I don't want her to wonder; I don't want her to think about anything at all but pleasing me. After all, I'm doing the same.

"I have a Christmas dinner tomorrow to attend for a client." The words escape my lips before I can think. Her forehead pinches and she's unsure why I'm even bringing it up. "I want you to come with me."

She stares at me wide-eyed and doesn't answer.

"A submissive doesn't question the commands." I pick my suit jacket up off the floor and wait for her response. "You know what to say Alena."

I wait with baited breath. This is about more than sex for me. And I damn well know the same is true for her. She just needs to give in.

"You came in here for a reason cherry." Her eyes dart to mine. "Let me give you what you need."

Her lips part with uncertainty.

"I want you. As submissive and more. I want you to

be mine."

Her eyes focus on my lips and I know I have her. If nothing else, she loves my touch. But I know there's more to it than that. You don't hold on to this desire and these feelings if there isn't *more* to it.

"Just say yes, Cherry. Let me collar you, like you really want me to."

She says the next words in the sweetest voice I've ever heard, "collar me, Joshua. I'm ready."

Epilogue

Alena

I twist my hands and struggle to move. I've been waiting here on the bed, tied down by my wrists and ankles for at least twenty minutes. In the six months that we've dated, Joshua has never made me wait this long.

I'm naked and horny and so ready for him to take me. But I lay here quietly and wait. I know he's going to come in and give me exactly what I need. And I trust him to do just that.

A small smile plays at my lips.

The only thing I really need is him. I sigh with contentment, feeling warm and safe. He's my security in life. I feel complete with him. I didn't even realize how much I was missing from life until he showed me.

My eyes slowly open and my pussy clenches as I hear the door creak open.

My chest flushes and heat travels to my cheeks. I'm spread and naked and I know he's seeing everything. But that's the way he wants me.

"Cherry, you're so damn patient," he says from behind me as he walks into the bedroom.

"For you," I answer with a smirk. Really, he's the patient one. It took me ten years to accept that I wanted this. Ten years for me to let him show me how much I'd love it.

The bed groans as he crawls closer to me. He's hiding something in his hand and excitement courses through me at the thought of what it could be.

"I got you a present," he says seductively. I smile broadly and let my teeth sink into my bottom lip to try to conceal my elation.

Ever since our second night together, he brings me little gifts while I'm tied up. That second night was Christmas Eve and he gave me a collar. It's beautiful and I love it. I wear the necklace, another gift from Joshua, outside of Club X, but inside and in the bedroom, I proudly wear my collar.

"What is it?" I ask.

"Uh uh, close your eyes." I smile sweetly at him, my

eyes darting from his handsome face to his closed hand.

I close my eyes and wait patiently. My blood heats and my breath stills as he leans over and slips a cold metal ring onto my ring finger. *Oh my god.*

"Marry me Cherry." Joshua says in a voice that has a hint of insecurity.

I keep my eyes closed. Still in disbelief.

"Say yes." He gives me another command.

I slowly open my eyes and stare back at him.

"You're mine, Alena. And I want you forever and for everyone to know it."

Tears prick my eyes and I nod my head. "I love you," I say as he bends down, kissing me sweetly. He breaks our kiss and says in the hot air between us, "you need to say yes."

"Yes," I whisper. He takes my lips with his and groans into my kiss. I have to pull away and struggle against the damn binds pinning me down. I just want to hold him.

A rough chuckle rises up his chest as he reaches over and unties my wrists and then my ankles.

It's then that I get a good look at the sparkling ring on my finger. It's a beautiful cushion cut with perfect clarity and at least three carats. I stare at it in awe.

"I had to tie you down and make sure you'd say yes."

I shake my head, my shoulders shuddering with a small laugh, "you had to know I'd say yes." I've never wanted anything more than this. My life feels truly complete. "You collared me for Christmas," I jokingly say back to him.

He shakes his head and looks at the gorgeous engagement ring on my finger. "For life my cherry."

Stolen Mistletoe Kisses

Chapter 1

Vinny

The brightly colored mouse face on the plastic phone in my hands stares back at me. I remember this toy, with its primary colors of red, yellow, and blue, and the loud noises the buttons make. I can't pull the little phone out, but I know there's a thin red cord that's connected so little tykes can drag it along the floor. I huff a small laugh.

Same damn toy I had as a toddler, twenty-five years later.

Some things never change.

I set the box back on the shelf and look over to my left. This aisle in the toy store lines up with the door to the back room, which in turn leads to the manager's office. That's right where I need to go. I'm just waiting on the perfect moment to slip into the back and grab the spare key. The manager slipped out already; he clocked out early even though the store's still open. I don't blame him, since it's dead. In this small town, everyone's done their shopping early for Christmas.

The owner and him are the only two with the keys to the registers, but now they're both gone and won't be back till after Christmas, and I know the keys are back there somewhere.

The old lady behind me finally tosses something into her cart, making a small racket and a squeak. I turn to look over my shoulder and watch as she pushes her cart away. I take the chance, looking to my right and left as I make my way to the "employees only" door and confidently open it.

As though I belong back here.

My heart's racing, and adrenaline is pumping through my veins. This isn't the first time I've done something like this. It's been years since I've jacked a car or stolen anything. Back then I was a thief for hire. I'm not proud of it. But now I stay on the right side of the law. I peek into the break room and see it's empty. Stockroom is next and there's a girl bending at the waist digging in a box, muttering about how the color of the dress on the doll isn't gonna matter. I keep walking until I find the door with the Manager's Office plate on it.

Bingo.

I test the knob and it doesn't budge. But that's alright. I may be a reformed man, but I still remember how to pick a lock. I stare at the door for a moment, then look back to the storefront at the end of the hallway as I shove a bent paperclip in the lock.

This isn't about stealing for me. It's about doing the right thing. Maybe it's the wrong way of going about it, but it's the only way I know.

The lock clicks and I'm quick to open the door, walking in as swiftly and quietly as possible and shut it behind me with a soft low *snick*. My heart pounds, and I can hear the blood rushing in my ears.

I stalk to his desk and check there first. I need the keys to the register. I need that cash. I know this old toy shop doesn't have a safe. All the money's stored in the registers, and I need that fucking key.

It's not on the desk. I open one drawer after another, sifting through all the paperwork and looking under the stapler and pens.

Where the fuck is it? I know he didn't take it with him. He's got the key to the entrance doors though and I wasn't able to lift that like I would have liked. My eyes look up and hone in on something shining on the bookshelf filled with binders.

A smile crawls across my face.

The tiny key that's been a pain in my ass the last week to get is hanging on a keychain, and I don't hesitate to grab it. Finally. The last piece falls into place. I shove it in my pocket, knowing I'm one step closer to completing this task. Nothing's going to stop me.

I put my ear to the door and listen for anyone coming. I don't hear anything, so I open it slowly and peek out.

The chick who was digging in the box is walking toward the door leading out to the rest of the store with her back to me. She's empty-handed and muttering to herself with her hands balled into little fists. She huffs a deep breath like she's getting ready to go to war over this doll. I shut the door and wait a moment, listening for the telltale sound of the heavy door opening and then shutting. *Click*.

Once the coast is clear, I sneak another look and make sure.

No one's there. My throat feels dry and my face is heated, knowing I need to make a clean getaway out of here and back into the store.

I lock the manager's office door behind me and make a beeline for my escape. As soon as I'm back to the customer area, I feel a slight sense of relief. But I need to get the fuck out of here. One rule I always lived by back in the day, you never stick around to find out if someone saw you.

There's no security in this place though. I know that for a fact.

If there were, I wouldn't have to do this. They would've caught that bastard in the act, and it wouldn't be left up to me to get justice.

I walk quickly toward the exit, through a few aisles of toy trucks and stacking blocks, but I stop before walking through the large automated glass doors.

Cary Ann's standing at the register. Sweet Cary. The sight of her makes me stop before I can leave.

I've known her most of my life since we grew up together in this small town, but scoping this place out has made me see her in a new light. It's been years since I really *looked* at her. And now I can't stop. She's not the little girl who'd fawn over me on the school sidewalks. She's a woman now.

Her tight, faded jeans fit her figure just right and make my dick hard as a fucking rock. They leave nothing to the imagination, and I can just picture how the curve of her ass would feel in my hands. I don't know how it's possible that I ever looked at her with anything other than lust; she's fucking gorgeous.

Her white tanktop is low enough that a bit of cleavage is showing, but the red cardigan she has partially buttoned up over it makes her look a bit more modest. I crave more. I wanna see more of that sun-kissed skin. Every inch.

She's always popping that bubble gum, blowing big, round, cherry-red bubbles at the checkout counter. *Pop!*

It's like she knows she's tempting me with her sweet innocent glances. I don't even know what she's still doing here; she's better than this.

She's got her degree in social work, and I know she doesn't want to work here at the toy store forever. This was a side job for money while she was at the university. She shouldn't be here.

I clear my throat as the front doors open and an older lady walks out, clutching her cardigan.

Cary's a distraction. And she's sure as fuck too good for a man like me.

I thought she'd be gone by now. In the weeks I've been staking this place out, I never thought she'd still be here. But Christmas is around the corner, and she's not showing any signs of leaving or even putting in her notice.

That's a big fucking problem for me. I'm stealing every fucking dime in this place on Christmas Eve. She can't be here, but she's scheduled to be the one closing. All alone, too. I can't pull a gun out and point it at my cherry. The thought of putting fear into those innocent baby blues breaks my heart.

But I'm not the villain here; Jimmy Morose, the owner, is a greedy thief. He's practically the fucking Grinch. All the money that was supposed to go to the orphanage, he's already stolen. I'm getting it back though, and that means emptying these tills at midnight on Christmas Eve. It's the perfect time, right when the annual Christmas Eve parade will be happening and the police will all be there on the other side of town. It's then, or never.

But Cherry's going to be here... A grin slips into place. I could just steal her, too.

Chapter 2

Cary Ann

He's here again, and he still hasn't bought a damn thing. Not that a man like him looks like he needs anything in this toy store. I think he's just coming to check me out. Or at least I thought he was. But he hasn't said a damn word to me. Maybe I'm just vain or getting carried away with the thoughts I used to have of him.

Vinny's a bad boy... or bad *man*, I should say.

I knew him growing up, and lusted after his I-don't-give-a-fuck attitude. He wore his leather jacket and rode that motorcycle everywhere. I wanted to be on the back of that bike. I wanted him to take me away. I shake off the thoughts and swallow down my childhood fantasies.

I was just a silly little girl. My parents would never have allowed it, and he was a few years older anyway. He wasn't interested in a girl like me. Besides, I'm better for it now. I have my degree in social work, and I've already nailed down the job of my dreams. I'm going to be making the world a better place.

I'm not saying Vinny would've held me back, but I'm damn proud that I was able to focus on school and my career.

And to be wise enough to know what's been going on around here.

Now Vinny's back, and he's tempting me. But judging by the puppy dog look on his face, I'm tempting him just as much.

My heart beats just a little faster, and my blood heats with lust. *Pop!* I blow out a bubble and hide my smile when I see him shake his head and smirk at me. My cheeks heat with a blush as I lower my head out of shyness and ring up the remote control car for the mom that's checking out.

"But I want it!" her little boy screams from the seat in his cart, and his loud shriek brings me back to the present.

He's a cute little guy in a snowman sweatshirt, jeans and little boots that look like they could take on a blizzard. But his high-pitched yells and him kicking the cart are driving me crazy. And giving me a headache.

"You want to just hand it to him, or do you want it in a bag?" I ask the mom. I feel bad that she's got two kids out here this late at night. That's gotta be a handful and even worse since they're obviously tired. She looks worn the fuck out. Her hair's pulled back into a ponytail and the little infant in her arms is trying to yank on her earring, which is a miniature Christmas ornament. I wince. That looks like it hurts.

The woman leans her head down so her baby isn't tugging on the earring, seething through her clenched teeth; the pain is evident on her face as she pries the little fingers off of the dangling jewelry. The little girl squeals with delight in her mama's arms and the woman gives the baby a small smile, but switches her to the other hip.

I don't know what good that's gonna do, since the little girl just focuses on that side's earring now.

"No thanks, can you bag it please?" she answers with a forced smile and leans forward to talk to the boy in the cart. "You have to wait, little man." Good for her for at least holding it together.

The boy comically crosses his arms across his chest with a pout, and I have to stifle my laughter as I ring her up.

Once she's done, the store's basically empty. And it's only a few minutes before close. Thank God. I'm spent. I'm ready to get out of here and grateful that so many people are shopping online. I yawn and cover my mouth, then look back to where Vinny was standing. He's gone, and the sight of the empty aisle makes a frown touch my lips. I don't know why, but I just want him to say hi. To just acknowledge my presence. He never did growing up, but I never talked to him either. I didn't have the courage back then. Now though... I need to suck it up and let him know I'm interested. I can do that. I should've already.

He's been in here three times this week, and he's never bought a damn thing. The knowledge makes my stomach twist in knots.

He's up to no good. I hate that I think that. That's what everyone said when he was growing up. They pretend like they don't know why he ended up doing shady things when they never even gave him a chance at anything else. From what I know, he's a good man now. He's got his life together. And I hate that I think anything negative about him at all. But why the hell does he keep coming in here?

I hated the way the parents and teachers all talked about him when we were younger, yet I find myself thinking he's gotta be up to something.

Or maybe I'm just projecting my own actions onto his behavior. My blood cools at the thought, but I can't focus on that right now.

I smile as I ring up the last two customers in the entire place. At least there aren't any more kids in here yelling. I've taken so much Advil the past week that I should really consider buying stock in them.

I'm leaving soon though; this job isn't forever. I just need to stay until Christmas. I have to. I need to be here and make sure everything goes the way it's supposed to on Christmas Eve.

With the store finally empty, I go through the daily closing checklist and take a peek down one aisle. It's a fucking disaster.

Cindy's crouched down, picking up dolls off the floor and shoving them back into place on the shelf. "I bet it was that little brat," she says under her breath when she sees me. I have to press my lips together and hide my grin. She's had a really hard day and given the fact that she only stayed on later because the manager ducked out early, I can see why she's pissed.

"I can take these if you wanna line up aisle three?" I ask her. I know she prefers the larger toys. They're mostly in boxes and easier to straighten out.

She sighs and looks up at me, shoving her blonde hair out of her face. "It doesn't matter really. I'm just tired and ready to go home." She looks fucking exhausted.

"Go ahead," I say with a shrug, "I got this." I don't

mind taking a little more work anyway. *Besides, it'll give me a chance to get things ready for Christmas Eve.* The thought makes my skin prickle with nerves.

"You are a saint, Cary." She rises slowly and stretches out before giving me an unexpected hug.

"Thank you," she says and then doesn't look back as she heads out the front doors to the parking lot. For this town, nine o'clock is late for any place to be open. But for the holiday season it's worth it to be open another three hours on Sunday. At least that's what Morose thinks, but he's a liar, a thief, and an asshole. Judging by the lack of business, you can add dumbass to that list.

I have to straighten two more rows, all the while wondering if I'm going to be able to go through with my plan, and then I turn out the lights and lock the doors. I've been sick over this. I can't stand it, and I want to make things right.

But I'm struggling with what I need to do. I'm not a criminal. And what I'm planning on doing is a crime. I run my hand over my face, feeling torn and exhausted as I walk to the parking lot. It's late, and the street lights are dim. My heels click on the pavement, and my keys rattle in my hand. I look at the ground as I carefully watch my step, avoiding the potholes in the parking lot that Jimmy Morose hasn't bothered to get fixed yet. The only sounds I hear are my heels, and I think I'm alone, but when I lift my head, I stop in my tracks.

Vinny.

He's leaning against my car, his motorcycle parked behind him.

Chapter 3

Vinny

I can at least get her number, I think as I walk out of the store. Take her on a date. Maybe then I can convince her to quit. Or better yet, wear her out and make her pussy so sore she won't be able to work on Christmas Eve.

The thought makes me smile as I take out my cell and text Toni. I let him know it's all set for Christmas Eve and then sit on my bike watching the little boy across the parking lot say "please" over and over again to the mom who looks like she's gonna snap any minute. She's got a cart full of toys by her trunk, a little boy kicking the cart for enjoyment while begging for something, and the baby in her arms is throwing a fit.

Last-minute shopping doesn't look like it's treating her well.

"You need a hand with that?" I ask her, walking away from my bike and over to her minivan. The night air is crisp, and my boots smack against the pavement.

"Please," she says as she looks up at me, but it doesn't last long as her infant arches her back and lets out a shrill cry. "I thought they'd sleep," she says with desperation cracking her voice. Poor mama. I feel bad for her as I reach in the cart and grab a few of the bags in each hand.

She opens the trunk and then the side door before placing her keys back in her purse. "My husband had to work late," she starts explaining, as if she owes me that, but she doesn't. I get it. Sometimes we do shit we wish we didn't have to. "And he was supposed to do the shopping for his side of the family, and he never did." She talks while plugging her little one into the carseat. I can faintly hear the clicking of the buckles.

The rustling from a plastic bag makes me look up, and I catch her little boy trying to grab one of the bags.

She shuts the door and comes around the rear of the van with her hands on her hips. "Jaxon!" she yells out. The little boy looks up with big wide eyes and his lips in a perfect "O." He's been caught red-handed. And he knows it. The look of fear is evident in his eyes and the entire thing makes me chuckle, but I turn away so he doesn't think this is funny. Little rascal.

She snatches him out of the cart and moves to the other side of the van to put him in his carseat. He can't be any older than three. He's silent the entire time and looks stiff, like he knows he's in trouble. At least he's not throwing a fit.

I load the last few bags in and shut her trunk with a loud clunk and start rolling the cart back over a few parking spots to the cart corral to join the rest of them.

I look back over my shoulder as I hear the door close.

"Thank you," the woman says with a look of sincerity.

"No problem," I answer back, giving her a little wave as I shove the cart into the others.

"Merry Christmas," she says, grabbing the keys from her purse and walking to the driver's door, her boots smacking on the pavement. As she opens the door, I can hear her little girl wailing. I cringe out of instinct.

"Merry Christmas," I say, but I don't bother raising my voice since I doubt she can hear me.

I haven't had many people tell me that this season. *Merry Christmas.* I'm not used to hearing it anyway. Same with the rest of the holidays.

I grew up alone, and I'm fine with that. But it's nice to hear holiday greetings occasionally. I can't deny that. The older I get, the more I realize how much I want it.

I click my phone to check the time, shaking off the

unwelcome feelings. Cary Ann's gotta be closing up soon, so I might as well wait for my cherry.

I tap the phone against my jeans, staring at the building. This is bad news. I shouldn't even be going after her, but I *want* her. Something about her is calling to me. I can't justify it. In fact, this can only complicate things. But still I lie to myself.

I can convince her to stay away. I can keep her out of danger by getting close to her.

That's enough to slip a smile across my face as I head on over to my bike and take a seat while I wait for her.

I get lost in my emails on my phone. Since I've been distracted with this heist, I've fallen behind on orders for my custom-made choppers. But I'm calling the delay a holiday break, and my customers don't seem to mind. They don't have much of a choice either. There's a reason they come to me. No one can build choppers like I can. If I'd known all those years ago that I could make good money doing this, I never would've gone down the path I did. I shove down the regret. The past is in the past, and I've moved on.

I look up as a sweet little thing strolls out of the store and walks straight to a beat-up, faded white Honda in the parking lot. It's not my girl, it's the chick who was getting all wound up in the back room. I smile to myself remembering how pissed off she was, and return to my phone, wondering if the customer even got the doll.

I stop what I'm doing when I feel her eyes on me. For a moment, I freeze. *Fuck.* I shouldn't be lingering out front. What if it seems suspicious? How fucking ironic would it be if I got caught because I was waiting for her? Something that has nothing to do with this shit I have planned.

The girl starts her car and sits there a minute, looking at me in her rearview before driving away. She looks back at me again when she gets to the stop sign and then pulls off as I meet her gaze.

No, that's not gonna happen. My cherry will tell them I was just waiting on her. I know she will. Yeah, that's just one more reason to pursue her. Now she's my alibi.

Every time I was here, it was just to see her sweet ass and work up the courage to ask her out.

I grunt a laugh, seeing as how that's sorta what happened, too. I'd feel pathetic over the thought if I really stopped to think about how this girl's got me twisted up in knots, but I stop that thought in its tracks.

It's the way she looks at me. I'm affecting her just as much and the moment she steps out of that store, I know I'm not gonna have any problems making her mine. As if accepting the challenge, she slips out of the building and locks the doors behind her.

I think about how easy it'd be to just lift them off of her. I could do that. Maybe I should. If we had the keys, it wouldn't have to be a stick-up; without them we'd be left to break a window, and that would trigger the alarm. That's something we don't want. The thought lingers in my mind, but it's quickly replaced by the sight of her lush ass in those jeans.

Damn, I can't wait to get her writhing underneath me. My dick is rock hard as her hips sway and she strolls toward her car. I get off my bike and wait for her. She seems lost in thought as I lean against her passenger side door. She doesn't even see me at all. She should be paying attention out here alone at night.

Fuck, my dick twitches in my jeans. We could fuck right here and right now, and no one would ever know. This town is old and small. Everyone's home this late at night. And this shopping strip is mostly vacant and on the edge of town. We could get away with it.

My cherry's not that kind of girl though, I know she's not. She's not gonna be giving it up that fucking easy. And I'm fine with waiting. For a night, anyway. And then I'll make sure she warms up to me.

She finally looks up, and her eyes go wide as she takes me in and stops walking in her tracks. I give her a cocky smirk and nod my head. "You finally got off?"

She blushes at my words, and it's only then that

I realize the double meaning. My sweet cherry has a dirty mind.

"Vinny, right?" she asks, swinging the keys in her hand and walking up to me full of confidence with a playful smile gracing her lips.

Fuck, I love that about her. Her confidence. I know she's a shy girl at heart, but she's got a way of putting it all out there for me. I fucking love that.

"Cary Ann," I reply and nod my head as I let my eyes roam down her tight body. I want her to see me appreciating her curves. It's pretty fucking cold out here, and her coat's hiding a lot of her body, but the plump part of her breasts is peeking up and flushed with the chill of the December night.

"What are you doing out here?" she asks as she moves around to her side of the car and I follow behind. She opens up the door and leans against it, giving me a generous view of her ass and taunting me. I adjust my dick real quick while she's not looking, and she actually wiggles her ass some. She definitely teasing me.

"Oh, don't tempt me," I warn her as she puts the key in the ignition and starts her car. It's not that cold that she's gotta warm her car up. It never gets that cold this far south, but I do appreciate the view.

She blushes and looks over her shoulder. "Oh yeah?" she says before sinking her teeth into her bottom lip. I wasn't actually considering fucking her against her car, but if she keeps this up that's exactly what's going to happen.

"Come on, Cherry," I say and lower my voice, "I'm trying to be good for you."

She straightens herself as I walk closer to her. She looks up at me, batting those thick lashes as she says, "I heard you were bad."

I stiffen at her confession, but she leans in and whispers, "That's what I like about you." Her hot breath tickles my neck as the sweet words touch my ear, and a playful smile spreads on my lips.

She pulls back with her eyes sparkling, and lust clearly present.

"Good. 'Cause I wanna take you out and show you a good time." I get right to the point before I do end up crushing her body against this car and giving us both what we want.

Her smile widens, and that shy side about her comes through as she brushes her hair out of her face and tucks it behind her ear. "I'd like that." A blush brightens her cheeks. "I was wondering when you were gonna ask me."

My brow pinches in confusion.

She gestures to the store and explains, "You kept coming in, but you never said anything." I swallow my nerves and smile back at her, but internally I feel like I'm suffocating. It's not good that she noticed, but this is the perfect cover-up.

I shrug it off and say, "I was just waiting till it felt right."

We both turn to face the entrance to the parking lot as the white Honda from earlier drives through and comes straight for us. The girl from earlier takes a look at me and then says, "Cary, you doing alright?"

Cary laughs a little, walking to her friend and bending over to lean into the window as she replies, "I'm fine, Cindy. Just getting asked out on a date," she says, staring at me over her shoulder and clearly looking pleased. It's a little irritating to be interrupted, but I have to admit it's a nice thing for her friend to do. I can't say that I blame her; I was looking a little sketchy earlier. The suspicious gaze she was giving me with narrow eyes turns into a surprised and somewhat excited look.

"Did you really drive all the way back here to check on me?" Cary asks with a hint of disbelief.

Cindy rolls her eyes and shrugs before saying, "Sue me for being a good friend and caring about your ass." She grins at Cary and gives me a quick wave. "Alrighty then, I'll leave you two to it."

A rough chuckle rises up my chest as she pulls away and my cherry walks back to me slowly.

"So, tomorrow night?" I ask her as the back lights from the Honda fade in the distance down the street, feeling cocky. My dick's already hardening at the thought of getting her under me.

"That's the night before Christmas Eve; I have a family dinner." Oh, yeah. I forgot for a moment. It's not like I have anything going on, but most people do.

She's looking all sorts of disappointed, like it really hurt her to tell me no. "Sorry. We decorate the tree. It's a family tradition."

"That makes sense." I don't have family traditions. You need a family in order to have them. Yet another difference, another reason we shouldn't be together. The thought takes me back.

I'm not planning a future with my cherry. I struggle for a moment to remember why I'm out here with her. Why I waited with the intention of seeing her and planning our little date. I need to get her out of the store on Christmas Eve. Yeah, that's the reason. I'm a fucking liar. I just wanna get her under me.

She shrugs and says, "It's early, and my mom's usually tipsy and passed out by eight." She sways from side to side, shrugging. "I can skip out. Meet you a little later?" Her voice practically purrs on the last line.

"Fuck, yeah. It's a date."

Chapter 4

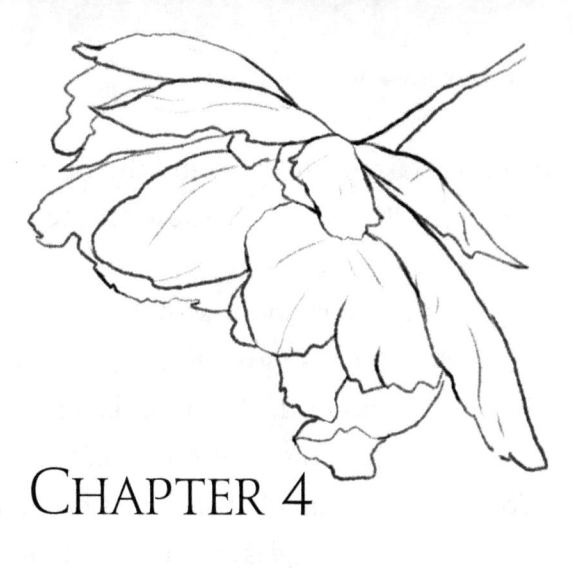

Cary Ann

This is stupid. I have butterflies and I'm nervous and I feel so childish, but thinking about Vinny reminds me how I used to feel about him. I'd walk back home from school while he drove away on his motorcycle, just dreaming about being on the back, my arms around his waist. Imagining how he'd kiss me outside of school. I huff a small laugh and bring my beer to my lips.

Times have changed, but I can't help feeling the nerves from way back then.

I watch as a customer rings the little bells scattered along the holly on the bar. That, along with Christmas music, is really making it feel like the holidays. The holly also has fake snow on it, and there's a snowman spray-painted with more fake snow on the front window of the bar, too.

It's cute, but some asshole is running his finger through it and pissing off the bartender, who I'm guessing is the one who made the artwork. I look straight ahead and just ignore him. The guy's drunk, and the bartender doesn't do anything but shake his head, then continues wiping down the glasses. I imagine he's gotta spray-paint a new snowman every night.

"No mistletoe?" I jump a little in my seat and almost spill my beer when I hear his voice. *Vinny.*

I give Vinny a small smile and set my beer down, trying to remember what he asked as my heartbeat calms back down. His voice is so deep and rough that it makes desire stir in my belly.

My cheeks flush when I finally realize what he said. *Mistletoe.* I'm a strong, confident woman, but this man brings out a shy side of me that I haven't felt in years.

I start picking at the label on my beer bottle and shake my head with my teeth sunk into my bottom lip. "Not here," I whisper in the sexiest voice I can.

I dressed the part tonight, wearing a deep red dress that clings to my figure. I know it's tight and a bit provocative for this bar, but I want to look good for him. I want to show off this feminine side of me. I want to show him that I'm a woman now, and that I want exactly what he has to offer.

Part of me feels self-conscious, while another part of me feels slutty. But I don't care. I want him, and I'm not letting him go without trying.

He takes a seat at the bar, looking up at the college football game on the TV behind the bar as he slides off his leather jacket. All he's wearing underneath is a clean crisp t-shirt that hugs his broad shoulders tightly, and a pair of faded blue jeans. Fuck, even in casual clothes he looks like a million bucks.

Suddenly the expensive dress I wore makes me feel cheap. I stop picking at the stupid label on the bottle and finally take another swig.

"You look beautiful, Cherry," he says in a deep low voice that's somehow directly connected to my clit. I turn to look at him when I feel those baby blue eyes on me.

I'm not letting him go without making it damn well obvious what I want tonight.

He's my Christmas present to myself. If that makes me a ho, then I'll ho ho ho myself right to his bedroom. Definitely his, since I'm still at my parents' house until I start my new job. I visibly cringe at the thought.

Vinny laughs, and then orders a beer. "What, you don't like my nickname for you?" he asks me.

I let out a small laugh and smile, feeling the light

buzz of the beer and accepting another as the bartender slides the glass bottles toward us on the bar.

"I like your nickname for me. It sounds dirty when you say it," I confess and blush violently at my own words and silently blame it on the alcohol.

He cocks a brow at me and leans in as he asks, "Is that so, Cary Ann?" His hot breath lingers on my neck and creates a shiver that slowly runs down my body, hardening my nipples. His lips barely touch the shell of my ear as he huskily says, "I didn't know you were a dirty girl... Cherry."

I laugh it off even though I'm all hot and bothered. I want him to know that I want him, but I'm not going to make it *too* easy for him.

"So what are your plans for Christmas Eve?" I ask casually, and then I remember my own plans. All the desire leaves me, and my mouth goes dry. I grip my beer a little harder. My heart races in my chest. I have to work, but more importantly, I need to make sure everything goes smoothly.

I need to stop the video camera footage first. My blood heats with anxiety. I'm not letting Morose do this again. That orphanage matters to me, and I know for a fact last year he did the same thing. The donations are truly needed, and that greedy fucker took it all. I saw the check he wrote to himself. I didn't want to believe it, but when I asked Mrs. Pilcavage if the check went through and she said she hadn't gotten it, my heart truly broke. She's an older lady and she believes what he tells her. It's so wrong. I can't stand it. I'm going to do the right thing, even if it costs me everything.

"Not much," Vinny says and shrugs and then seems to stare off at the television for a moment. I have to get my shit together. I take a deep breath, trying to calm myself down.

I've never done anything like this, but I'm not going to let anything stand in my way of making sure I take every cent from the registers and giving it to the orphanage where it rightfully belongs.

And on top of that, I have proof of what Morose did so he goes to jail for being the thief he is. But I'm not waiting on the law. I'm making sure those kids have the best Christmas they've ever had.

The last thought fills me with conviction.

Anger courses through my blood, but the sight of Vinny staring back at me changes it to something else. Something stronger, something hotter that I can't deny.

This shit is for me to worry about tomorrow night. Everything's going to go down perfectly. So tonight I'm going to relax. With *him*.

"So nothing for Christmas Eve then?" I ask casually and then set the bottle down on the bar. I remember he's from the orphanage, and my heart hurts a little. He grew up there for a few years before his aunt finally took him in. I can't believe I forgot. I take another drink to stop all the emotions from creeping up on me.

I have to change the subject, fast. "You looking forward to anything for Christmas?" I ask him.

He looks above me at the holly and asks again, "Mistletoe?"

I laugh a little, making my shoulders shake some.

"How about a kiss then?" he finally asks me, leaning in.

I smile shyly at him, but I'm not shy about this kiss. I'm more than happy to give it to him. I want *more* though.

I lean in slightly and he goes for it, but I put my finger to his lips and stop him. His eyes slowly open and they narrow at me, as if daring me to deny him. The hidden threat lying there in his baby blues ignites that desire full force.

"I'm gonna need you to take me home first," I whisper against his lips.

I gasp at the heat that blazes in his eyes. "That can be arranged, Cherry," he says. "Finish your beer, and then you're coming home with me."

Chapter 5

Vinny

I can't rip this dress off of her fast enough.

Her fingers kept inching closer and closer to my dick while I drove her back here. We left her car at the bar and she rode with me on the back of my bike, her warmth on my back and her breasts pressed against me. I was already hard just feeling her curves, but then those hands...

My cherry is a naughty girl, and I fucking love it.

Her nails gently scratched at the waistline of my jeans until the tips of her fingers were buried inside.

"Cherry," I admonished her as we pulled up to a red light. But all she did was lean forward, taking my lips with hers and moaning into my mouth.

Fuck, my dick twitches thinking about how I wanted to take her right then and there.

I slam her back against the wall of my foyer, kicking the front door shut behind me and struggling to get these fucking clothes off. I should get a damn medal for waiting until I got her home behind closed doors.

Her lips press to mine, molding to my easy pressure as I slip my tongue into her hot mouth. She kisses me with a passion I've never had with anyone else as my hands roam her body.

I grip her ass in my hands and pull her up to me, her legs wrapping around my hips like a good girl.

Fuck, if I'd known how much she wanted me, I would've skipped the bar entirely. I pick her up and walk to my bedroom. No shame, and no fucks given. We're both adults with needs, and I'm ready to strip her down and relieve all this sexual tension between us. My hand's up her dress and caressing her smooth skin, while her nails dig into my shoulders and her other hand grips my hair.

"Vinny," she moans my name. I take the break in our kiss to graze my teeth down her neck and leave open-mouth kisses all along the exposed skin. As the front of my legs hit the bed frame, I throw her ass down on it and smile when she lets out a playful squeal.

I'm quick to take off my shirt and then reach over for

the light on the nightstand. I slowly unbuckle my jeans and look back at my sweet cherry on the bed.

She's looking all kinds of hot and bothered, and a little shy, too.

She's still wearing her dress although her heels are gone, lost somewhere between the foyer and the bedroom.

"Take that off, Cherry," I say beneath my breath, looking at her with obvious hunger in my eyes.

She looks to the light switch and visibly swallows. "Can we turn the lights off?" she asks softly. Her confident energy is gone, and her insecurity is coming through. A part of me wants to give in and let her have whatever she wants, just grateful that a girl like Cherry wants to be with a man like me. But that's not happening. I wanna see her.

"No," I shake my head, holding her gaze. Her expression falls slightly and I shove my pants down and stalk over to her, buck naked. The bed groans as I crawl closer to her, my dick hard and ready. "I wanna watch your face when you cum on my dick, Cary."

My dirty words make her mouth fall open into a beautiful "O."

"Off," I give the command and she shimmies out of her dress and then hesitates to unclip her bra. But a cock of my brow has it coming off of her, leaving her in nothing but a skimpy pair of lace undies.

And those have got to go, right fucking now. I lean forward enough to shove my thumbs through the lace and tear them off of her.

I shouldn't have done it, but she'll forgive me. She gasps, but she doesn't protest. Her breathing is coming in short pants and her pale pink nipples are pebbled. She's fucking gorgeous.

I toss them off the bed and grab her hips in my hands, angling her pretty little pussy and taking a languid lick.

Fuck, she's so sweet. Just like I knew my cherry would be. Her fingers spear through my hair and she pushes my face into her pussy. I smile into her tight cunt at how greedy she is. I take her clit in my mouth and suck, making her squirm under me.

She needs more, and I know it. She's trying so hard to get herself off. But she needs me. I massage my tongue on her throbbing clit and I'm rewarded by the sweet sounds of her moans spilling from her lips.

I finally take my hand off her ass and shove two fingers into her pussy, stroking her G-spot and fucking her just like she needs.

"Yes!" she cries out, rocking her pussy into my face. I pull away and pin her hips down, staring at her with a serious expression on my face.

"You need to be a good girl, Cherry," I say and she looks up at me, her breath ragged. "Stop moving your ass, and stay still for me." I'm serious, too. I don't mind her riding my face, but right now I want to be the one controlling her pleasure.

"Yes, sir," she says back breathlessly, and it nearly floors me. Fuck yes. My dick's leaking precum, and I need to get her off quick so I can get inside.

I dive back between her legs and ravage her pussy like a starving man.

Her fingernails scrape along my scalp, but she's holding still for me, even as her back bows with pleasure. *Good girl.*

I suck her clit and push my fingers in, pumping in and out until her thighs are squeezing around my head. I move my face away, licking my lips and looking up her body to find her heated gaze.

"Cum for me, Cherry," I whisper the command, pressing my thumb down on her clit and she ignites under me. Her head falls back as she lets out a strangled cry and then moans my name. She's the most beautiful sight I've even seen. Her thighs are still trembling as I push her legs farther apart so I can fit my hips in between and line my dick up.

I slam into her before she has a chance to come down from her high, and her back arches from the intensity.

I groan in the crook of her neck, completely buried to the hilt and let her adjust to my size. She's so tight.

She's soaking wet for me, but she's so fucking tight.

"Vinny," she moans my name again, and the soft sound spurs me to move. I grip her hips and thrust my own in a rhythmic pace, watching the looks of pleasure play across her gorgeous face.

The dim light in the room makes her soft features look even more beautiful.

"Look at me, Cherry," I whisper as I pick up my relentless pace, nearly out of breath.

She stares back at me, eyes half-lidded and her gorgeous lips parted. "I wanna watch when you cum this time."

She nods her head although she doesn't say anything. She looks like she's lost in pleasure and on edge, and I'm ready to push her over a second time.

I pound into her tight cunt over and over. The bed groans with each thrust and the harder I fuck her, the harder the bed hits the wall. But it only fuels me to take her further, to push her limit higher. I lean forward, nipping her lips and staring into her lust-filled eyes.

My spine tingles, and my toes curl.

Fuck, my balls draw up and I know it's coming. I hold my breath as I fuck her harder and faster. Mercilessly pounding into her and desperate for her to find her release with me.

Her neck arches and her fingers dig into me, but

she never stops looking at me. She's so perfect. Finally, her mouth opens and I hammer into her just two more times and her tight walls are spasming on my dick.

The feel and sounds of her own release push mine over the edge. My body ignites with pleasure, tingling over every inch of skin as I fill her tight walls with my cum in thick, hot bursts. Waves of heated and numbing pleasure crash through my body as she trembles beneath me, shaking from the intensity of her own release.

I lean forward and kiss her sweetly. She moans into the hot air, holding me close to her, and everything in that moment feels right. It settles something deep inside of me, and when I pull away, it's still there.

I don't know what it is, and I try to shake the unfamiliar feeling as I walk to the bathroom and clean myself off before grabbing a washcloth for her.

She's still lying curled on her side in the bed, looking absolutely beautiful and vulnerable with her eyes closed as I wipe up her thighs.

She lets out a small satisfied sound as I clean her up and pull the covers around her. But that action seems to break whatever sensual spell she was under. She sits up with her eyes wide open and looks around the room the second I get off the bed.

She's looking for her clothes. She's already leaving? Damn, that's a first. I try to ignore the feeling in the pit of my stomach.

I walk to the bathroom and toss the cloth in the hamper as she starts gathering her clothing.

"You wanna stay?" I offer. I want her to. I wanna have access to that sweet body all night and wear her ass out.

The thought reminds me that she's working tomorrow. Shit.

Fucking her was a beautiful distraction, but the reality is slowly creeping back in.

"I'll make you pancakes in the morning. Give you a little sausage, too?" I try to make light of it, but I'm already feeling the high wearing off. I wanna just rewind, back to when it was just us enjoying the feel of each other.

"That thing is anything but little," she says comically, looking back up at me as she tosses her torn underwear into the trashcan by the desk.

A grin slips across my face. It's almost like tomorrow doesn't exist. Like what I have planned isn't important at all. But it is. It's life changing. Not just for me, but for those kids.

"So you staying over?" I ask her again. I want her here. I need to keep an eye on her, and I don't like the idea of not having control of that aspect tomorrow.

"I can't. I need to wake up early."

"For work?"

"Yeah," she answers. Fuck. I don't want her to go in. It would be so much easier if she wouldn't.

"I don't think you should." I try to say it teasingly.

"I don't think you should tell me what to do," she says with a smartass tone while slipping her heels back on. Her snappy response makes me walk straight to her and grab that ass of hers, pulling her over to the bed. She gasps as I toss her body down and I cage her in, her small body trapped under mine.

"And what if I want to?" I ask her, staring into those baby blues.

She's breathless and her eyes are heated with desire, but she pulls away. Damn. This time I let her go.

"Sorry, Vinny. I've gotta work tomorrow." She slips out from under my arms, and I groan in disappointment. My dick is so fucking hard again already.

"You gonna leave me like this?" I ask her, gesturing to my obvious hard-on with a grin. "Come on Cherry, I didn't think you'd do me like that."

She gives me a wide smile and leans in, putting her knee on the bed and planting a kiss on my lips.

"Maybe tomorrow?" she asks, vulnerability shining in her eyes. "Late tomorrow night?" She kisses me one more time. "I get off, and then you get off?" she asks, looking straight at my dick.

Fuck, I want that. So damn bad. But tomorrow

night... she might know. There's no way she's not gonna recognize my voice. I gotta figure this shit out.

"You alright?" she asks with concern obviously written on her face and laced in her voice. I realize then that my expression has turned.

"Yeah, yeah Cherry." I give her a small, chaste kiss, my hand cupping the back of her head. "I'll take you back and see you tomorrow night."

Chapter 6

Cary Ann

Ever since I grabbed the duffel bag, my heart's been beating out of my chest. I have that ready, along with the tape with the evidence on it. I already wrapped and addressed the tape so all I need to do is mail it, and the video footage has been stopped. I removed that tape altogether and got rid of it, so they'll have no idea it was me. There's nothing stopping me from opening up every register with my PIN number and emptying out the drawers. There aren't even any more shoppers left. For the last twenty minutes this place has been dead. I'm waiting until we're closed though, just in case.

Being open on Christmas Eve is a fucking stupid

thing to do in a small town. Everyone's done their shopping and they're either at the annual parade, or hunkering down and telling their kids Christmas stories as they try to settle them down for bed.

If I wasn't planning on using this situation to my advantage, I'd be pissed that I had to work.

But here I am, prepared to right a wrong and steal this money back. I click the button on my phone and see it's eight. Closing time.

I'm staring at the two cars in the parking lot that aren't mine. They need to leave and get out of here so I can do this and get it over with. I don't know why they're here. Nothing else is open on this strip, and the owners don't seem to be coming in. My palms are sweaty, and my heart's racing. I just want this to be over with. I'm sick to my stomach over it.

I tear my eyes away from the parking lot. I just need to stay calm and do everything with ease.

I close my eyes and take a deep breath, calming myself.

But then my eyes snap open and my heart sputters faster in my chest. Someone's come in. Fucking hell. My nerves can't take this.

I slowly turn, expecting to find Mr. Morose there, ready to thwart my plans because that would be just my luck, but instead it's worse. I'm frozen in place. Fuck. My heart slams against my chest so hard it hurts.

Much worse.

I should scream, but my lungs are paralyzed in my chest, and my legs are shaking. I grip the counter to stay upright as two men in black ski masks walk through the door and the second one locks it behind him.

Oh my God.

I shake my head in disbelief, every ounce of strength replaced with fear. My legs feel weak, and my body feels freezing cold.

"Stay," the first man commands, and some small part of me notes his very deep voice. They each have a gun in their hands, but neither are pointed at me. They have on gloves and masks and all black clothing. Oh shit. No! This can't be happening to me!

My eyes dart to the parking lot as I take in a shaky breath. Both cars are still there. Fuck. I bet they belong to them.

I shake my head, wanting this to all be make-believe.

"It's gonna be alright. You just need to listen and do what we say, and this will all be over with as soon as possible," the man on my left says calmly. His voice is lighter, and sounds more southern.

With the ski masks on all I can see are his deep chocolate eyes. Both men are tall, with broad shoulders. The one on the left is heavier than the other. Internally I start to track all the features that can be used to track these assholes down. I stand a little straighter, feeling my determination come back to me.

I'm not letting them get away with this.

The man on my right slaps a large black backpack on the counter as the man on the left says, "Just put the money in the bag and we'll leave." I stare at the black backpack, feeling the anger rise in my body as my hands ball into fists.

This money was supposed to be for the orphanage. I seethe in a breath through my clenched teeth and shake my head.

"No?" the man to my left says incredulously. He moves the gun from one hand to the other, and while it's still not pointed in my direction, it does the job of instilling fear in me. My heart thump, thump, thumps.

"Look sweetie, it's real easy. You just empty the cash out of each of the registers, or we will."

I shake my head again, feeling tears prick my eyes. The man on the right is stock-still, just staring at me with his pale blue eyes. "I won't give you my PIN," I say in a cracked voice.

This is stupid. It really is. But I can't let them do this.

I can't let yet another person steal from these kids. It belongs to them, damn it! They *need* it. Not these assholes who thought they'd rob a store on Christmas Eve.

The thought makes me even angrier, and I almost

lose my shit. But the man on my right walks closer.

"This doesn't have to be a fight," he says beneath his breath. So low, but he sounds so familiar. He looks to his partner and adds, "We don't wanna hurt you."

Tears leak from the corners of my eyes, rolling down to my cheeks and I angrily brush them away.

"Besides, we've got the key," the man on my left says confidently as he holds up the manager's key. What the fuck? My face scrunches up in a mix of sickness and irritation.

They don't even need my PIN. Shit, I'm going to have to physically keep them away, and that simply isn't going to happen. But I still have to try.

I shake my head and outright refuse. "No," I say with a strength I hardly feel. "I won't let you." I close my eyes and try to summon the courage to continue fighting them.

When I open my eyes, I instinctively take a step back, the small of my back butting against the counter and forcing a small scream from my lips.

Oh fuck, he's pointing the gun right at me, and my heart stops entirely. His chocolate brown eyes stare back at me, daring me to resist further. I put both of my hands up as fear grips me. I don't wanna die. I take in a shaky breath.

"Don't you fucking point your gun at her!" the man on my right snaps. My heart stills, and my hands slowly drop. I do recognize his voice. I shake my head, not wanting to believe it.

But the second he looks back at me, I know it's him.

"Vinny?" I whisper.

Chapter 7

Vinny

It's a fake gun, but Toni's scaring the shit out of my sweet cherry. I'm gonna beat the shit out of him.

I'm gonna spank Cherry's ass, too. Money isn't worth putting herself in danger. What the hell is she doing?

I was starting to feel like everything would be fine. We'd just have her step aside, grab the money and get the fuck out.

Easy peasy. I've got the two junkers out front to throw her off, and the cops too once they get here. They can't be traced to anyone, and everything would've been fine.

Shit, I was looking forward to consoling her tonight.

I know my cherry's strong, and she's wanting to do the right thing. But she shouldn't be risking her life like this.

My heart beats faster as she shakes her head no again. She's terrified, and all I wanna do is pull her into my arms and calm her down. I wanna let her in on what's going on. But she's not going to understand. She might not even believe me if I told her the truth.

The very thought that she'd think I was lying and that I'm no good makes my heart hammer faster in my chest.

I can't let that happen. I don't want this to come between us. There's something here, and I want more of her. I can't let this shit get out of hand.

"No," she says as she looks Toni in the eyes. Damn, my girl has some balls on her. "I won't let you."

She closes her eyes, and Toni raises the fake gun in his hand.

Fuck that. He's not going to scare her. I can't let him fuck her up like that. I've had guns pointed at me before. I won't let her go through that shit.

"Don't you fucking point your gun at her!" I scream at him, reaching over and smacking the gun away. I can't hear anything but the sound of my heavy breathing, I'm so pissed. He should know better than that.

I start to tell her to run, to get the fuck out of here before she gets hurt, to do anything but stay here, but she whispers, "Vinny."

My blood runs cold and I stare back at her, slowly facing her and watching the disbelief grow in her gorgeous eyes.

My palms feel like ice. Shit, this is the worst possible outcome.

She knows.

I raise my hand up, trying to calm her as she seems to get over her fear and starts shaking her head even stronger and harder than before.

"It's not what it looks like-" I start to explain myself, but she cuts me off.

"Are you fucking kidding me?" she practically spits out. She must really fucking trust me because all traces of fear vanish, replaced with rage. I was not expecting that. "Are you fucking serious?!" she yells at me.

She's pissed.

"Shit, shit," Toni curses behind me.

"Cherry," I say in a low voice. It's a warning. I know she's angry, but she needs to calm her ass down.

"You aren't taking this money! It's for the orphanage!" she screams as she walks around the counter to get in my face. "You of all people-" she starts to rip into me, but I cut her off, gripping the hand that she tries to shove into my chest. I need to tell her the truth, and she's not gonna like it, and she may not even believe it.

But she's gonna fucking hear it.

"It's not gonna go there," I say as she stands toe-to-toe with me. Completely forgetting the fact that Toni's right there, watching us go at it.

"The hell it isn't!" she yells back. "Take your mask off and talk to me!" She tries to smack my chest with the other hand, but I grab that wrist too and hold her still.

"Stop it, Cherry," I tell her in a low voice, with a threat just barely there. I'm not above grabbing her ass and taking her out of here like a toddler having a damn fit. Toni can handle this on his own. "The video surveillance is running, and I can't let them see my face." I know there's no audio, but there's video at least. I know that much. And even though I know Cherry knows, I still have faith she won't tell them.

"Fuck, man!" Toni yells behind me, slamming his fist down on the counter and pacing a bit. He needs to calm down.

"Everyone, just calm down," I say loud enough for both of them to hear.

"I already cut the feed. You're going to have to fucking kill me." Cherry pulls her hands out of my grasp. "I worked too damn hard to make sure the kids get what they need."

I try to take in what she's saying, but it doesn't make sense. She crosses her arms across her chest, looking at me with tears in her eyes. She's trying to be strong, but the weight of what she just said is wearing down on her.

I tilt my head and ask, "What do you mean you 'cut the feed'?"

She rocks on her back foot and looks away. Fear is creeping in. She's trapped in this store, and she's just said there's no feed. *Cherry*. She really does need me to spank her ass raw. What the hell is my sweet cherry doing admitting shit like that? She's not very good at staying out of trouble.

But then again, if she was, she wouldn't have been with me.

"Tell me." I give her the simple command, and that gets her attention.

"I can't let you steal this money." She says the words simply in a soft voice etched with pain. Conviction is there as well. I know why. She thinks this money is going to the orphanage like it's supposed to. But it's not.

"I'm taking this money to the orphanage," I tell her, staring into her soft baby blue eyes. "Morose is stealing." I take in a heavy breath as her eyes widen. She's gotta believe me. "It has to go there, Cherry. Just let us take it to where it belongs."

She blinks a few times and her breathing comes in short pants. "I swear to you, just let us take it to the orphanage."

"No fucking way," she says, and then my cherry takes

two steps closer to me before she does the last thing I thought she would. She wraps her arms around my neck and presses those sweet lips to mine, moaning into my mouth.

I'm shocked, but she feels so damn good, I fall under her spell, letting her kiss me and setting the gun down on the counter behind her so I can hold onto her small waist, pulling her closer to me.

I could do this all night, but we can't. I try to pull away, but she just holds me tighter. My greedy girl. She doesn't let up until Toni snaps from behind me, "What the fuck is going on?"

Chapter 8

Cary Ann

I pull away and look at Vinny's friend. The smile on my face dims as I catch sight of his gun again.

I take another step back and look between the two of them.

"You cut the feed?" Vinny asks me.

I nod my head and reply, "Yeah." My heart is just too full knowing Vinny was doing exactly what I was planning on doing. I feel safe with him. Which doesn't make sense with his friend freaking out. It makes me really uneasy to see the guns.

"What the fuck's going on, man?" The guy pushes on Vinny's shoulder as Vinny takes his mask off.

"She's cool, Toni."

"So you were gonna rob me?" I ask Vinny, ignoring the prickle of fear running through me. I keep looking at Toni. I don't know him, and I don't like that he's here. For some reason it's so easy to forgive Vinny. Especially knowing why he was doing this.

"I didn't want to." He wraps his arms around my waist and pulls me close to him. My small hands land on his chest. "I didn't want you to be scared."

I scoff at him and refuse to admit how worked up I was and say, "I was pissed, not scared." He smiles down at me, like I'm being cute.

I look back at his friend who finally pulls the mask off of his face. He looks vaguely familiar.

"She your girl?" he asks with his brow pinched. "Would've been easier if this was an inside job," he mutters.

He shoves the mask into his pocket and walks over to the nearest register. Vinny's grip on me tightens as I try to pull away and watch Toni.

"So we're robbing this joint together?" Vinny asks me with a smile and then kisses my nose.

I purse my lips, not sure if I trust the fucker at the register.

"It's right across the street, baby. We've got twenty minutes before the parade goes through. We take the cash and slip it through their mail slot in the door." I nod my head. That's better than the plan I had, which was to drop it off in the early morning. Now is better. Get the cash and move it from one place to the next as quickly as possible.

I look at Vinny, and I'm pretty sure I know why he's doing this, but I don't know Toni's story. I watch him as he shoves the money into the bag. Vinny's completely at ease, and obviously trusts him.

"Why are you doing this?" I ask as Toni closes the first register and moves to the next. There are only three in the entire store. So this won't take long.

"I went there once." He looks up at me. He's got a baby face although he's built like a man. "To the orphanage. Without Mrs. Pilcavage I wouldn't be standing here today. There's no doubt I'd be locked up." He opens the next register with the key. "Those kids aren't gonna have the life I had." There's a hint of sadness in his voice.

"You trust me, Cherry?" Vinny asks me, pulling my eyes away from Toni.

"I don't know," I whisper although everything in me does. I shouldn't. I know I'm naive, but I do. I trust him.

"Shoot me, Toni," Vinny says, and my heart stops. Toni laughs and picks up the gun.

"Stop!" I scream out, pushing Vinny hard in the chest, but he's a powerful man and my strength doesn't do a damn thing.

My heart pounds as Toni pulls the trigger over and over again.

It takes a minute for my racing heart to settle. He's gotta be fucking kidding me.

"It's a squirt gun," Toni says before looking at his watch and then heading to the third register, "but there's no water in it."

"I knew you'd be working," Vinny says. "I couldn't bring a real gun, I couldn't risk even the slightest possibility of you getting hurt."

My heart clenches in my chest. I swallow thickly, not liking how strongly I feel toward this man. It's too fast, too soon, but all I wanna do right now is run away with him.

The last register closes shut with a large clank.

"It's not everything that was donated," Toni says, "but it's close." He zips up the backpack and clicks his phone to life.

"Fifteen minutes," he announces, throwing the bag over his shoulders and looking back at Vinny and me. "We gotta get this over there."

Vinny looks down at me, and I know he's going to tell me to stay here. But that's not happening. No fucking way.

"Cherry-" he starts, but I'm not letting him finish.

I shake my head and say, "No, I'm coming with you."

Vinny's eyes are hard, but the moment is broken by the laughter coming from Toni.

"Yeah, she's definitely your girl," Toni says.

Vinny puts his hand on the small of my back and leads me toward the doors as he says, "Let's go then. We gotta make this fast."

"Leave the keys on the counter so they know it wasn't Cherry," Vinny says, and Toni nods. He leaves the keys and then slips a note under them. I walk over and reach down to touch it, but Toni stops me, grabbing my wrist.

"No prints," he says easily, and I nod my head. I suppose they'd run fingerprints on employees first. I could see that.

"What's the note say?" I ask him.

An asymmetrical smile kicks the corner of his lips up. "Merry Christmas, Grinch."

Chapter 9

Vinny

She keeps watching Toni and I can practically see the wheels turning in her head. She doesn't trust him.

"Yo, Toni," I call out to him as we walk past the two cars we planted and head through the parking lot to the other side of the vacant strip mall. We drove Cherry's car around the block first. It added on a few minutes to the walk, but I don't want her car out front just in case they find the money gone before Thursday morning. I can't be too careful. It was awkward as fuck driving in the car. She's tense. But she'll be better once this is over with.

The orphanage is close. A five-minute walk if we

step on it, and that's the perfect amount of time. But I don't like the way Cherry seems to be so damn uneasy. The faster we get this shit done, the better.

Toni takes a look over his shoulder, he's leading the way. We have to go this way to avoid the cameras. The direct path goes right through the convenience store, and there's surveillance in that parking lot. So we're gonna avoid that and take the long way around.

Cherry's keeping a safe distance from Toni. I wish she'd knock it off, but she has no reason to trust him.

"Whatcha want, Vinny? I'm not slowing down," Toni answers as he hops over the chain link fence on the edge of the parking lot and turns to wait for us.

It's a clear shot from here on over to the other street.

"Give her the backpack," I tell him. He looks at me with a bit of confusion as I swing my legs over the fence and hop over easily. My sweet cherry is struggling a little. She's on the petite side and I've got my hand out for her ready to brace her body, but she's gripping the chain links of the fence.

"Alright sure, it's a little heavy though." He walks quietly over to Cherry as she tries to right herself. She almost landed on her ass, but I've got a good grip on her waist.

"Here little mama," he says, holding it out for her to take. We're hidden behind the bushes, but as a car passes, we all freeze. No one's out this late on Christmas Eve unless it's to go to the parade on the other side of main street. There aren't any houses over this side of town either. The orphanage is basically on its own on the outskirts of town.

I hold my breath as the car passes, the lights from the headlights peeking through the bushes. I step in front of Cherry and Toni huffs a small laugh at me.

"Calm down, we're home free." He looks relaxed and happy. Truthfully, this is an easy heist. We're so close to being done. I can taste it.

The car passes without incident and Cherry reaches for the bag, her eyes on Toni.

Her expression falls as he drops the full weight in her hand and she hunches forward to get a better grip.

"Holy shit," she mumbles and then shakes her head, shoving the bag back at Toni. "You take it."

Toni looks up at me, and I give him a nod. I just wanted her to see that it's not about the money for him.

It was never about the money. It's about the fact that the town wanted those kids to have a chance. That money isn't for toys. It's for the electric bill, the hot water. It's to put food on the table and shoes on their feet. I know how much those simple things in life can make a difference. And I know that Mrs. Pilcavage is struggling and that she's worried about the money that was supposed to come from the donation, but never came.

My anger rears up inside of me and I lead the way, my hand splayed on the small of Cherry's back. "Let's go," I tell them.

I crouch beneath the low-hung branches of the trees across from the orphanage and look both ways. No one's here, and all but one light in the whole house is off. I look for a sign that someone's watching, but there's no one here and no one looking.

Quickly, we cross the street and head straight over to the side door on the house. The outside light is on, so if someone comes, they'd see us instantly.

"Hurry." Cherry's fear is evident in her voice as Toni swings the bag off his shoulder and quickly starts shoveling the money through the slot. I take Cherry by the waist and lead her in front of him, the two of us blocking anyone from seeing him.

"You look like you're up to no good," my cherry says in a low voice. And I think she's playing with me with that smartass mouth of hers until she pulls on my jacket. Oh shit, I almost forgot about the all black I'm wearing. I quickly shuck my sweater off, I was hot anyway, and toss it into the trashcan out front.

"Toni, you too." He rises from his position, shoving the last bundle through the slot and then the card wishing a Merry Christmas and Happy New Year to all the kids at the orphanage. I know Mrs. Pilcavage, we both do. She's a good woman and when she wakes up tomorrow and sees that money, she's gonna cry with joy and relief. I know she will. It makes me proud to be able to give her back a sense of peace that she gave me all those years ago.

The town clock chimes as Toni stands up and chucks his black jacket off, revealing a beige thermal underneath, shoving the jacket and the backpack both into the trashcan. We toss our gloves and ski masks into the next trashcan and keep walking.

No more evidence. It's done.

I finally feel like I can breathe. The three of us stroll down the street, heading toward the main road where we'll meet up with the parade and blend in. I wrap my arm around Cherry's waist, but she pulls away and runs to a blue metal post office box on the corner of the block. She pulls a small package out of her purse, covered in brown wrapping paper with an address written in black sharpie.

"What's that?" I ask as she drops it into the box. She smiles and says, "The video surveillance of Morose." Pride's written on her face.

I huff a laugh and say a prayer that Morose pays for what he did. At least we've done everything we can do. The rest is in the law's hands.

"You alright?" I ask her as Toni walks ahead. He's got his hands shoved in his pocket and he's breathing easy. I am too, if I'm being honest. Cherry's not, she seems tense and she's looking every which way like someone's just waiting to get us. She gives me a small nod, but I know she's still a little shaken.

I'm a reformed man, but this isn't the first time I've gotten away with this shit. It'll be the last though. I don't need this in my life. Toni turns back to look at us and gives me a nod when Cherry leans against me, wrapping her arm around my waist.

Toni doesn't need it either. This was the last heist for us. It's a good way to end this career.

I look down at Cherry as we stop on the corner, finally seeing the parade just two blocks down. A Christmas elf from the bank is leading the way.

"You think it's going to be alright?" she asks me.

"It's gonna be perfect." I kiss her hair and she seems to relax a bit. "I promise you," I whisper.

The crowd from the parade appears, and the three of us keep on walking. Soon we'll be blending in with them. Just another block to go.

Cherry stops walking as Toni jogs across the road. I turn to look at her, wondering what she's doing.

I look down at my sweet cherry and she points up.

Right above us on a street light is a bit of mistletoe. I

let out a huff of a laugh and look back down at her. She's got a sweet smile on her lips.

"I'll give you that kiss if you stay with me tonight," she says softly.

"You already owe me a kiss," I tell her, cupping her chin in my hand.

"I owe you more than that," she says, batting her lashes. I lean down and take her lips with my own. The sounds of the parade are getting closer, but I don't stop kissing her until we're surrounded and the music and cheers envelop us.

She looks up at me with those sweet eyes when I pull away and I know she's feeling vulnerable and scared, but I'm gonna make everything alright. For her, I'll make it all up to her.

"Merry Christmas, my sweet cherry."

Epilogue

Cary Ann

One Year Later

"You have the biggest smile on your face, Cherry." I hear his voice from across the bedroom. I blush at Vinny as I sit up in bed and rub the sleep from my eyes.

"I'm just happy today," I say easily. I'm so full of warmth and so excited. I love this time of year.

He crawls on the bed closer to me, balancing a cup of coffee in his hand. Peppermint coffee, my favorite this time of year. *Mmm.* I reach out and take the hot mug from him, giving him a sweet kiss before taking a sip.

Coffee is my life source now.

I work nonstop, but I love it. Being a social worker

has made me feel like I'm finally giving back in the way I was always meant to. I feel complete in my career, even more so with Vinny in my life.

My engagement ring clicks on the ceramic mug and the bright light from the morning sun shining through the windows makes it sparkle. Every time I look down at the ring, I feel whole. I love Vinny more and more with each passing day.

Ever since that night, we've exposed ourselves completely to one another. I never believed in love at first sight, but all those years ago, that feeling in my chest was special after all. It had to have been love for us to fit so perfectly together. I know it.

We're gonna start trying to have a baby on New Year's Eve, but the wedding comes first. *A Christmas wedding.* The thought makes me practically shake with delight.

I set the mug down on the nightstand as he curls up next to me, pulling my back into his hard chest. My ass nestles into his crotch and I wiggle a little, wanting him to know that I want him.

I always want him.

His rough chuckle vibrates up my back, and his soft breath tickles my neck.

"Careful what you wish for, Cherry," he warns.

I bite my lip and roll over in his arms.

"So what do you want for Christmas?" I ask him. I

already know the answer though. He told me he wanted to donate toys to the orphanage, so that's going to be our tradition every year. And that's all he wants. Even for our wedding, in lieu of gifts we asked for donations to the orphanage. Especially now that my work deals with a few of the kids there.

No one ever found out what we did last year. We got away without a single soul knowing, and Morose went to jail for the crimes he committed.

Sometimes everything just works out perfectly.

"I already told you," he says softly before leaning in for a kiss.

I smile against his lips.

"All I want is you," he says again, and it makes me feel so full of love.

I brush his hair away from his face and say, "I love you, Vinny."

I whisper the words, and I mean them with everything in me.

He kisses me sweetly and says, "I love you too, Cherry."

About the Author

Thank you so much for reading my romances. I'm just a stay at home Mom and an avid reader turned Author and I couldn't be happier.

I hope you love my books as much as I do!

More by Willow Winters
www.willowwinterswrites.com/books

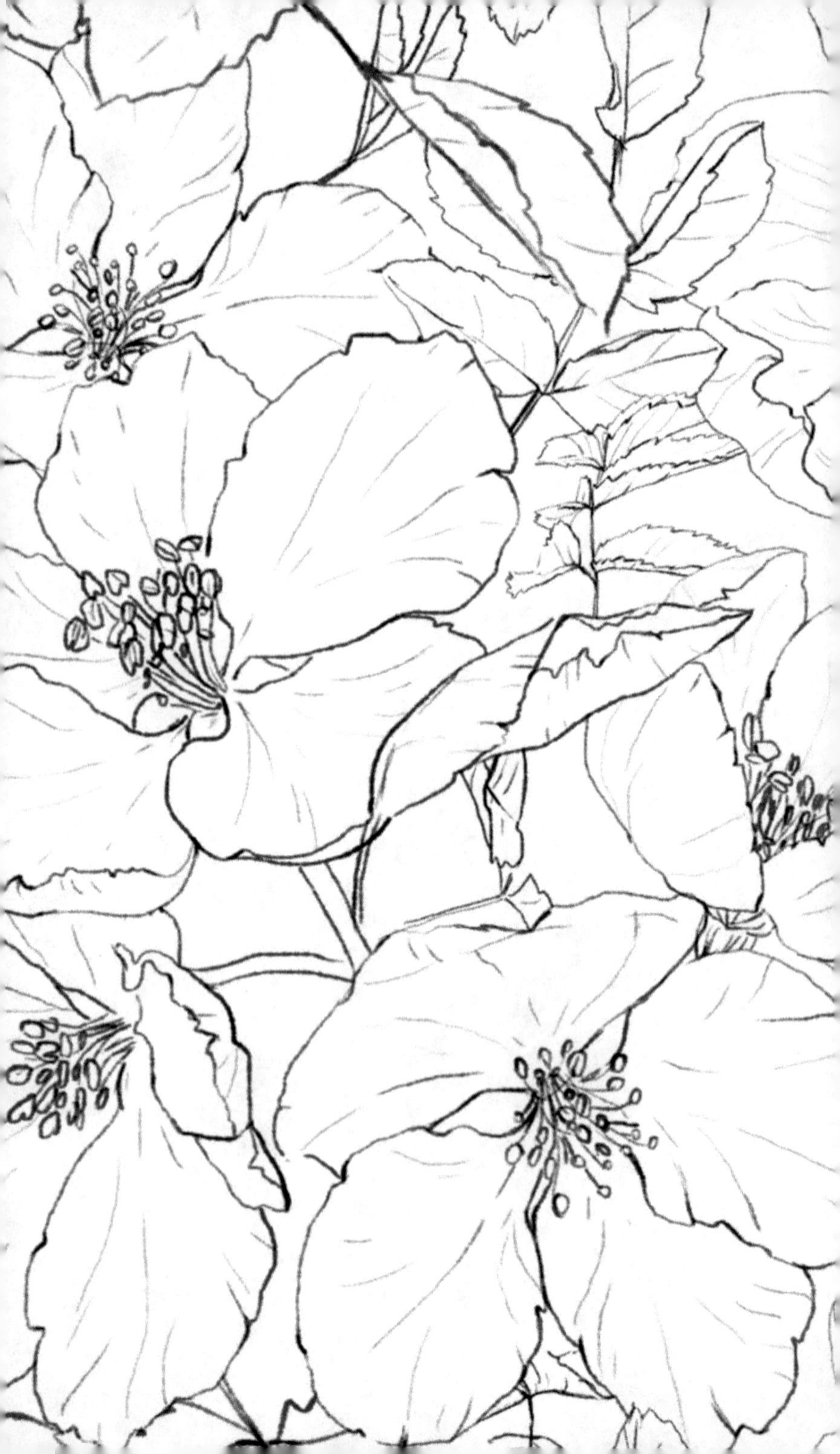

CPSIA information can be obtained
at www.ICGtesting.com
Printed in the USA
JSHW081719040623
42689JS00003B/18

9 798885 920636